The Phantasmagorical Imperative

and Other Fabrications

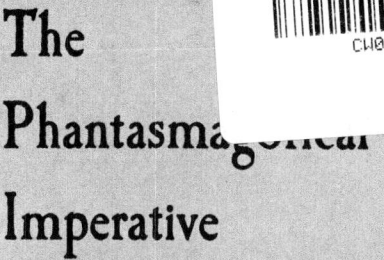

by
D.P. Watt

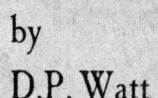

All stories
© D.P. Watt 2014
www.theinterludehouse.co.uk

Drawings
© Andrzej Welminski
www.welminski.pl

The Interlude House
2015

For Bob Brocklehurst and Nick Freeman,
who have, each in their own way, sought to know me

Fête nocturne

Cette fête lie les étangs
Au fulgurant charroi des astres
Avec ses cornes d'abondance
Où roulent nos pensers brillants.

Quelque part entre terre et ciel
Elle vide ces déchets d'âmes
Que d'aucuns dans la nuit en flammes
Prennent pour des cygnes volants

Et nous paternes assistants
De la transfusion de nos moelles
Voyons fondre aussi les étoiles
De nos rêves exhilarants.

                          Antonin Artaud (1923)

Contents

Foreword – Victoria Nelson ... 9

The Phantasmagorical Imperative ... 13
Laudate Dominum (for many voices) ... 43
By Nature's Power Enshrined ... 63
Holzwege ... 83
Dehiscence ... 99
The Ten Dictates of Alfred Tesseller ... 143
...he was water before he was fire... ... 203
14ml of Matt Enamel #61 ... 221
Vertep ... 239
A Harvest of Abandon ... 259

Afterword: 'As If' – Eugene Thacker ... 273

Foreword

The Phantasmagorical Imperative and Other Fabrications is D.P. Watt's wonder cabinet of obsessive, carefully written supernatural stories told by a breed of bachelor narrators who are a cross between M.R. James's buttoned-down antiquarians and H.P. Lovecraft's high-strung, slightly hysterical misfits—with a dash of E.T.A. Hoffmann and Bruno Schulz thrown in. The collective fate of these characters is to bend matter or be bent by it into strange new dimensional realities, *viz.*:

Eugene, a bookish recluse in a small Cornish town, encounters a traveling show advertised by a poster borrowed from Kafka. After a magical performance that all in the audience perceive differently, the master of ceremonies instructs Eugene in the art of transforming and he is moved to try it out immediately on his own household: "Everything was being remade, and each form begat other forms; animals desiccated into minerals before his eyes, saucepans became humming-birds, water evaporated into spices and the wallpapers dripped into puddles of oil that then exploded in pillars of flame"— the final transformation being, of course, the one Eugene enacts upon himself.

A man who is 'utterly reliable in all matters but those of the heart' embarks on a 'wild camping' trip in Scotland's Argyle Forest, where he encounters a mute *homo ferus* who charms a flock of 50 swans out of the water and shows him the wonders of the forest. At the end of the summer his secret sharer disappears with the swans when they turn into their true forms in the deep water of spirit, leaving the man left behind on the shore to await his own transubstantiation.

Two humans enact a Punch and Judy murder on each other at the command of the 'great elemental' that inhabits a jack-in-the-box. A Mechanical Marvel Museum features an organ with a small human voice.

A model train enthusiast works feverishly through the night so that he may take a visiting friend on a magical ride glowing with the fresh enamel paint their proud creator/demiurge has bestowed on the "rich, unchanging landscapes" flashing past the windows of the tiny train compartment they inhabit.

Reversing a stereotype, an English émigré in Poland refuses to sell the simple treasures of his junk shop to tourists and winds up on the street with a chest full of mundane but evocative objects, all of which have accumulated the most astonishing stories and each with its own exotic flower talisman.

Other curiosities besides these lurk in Watt's own chest of stories. Like his narrators, he has conjured worlds within worlds in a Schulzian quest for spirit in matter, for the souls of inanimate objects. As the showman Maximilian of the title story puts it, 'There are no gods or devils, angels or demons, simply the things of the world and their beautiful, endless interdependence—their eternal flow and mutability.' End result: not horror but magical metamorphosis.

– Victoria Nelson

There's many a
 strange thing on
  this earth,
So says each
  world-ranger,
But, of all the strange
  things to be seen
why —

I'm a little stranger!

The Phantasmagorical Imperative

> 'Act only according to that maxim by which you can
> at the same time will that it should become a universal law.'
> Immanuel Kant, *Foundations of the Metaphysics of Morals*

Werrow is one of *those* Cornish coastal villages, the kind that appears on holiday programmes about getting away from it all for a week or two; spending time with the kids, *outdoor* pursuits and the like. Its quaint cottages tumble down a steep cliff-side, the single-track road zigzagging its way through them in a fashion that makes visiting motorists marvel at how it still functions in the 'modern age'.

Everything in Werrow speaks of eternity; the harsh cliffs, the savage waves, the dwellings determined against the elements. But that eternity is also one of glacial ruin and Werrow wears these gentle marks too, although little noticed by the crowds that throng its streets in summer;

then, everything is alive with the urgent heat of holidays and the thrilled squeals of children by the water's edge. Only in winter are the crumbling rocks and thin cracks in every wall more apparent as everything slides, inch by slow inch, into the sea. It was this majestic, idle decay that brought Eugene Miles to live there.

I. Transition from oblivion to epiphany

Eugene Miles had for many years been a reclusive autodidact, obsessed with an interior world of books and ideas. Content with his own company and little interested in the opinions of the living—rather the intellect of the dead—his fifty years had been given over to *quiet* pursuits. He had lived very simply, writing and reading, in his small Oxfordshire cottage inherited from his mother when he had not even left university. He needed little by way of income and had survived on a few hours a week at a nearby supermarket. With the forced purchase of his cottage to build a new bypass for his growing town he had decided it was time to seek new surroundings, and what better than the idyll of a Cornish village: Werrow.

He had been named after Eugène Delacroix—through the subterfuge of his father, who had been an art historian of a sublime romanticist persuasion. Seeing Eugene shortly after birth he remarked that his podgy body reminded him of Delacroix's lithograph of 'Mephistopheles over Wittenberg'; lumpy and demonic. So rather than the agreed name for the child—Richard—his father had filled in the forms and named him Eugene. His mother's remonstrations were for naught though and Eugene he remained. But many deep passions, or obsessions—as every student of the world knows—end in tragedy and so it was with Eugene's father, for whom the world became only a grey and useless tracing of the wonder he found in paintings, who had taken his own life on a clear winter evening with an old cut-throat razor, a warm bath and a bottle of single-malt whisky.

Eugene had been little affected by the passing of his parents. Everything in their world had taken place at a distance and formality quite unusual in the modern world. Love was a subject of literature and art, passion was manifest in the work of the mind and the translation to the canvas—never in the home.

So Eugene had cultivated a manner which might only be described as 'being beside himself'. To most that encountered him the real Eugene was elsewhere—never truly engaged in the conversation he might be having. He found everyday encounters troublesome and wasteful—an excess of futile interaction. And the world's pleasures—if such they be—similarly eluded him. Television seemed to him a modern opiate, without the potential revelatory dream-visions. Travel and holidaying were only a sticking plaster on the festering wound of corporate stooges that had sold their time to fund a life of plastic gimmickry and gadgets. Similarly he found the theatre an idle irrelevance, more the domain of narcissists and decadents. However it is only so long that a soul can endure such asceticism and soon he was to discover the thrill of performance when *they* came to Werrow.

They were *Phantasmagoria*. Their poster appeared in the little village one crisp February morning. It read,

The Phantasmagorical Imperative...

We are *Phantasmagoria*—the flux of phenomena.

We are here to entertain! We are here to teach! The world is the object of our enquiry!
You will not be disappointed in the accomplishment of our rheological marvels.
We are—and you are too!—*unique*, but infinitely divisible!
For *one night only* and never again!
So, come; witness the wonders of *Phantasmagoria* tomorrow!

If you miss your chance you will miss it forever!
Never again will such tremendous opportunity for the revelation of transformation be performed in such a beautiful locale.
We pity the heart that would suffer the regret of missing *Phantasmagoria*.
Everyone is welcome!
So, come; bring your beloved, bring your children, bring your parents, bring your lovers, but come, come!
Let nothing distract you from attending to the beauty of

ature*Phantasmagoria*—feats and doings unparalleled in human history

But hurry, so that you get in before midnight!
At twelve o'clock the doors will be shut and never opened again!
You will not be disappointed!

Eugene read it in the early afternoon, pinned to a telegraph pole by the bus-stop, after his daily trip to the bakery. A small group of locals were stood about excitedly discussing the show. Eugene was not impressed. It's absurd echoing of the hyperbole of 18th and 19th century charlatans, mystics and other performative buffoons immediately set him against the show.

But, contemplating it further on his short walk home, surely such grandiose (and somewhat parodic) claims were rather against the spirit of these times—riddled as they were with hollow sincerity and bloated with hordes of hopeful parasites eager to be adored for talents they did not possess innately and were incapable of acquiring through any disciplined training. Yes, this poster (now quite charming) spoke at least of confidence—and humour—and sounded, to Eugene, quite an antidote to the banality of gameshows and stand-up comedians that haunted the television screens and fading theatres; he might even go along.

Eugene's only real involvement in the local community was through his regular appearances at the local pub, 'The Anchor'. Even there few would engage him in anything beyond a grumbled, 'alright!' It suited him well though. He came for a drink, not conversation. But tonight, the pub was packed, and the one subject that he heard echoing from one group to the other was *Phantasmagoria*. After buying his beer, he headed to the lounge, in the hope of finding a seat. In the corner, by the jukebox, he spotted John Lyle, alone at a small round table.

The Phantasmagorical Imperative...

John was one of the men—in Werrow, or elsewhere—that Eugene had any time for. He had been a carpenter since leaving school, running his own business. A few years previously he had had to take work with a joinery firm in Falmouth, some thirty miles away. He hadn't wanted to do as most other local tradesman had: develop some sideline to cash-in on the tourist season. No, his interest was wood, and solely wood.

'So, you goin' along to this show then, tomorrow night?' John asked, pulling out a stool for Eugene.

'I doubt it,' Eugene said, grumpily. 'It'll just be nonsense. I hate the theatre, in all its guises, to be honest. I don't know why they bother. Everyone's supposed to "share in the experience", "suspend disbelief" and all that blather. I'd rather read a good book, on my own terms. Anyway, they probably won't show up. Whoever put those posters up will have gone back and told them it isn't worth bothering coming to such a small place—especially out of season.'

'God, you're a miserable bastard,' John laughed. 'It's not some local amateur dramatic group doing their version of *Macbeth*, with knitted chainmail and wooden swords. It's gonna be some kind of circus show isn't it. You can't say that circus folk are all fakes now can you? I'd like to see you breathe fire, or juggle, or walk the trapeze. Mind, you could use that face of yours to turn milk sour, that's for sure. Come! See the *Great Eugene*—the world's most miserable man, guaranteed to curdle your cream and turn your wine to vinegar. You want another pint?'

Eugene nodded and handed him his glass after draining the last few dregs.

He had a point. Eugene was himself engaging in something of the amateur theatrics—playing his part in Werrow as *the outsider*, holed up with his books and tired soul.

John returned with more drinks.

'You know,' John said, 'I really wonder why you wanted to come here. Was it just so you could fight everyone and pose around as the great intellectual? I haven't read as many books as you have, but if they make you this miserable I don't think I want to.'

'Alright, John,' Eugene said, not wanting this analysis to probe much deeper, 'I'll come to the bloody thing if it makes you happy. Thanks for the pint.'

'If I knew buying you drinks would get you to socialise then the beer would be on me from now on,' John said, grinning.

'No it wouldn't,' Eugene replied, 'because for every ounce of grumpiness in me, there's a pound or two of stinginess in you. It'd cost you a fortune.'

'That's true enough, on both counts,' John said. And they laughed the kind of laughter of warmth and truth.

∞

'For *one night only* and never again! If you miss your chance you will miss it forever! Everyone is welcome! At twelve o'clock the doors will be shut and never opened again!'

In the middle of the night Eugene awoke.

The poster for *Phantasmagoria* had been screaming its call through his dream world. It reminded him of something: 'The Nature Theatre of Oklahoma' from Kafka's *Amerika*!

He hurried through to his study to find the book.

He paused a moment before turning the light on to watch the night sea fold its frothy waves against the pebbles of the shore. His ears hardly heard the churn of the waves anymore, after years of living by them—that relentless, gentle shh, shhh, shhh that pulls the listener deep into sleep, like some babe in its mother's arms.

He found the book quickly. His bookcases were filed alphabetically by author.

He flicked through the pages. There it was, 'The Oklahoma Theatre will engage members for its company today at Clayton race-course from six o'clock in the morning until midnight. The great Theatre of Oklahoma calls you! Today only and never again! If you miss your chance now you will miss it forever! If you think of your future you are one of us! Everyone is welcome! If you want to be an artist, join our company! Our Theatre can find employment for everyone, a place for everyone! If you decide on an engagement we congratulate you here and now! But hurry, so that you get in before midnight! At twelve o'clock the doors will be shut and never opened again! Down with all those who do not believe in us! Up, and to Clayton!'

This clear quotation was enough in itself to convince Eugene to go along to the show. But then, as he'd thought over drinks with John, they probably wouldn't even turn up—that's usually the way of the world when you really want something.

II. Transition from cabbages to candy-floss

The *Phantasmagoria* players did appear. Early the following morning a group of children had been waiting up on the moor to see if they would. Apparently out of the morning mist wagons materialised, drawn by sturdy shire horses. They were accompanied by arched caravans in an old gypsy style. The travelling players were setting up in a field about a mile from the village. *Phantasmagoria* had arrived!

At around midday some of the adults had gone to verify the story—it was true. A colourful tent had already been erected and the wagons were circled around with a flurry of activity as the players prepared for their performance.

You could not go anywhere in Werrow without hearing of them. By two o'clock Eugene had already been told about their arrival twice in the post office (once in the queue by Mrs Perry, collecting her pension, and once from Mr Callow at the counter) and in the bakers he had to wait behind another queue of people, collecting their lunchtime sandwiches, all chattering about the show. On his way home John, from the pub, stopped him and joked that the 'no-show' he'd predicted hadn't quite happened. It was quite an event to have these performers in Werrow—didn't he think.

But Eugene hadn't really thought much further than the archaic wording of the advert and the echoing of Kafka's 'Nature Theatre of Oklahoma'. But he was intrigued enough now and confirmed he would be there.

John grinned and slapped him on the shoulder, 'You'll love it, mate. We all will.'

Eugene very much doubted that. It would be some worn out circus nonsense; a few shabby clowns (alcoholics, no doubt) and the usual rabble of misfits attempting minor displays of physical prowess. He wasn't sure if they'd banned using animals now in the circus—they probably had. If not there might be a mangy lion or arthritic camel to entertain the kids. The kids—would there even be any children there at midnight? It seemed a strange time to have the show.

But deep in his heart he was looking forward to it. And as darkness descended across the little village his excitement grew.

At around eleven o'clock he left the house and joined the straggle of people heading up to where the troupe had set-up. There were quite a few families really, and ahead he could see more. The night was clear and bright, and there was a real sense of thrill about the place for once.

The tent was smaller than he had expected. Although travelling like this, with horse and cart, it would be almost impossible to erect anything much larger. Why on earth didn't they use modern vehicles—they'd be able to get a much larger audience, and move around the country more efficiently? It was probably some Arts Council initiative or an attempt to recreate entertainments from the past—living history they called it, didn't they.

There were a few smaller tents gathered around the larger one, and a few stalls selling snacks. The performers seemed to mingle with the rest of the crowd, with little to show them as different, apart perhaps from their youth. Those that Eugene could identify (mainly because he had not seen them about Werrow before) were in their early twenties, maybe even latter teens. They all seemed busy, carrying great armfuls of props and gear around the camp. The whole place was lit with burning lamps staked around the showground and their fuel scented the night air with a sense of work and purpose.

Eugene saw a queue at one of the smaller tents and followed it to peer inside. There was a fortune-teller sat at a table laid with a velvety red cloth, theatrically presenting tarot cards to her client—Mrs Lyle (John's wife), who looked on in awe. The little tent was stuffed with the paraphernalia of the charlatan; crystal balls and mirrors, incense burners and candles. Again the woman playing at divination could have been no more than twenty. She looked up from the cards momentarily and fixed Eugene with her round, brown eyes, 'And this is the three of wands; look for positive change in the near future.'

Clearly the troupe had to supplement their performances somehow, and Eugene thought there was little harm in such useless childish games.

He continued to wander about the few caravans and stalls. More villagers were arriving—almost all of Werrow were here.

One of the snack stalls was a great wooden barrel from which a tall man was winding great sticks of candyfloss. Eugene thought how ingenious it was to conceal the appliance for producing this sickly treat within an old barrel—they certainly worked hard to maintain an authentic 'olde worlde' atmosphere to the show.

Ian Banks, a local policeman, was at the stall with his daughter Emily. Her eyes were wide in fascination as the man whirled the little stick around and produced a great tower of fluffy pink fibres from the barrel. The little girl took her stick of candyfloss and bit into it. She laughed as the sugary strands turned to gooey blobs of red syrup around her mouth and on her nose.

'How do you make it?' she asked the tall man behind the wooden drum.

'Oh, that's very simple, my dear,' he said, bending down to her. 'We weave it from the sweet currents of the air.' And he swirled his hand around her head and produced a green strand of candyfloss from nowhere that fluttered away on the breeze with a flick of his fingers.

Ian Banks laughed as Emily gazed in awe as the candyfloss, delicate as a web, danced into the night sky. It was a wonderful trick and one that any street magician would have been happy to effect—most importantly though, it made Emily joyous.

There was a different atmosphere here—true relaxation and celebration—something Eugene had not experienced in years. Here there was a genuine spirit of joy among the townsfolk, almost as though an enchantment had been cast upon them. It would not surprise him in the least, Eugene thought. These travelling players were so out of place that it almost felt they had stepped from the pages of some fantastical tale—stage magic would surely be the least of their abilities. Eugene chuckled to himself at this silly whimsical thought. But there was something strangely different about them all; as though they were not simply out of *place* but deeply, and profoundly, out of *time*.

Then, the bells of Werrow's little church chimed out midnight across the cold night skies, and on the final chime a trumpet sounded a fanfare from the entrance to the main tent. People hurried over to make their way in, worried in case they should miss the show.

Inside low wooden benches were arrayed on a set of rostra to the left and right of the entrance. At a glance Eugene guessed they might seat about sixty. It would be a tight squeeze. He headed to the left and sat in the centre of the bench on the back row. Once everyone was seated eight of the troupe appeared and passed through the rows exchanging short ticket stubs for a pound from each person. A pound, Eugene thought, how on earth can they make it pay?

Opposite the crowd was the 'stage'—merely an open area of barely trodden grass of about the same size as the audience's benches. It was lit by a few lanterns, of a similar style to those outside. These however had been fitted with back shutters that functioned to cast the light back into the performance space, rather in the manner of old footlights.

A young man entered in a long black tail coat, top hat and great black boots, his face dark with thick lines of heavy make-up. He carried a long cane and strode up to the lights. He must have been nearly seven feet tall and seemed to fill the tiny space.

'Good evening, ladies and gentlemen,' he began. 'I am the *Marvellous Maximilian*, your host for this performance of *Phantasmagoria*.'

There was a ripple of applause, and some cheers from some of the younger children. Clearly the Werrow crowd were eager to join in the fun.

'Without further ado I introduce to you our players for the evening,' Maximilian announced, sweeping his arm towards the curtain behind him. 'The Incredible Troupe of Fantastical Phantasmagoricists.'

The same people that had gathered the money only a minute or two before filed in. Each of the young performers was heralded, in booming fairground voice, by the *Marvellous Maximilian*, their ringmaster; the *Amazing Anna*, the *Great Gary*, the *Incredible Ian*, the *Miraculous Mary*, the *Renowned Rebecca*, the *Splendid Sarah*, the *Tremendous Timothy*, the *Wondrous William*—with an extravagant alliterative adjective accompanying each. The antiquated mode of delivery, and the exaggerated nomenclature, was juxtaposed by the ordinariness of the names and their general attire. Only the *Marvellous Maximilian* sported what might be considered a costume; the rest were dressed quite casually in jeans and jumpers, and other everyday wear.

Then the performance began with immediate and striking effect.

Each of them produced a simple stick from their pockets and proceeded to transform the item into various different forms; now a lit candle, a colourful plastic ball, a rabbit, a series of handkerchiefs—knotted together. It was fairly standard magicians' fare. What was quite remarkable was the real skill that each displayed in their sleight of hand. There appeared to be few places where these other objects might be concealed, and to do the tricks in such close proximity to their audience would surely rely on a variety of ingenious stage contraptions to hide these things—none of which were present.

It was difficult to keep track of what was happening, as objects seemed to proliferate and fill the space. A moment before there would be a wooden bucket from which water was being ladled, turning one's gaze away for an instant, and then returning, one found a rocking chair, or a tin bathtub. Interspersed with these transformations were turns of a more recognisable format, but each involved some manner of change in the objects used. Juggling balls became fire batons, only to be replaced seconds later by eggs that suddenly burst into clouds of red and orange smoke.

The crowd were enthralled. Eugene remained, for a while, more analytical. He guessed that the trick relied on the chaos of the multiple performers—but how could they be sure each member of the audience would be looking away while they effected the swift substitution of the objects? And many of these changes occurred, as in the case with the juggling, in mid-air.

As with many magical illusions, Eugene thought, one is best to give oneself up to it and then attempt to unravel the process later—a true observation of many things.

Occasional 'star turns' were offered, where one or two of the troupe would take centre stage while their colleagues watched. One of these involved the *Great Gary* and *Miraculous Mary*. They carried a small log to the footlights and then stretched what appeared to be a blue silk scarf between them, across the log. Bam! It transformed into a double saw and they set about sawing off chunks of wood. As each fell to the ground it became something else entirely; a thin slice became a gramophone record, a larger one a dinner plate, another a wheelbarrow wheel. Once the sawing had ceased and the log was gone these objects were then thrown about the tent to other performers who each, in turn, transformed them into other things; the wheel became a clockwork toy, the record stretched into a trumpet and the dinner plate became a chicken that then strutted freely about the place for the rest of the show, pecking at the grass.

The final scene saw the *Amazing Anna*, who Eugene recognised as the fortune-teller from earlier, bring on a longbow and stand defiantly before the crowd staring at them.

The oohs and ahhs had given way to a tense silence.
What would she do?

Her fellows each gathered a blade of grass from the ground and brought them to her. And then, with incredible speed she grasped each one, which then sprung into a wooden arrow and loosed them at the crowd. There were terrified shouts as each arrow shot from the bow, but the instant each they set forth towards their target they became sparrows that circled the tent attempting to discover an exit. With the final arrow she paused a moment and levelled her aim at Eugene.

Those wonderful brown eyes.

The arrow was loosed, but did not instantly transform.

It roared across the heads of the crowd, still heading straight for Eugene. The crowd followed its arc with a gasp. Eugene did not move.

Then, only feet from him, it soared into the air—a white dove!

'And that, ladies and gentlemen,' Maximilian roared, 'concludes *Phantasmagoria*. We wish you a safe journey home and every happiness in the future.'

The performers exited through the curtain at the back of the tent, bowing as they went. Some of the audience were on their feet and cheering.

On the trampled grass before them there remained the most surprising array of objects. It looked like the remains of a car boot sale; boots and bags, books and flowers, musical instruments and metal poles. Everything imaginable lay here and there, and above them chattered many birds, eager to find their way out into the freedom of the skies.

The performance had lasted barely half an hour. The audience waited around a few minutes, after they had finished applauding, clearly mesmerised by what they had seen. Then gradually people began to file out in a strange, almost reverent silence.

None of the performers were to be seen, and all the oil lanterns had been extinguished. The only lights were the moon and the bright stars and the few twinkling lights that indicated their village in the distance.

The procession of Werrow villagers headed slowly back home. Many had brought torches with them and it struck Eugene how such lines of people might have snaked across the moorland in times gone by, returning from some ancient ritual to the safety of their coastal homes. There had been no sacrifice, or arcane rite, but something had happened that gave the event a solemn and religious air—a communion of enchantment. For that was what it had been surely, Eugene pondered. It had been an excellent display of conjuring and stage magic—a genuine *entertainment*.

But as they approached the village people began to talk and soon an excited murmur spread through the crowd, as each recounted their favourite moments of the performance, describing in detail how a bird had flown into a cage and emerged as a skein of golden wool; how five bricks thrown into the air had disintegrated into a shower of water droplets, only to fall to the ground and burst into purple smoke.

But each of these moments, described with great eagerness by its teller, produced only confused responses from each listener, who seemed unable to recall those particular feats. So instead they described their own favourites; again, to the incredulity of those listening.

Indeed Eugene, who had been listening to many of these conversations, could not remember a single one of the transformations others recounted. It soon became apparent that the entire village had each seen quite a different performance to that of their fellows.

Eugene turned and made his way back, through the crowd of chattering villagers, towards the camp of the *Phantasmagoria* players. There was much more to this performance than the demonstration of remarkable conjuring skills.

III. Transition from being to becoming

There were still a few of the performers around busy with taking props and lanterns about the small camp. Faint glows illuminated the curtains of most of the caravans and low voices could be heard from them; laughter and the clinking of glasses.

Moving as stealthily as he could (he felt for some reason he should not be there) Eugene made his way about until he came to the small tent where he had seen the fortune-teller. The tall man that had been at the candyfloss wagon emerged from it with a wooden tea chest and headed off to one of the wagons; Eugene ducked back into the shadows.

He heard Maximilian's great booming voice from within—as loud and full as though he were in a show. He was singing '...I know you now, I knew you all along, / I knew you in the dark, but I did it for a lark, / And for that lark you'll pay, for the taking of the donah...'

When he was sure nobody else was about Eugene crept towards the tent and peered inside. There was Maximilian packing the last few items away into a smaller wooden box. These seemed to be the fortune-teller's more delicate props; the crystal ball, the cards, leather-bound books and an animal skull.

Eugene cleared his throat at the opening to the tent, for fear of startling the man.

Maximilian looked up from the box but did not seem too surprised to see him there.

'I am sorry to disturb you, as you and your colleagues are busy packing up,' Eugene said. 'My name is Eugene Miles. I'm a... well, I live here... and... I came to see the show the evening and I wondered if I might take a few moments of your time to discuss something with you?'

'Why certainly, Mr Miles,' the 'marvellous' Maximilian said, pointing to a wooden chair opposite—

The Phantasmagorical Imperative...

one of the few remaining items in the tent. 'Why don't you take a seat and we can have a little conversation.'

The table was still spread with the red cloth he had seen the fortune-teller lay the tarot cards upon. He picked a little nervously at the edges of it, like some naughty child about to confess their crimes to a stern parent.

Maximilian kindly broke the silence.

'Did you enjoy our show?' he asked. 'It is short but packed with marvels, we believe.'

'Oh, it most certainly is,' Eugene said, enthusiastically. 'And it is precisely that I wish to discuss with you.'

'What, its brevity? Have you come to ask for your money back my friend?' Maximilian laughed. It seemed to Eugene that the laugh resonated right through him with a great depth of sound that seemed to billow the tent's canvas.

'Oh, come, come, my friend,' Maximilian said, after his laughter had subsided. 'I am joking with you. There is no need to be nervous. What is it you wish to know?'

'I wondered why you'd chosen the quotation you had, from Kafka, for your advertisement,' he asked. 'It's certainly enticed me along and I just wondered if there was some particular significance you found in the work.'

'I must confess I have never read this book, *Kafka*,' Maximilian replied.

'No, Kafka is the writer, Franz Kafka,' Eugene said. 'The book is *Amerika*, although most people know *The Trial* and *The Castle*.'

'I know nothing of this writer, or his work, I'm afraid,' Maximilian said. 'I am very sorry to disappoint you. Our show is merely *our show* and we have advertised it with this poster for many years.'

'Well, not to worry, it just seemed that the wording was so similar I thought there must be some reason to have used it. It must just be a coincidence,' Eugene said.

'Oh, there are never *just* coincidences, Mr Miles,' he replied. 'I would have hoped our little show went some way to demonstrating that.'

'Your show, yes, certainly...' Eugene stuttered, 'it's quite... quite... remarkable. Such skilled performers—how did you come to assemble so many magicians? I assume it is your troupe.'

'Oh, we aren't magicians,' Maximilian declared.

'Well, conjurors then, whatever the term might be,' Eugene said.

'We aren't conjurors either,' Maximilian said bluntly, drumming his thin fingers on the table.

'Whatever you might call yourselves,' Eugene said, becoming a little irritated. 'I wonder how you might explain the fact that all the locals are now returning home with quite different accounts of what happened here tonight. I'd call that rather odd wouldn't you?'

'Not at all,' Maximilian said. 'That's perfectly natural when we initiate the sort of transformation you have seen tonight. Many people have quite varied reactions—let us remember that sight is also a product of the iridescence of materials; as things bend and reform there is naturally some difference in the reception of the event in any given number of observers.'

Eugene hadn't the slightest idea what the man was talking about.

'Let me show you again,' Maximilian said, producing the crystal ball from the box. He spun it about in his hands and then it disappeared. He produced it again a few seconds later from beneath his top hat. 'That is stage magic, my friend. It is nothing particularly impressive—merely agile fingers and suitable gullibility on the part of one's audience, if you'll pardon the phrase. But it is not this you have come to see is it?'

Eugene shook his head.

Maximilian flicked the polished ball across the table. It rolled towards Eugene over the rich red cloth, spinning little refracted images of himself and Maximilian as it did so. And then it vanished again.

Eugene looked up in astonishment—that was no sleight of hand, he wasn't even touching it.

Maximilian stared back at him intently and said, slowly and softly, 'Look again.'

He duly did.

There, scuttling across the velvety table-top was a woodlouse—heading on the same trajectory the ball had been travelling along.

'Why that's ridiculous,' he stated firmly, folding his arms with a childish shrug.

'No, it is far from ridiculous,' Maximilian said, mirroring Eugene's aggression. 'It is simply the truth.'

'But, these are just parlour games,' Eugene said defiantly. 'You don't expect me to believe that you just transformed a crystal ball into a little bug before my eyes do you? This is just a good trick—and I must congratulate you there, one of the finest I've ever seen—but a trick nonetheless.'

'Oh, I don't *expect* you to *believe* anything,' Maximilian replied, placing his hands flat upon the table. 'I'm not some little god, asking for your faith and offering you no evidence. This thing I have shown you is nothing magical or mystical. I do not want to see you dressed in ludicrous robes and chanting to the congregation. This is simply *the world*—its *form*!'

Eugene stared at him. His entire outfit—the hat, the tails, the cane, the heavy make-up—said 'this man is tricking you' and yet his voice and eyes spoke only of the truth.

'Repeat the trick then,' Eugene said.

'I can demonstrate the *event* again, certainly,' Maximilian said somewhat despondently. 'But I must assure you, it is no *trick*.'

'Repeat the *event*, then,' Eugene said, 'but *this time* under *my* conditions.'

He realised this last remark sounded quite sharp, even insulting. There was a pause during which Maximilian glared at him, clearly irritated.

And then he laughed again.

'Certainly, my sceptical friend... would you like me chained up... in a great tank of water... or something like that?' Maximilian said, spluttering the words out between great giggling breaths. 'Or perhaps a glamorous assistant might be able to hold me down... no, no, she could pass a metal hoop around me... to show there are no wires. I will call for Anna—the one you like—shall I?'

And the laughing went on, and on, until it seemed that the very seconds were even mocking Eugene as they transformed themselves to minutes.

The Phantasmagorical Imperative...

'I have a better idea,' Maximilian said finally. 'You shall do it yourself. Pass me the little creature.'

Eugene brushed the woodlouse into his palm and passed it over to Maximilian. It had curled into a little ball.

Maximilian rolled the woodlouse back and forth in his palm until it suddenly sprang back into the crystal ball. He passed it back to Eugene, whose expression was as amazed as it was suspicious.

'Now you do it,' Maximilian said.

Eugene held his hand out and concentrated on woodlice. How absurd, he thought, without even some instruction in how to perform the trick, here he was attempting to turn a block of glass into a living creature.

'It must be in motion,' Maximilian said. 'Move your hand slightly so that the ball begins to rock back and forth a little.'

Eugene did as he was instructed. The crystal ball rolled awkwardly back and forth across his palm.

'Now focus on nothing at all,' Maximilian said. 'You must allow nothing to interfere with the simple function of materials—with the endless flow of objects.'

As Eugene attempted to clear his mind it seemed as though his own memories were vanishing. He struggled to remember his father's features or his mother's voice. The table before them and even the tent seemed to take on a strange quality. The village of Werrow and the Cornish coast fell into a vast white emptiness that billowed in great gusts. His entire consciousness dissolved and reformed in moments.

The crystal ball collapsed into a heap of dry sand; the grains spilling through his fingers in a delicate trickle.

Eugene sat there shaking, with the horror and bliss of the initiate.

'I repeat—this is *simply* the *form* of the *world*,' Maximilian said, wearily.

Eugene was tired and incapable of fully comprehending what had happened to him.

'You are trying—I see it now!—you are trying to tempt me,' Eugene said defensively, standing up from the table and shaking the last grains of sand from his hand. 'There is something diabolic about *this*... something dark... *unwholesome*... I do not have the words for it...'

Maximilian smiled back sadly.

'I am not a religious man—well, not previously,' Eugene continued. 'But what I have seen here this evening I am prepared to believe. And I use that word again—*believe*. I have seen it with my own eyes—I have felt it—and I *believe*. But, *in* it—and *from* it—I can find nothing *good*.'

'Really, my friend, have you heard nothing I have been saying?' Maximilian said. 'There are no gods or devils, angels or demons, simply the things of the world and their beautiful, endless interdependence—their eternal flow and mutability. There is nothing terrible in that, surely? If you consider the collapse of the corpse into its chemical components—that is certainly a horrible image for those obsessed with base materiality, even for many of those with their eyes set on eternal life—recall the horror of the dissection table; a *fate worse than death*! But, for those of us of a more *mature* and, I might hope, *theatrical* disposition we might even consider it beautiful, no?'

'*Beauty*,' Eugene said, 'is that all you are seeking?'

'Oh, far from it,' he replied, 'far, far from it. But I see our conversation is in danger of spiralling into useless repetition. You are capable now of finding the subtle rhythm of the world; and that is enough—use it as you will.'

He stood and pushed the plush drapes of the tent aside. A cold wind rushed in stirring the red tablecloth around Eugene's knees. He thought he glimpsed delicate tendrils of flame at its edges—perhaps even the elements were in transition.

'I see my people are almost done packing up our show,' Maximilian said despondently. 'They will need to collapse this tent now and then we will be on our way before that storm comes in from the sea.'

Eugene rose and made his way out into the chill night, with its clear sky and bright stars—each twinkling now with incredible possibilities that he dare not believe.

'Well, I thank you for your time, and for your wonderful performance earlier,' Eugene said, offering his hand. 'I must say it was remarkable... truly remarkable.'

Maximilian shook his hand and looked long into his eyes.

'Oh no, sir,' he said. 'I can assure you—it was nothing, *nothing* at all.'

And with that he turned sharply, his tailcoat sweeping theatrically about him, and went back into the tent.

A number of the players were stood about with hammers and poles, taking to pieces the final sections of the camp and loading them onto the wagons.

Eugene surveyed the scene one last time, hoping for another glimpse of the 'amazing' Anna. But she was nowhere to be seen.

He pulled his coat tighter about him, against the increasing chill wind and headed back into Werrow, musing on the truth of what he had witnessed.

∞

Back at home he did not even try to go to sleep. It was nearly 3 o'clock in the morning and he decided it would be good to allow the night's events to percolate through his mind a little whilst reading. He would watch the sun rise—something he always loved to do.

He sat there in a tattered leather chair with an old book in his hand, a volume of *The Great War* by Churchill, but he was not really paying attention. As the peculiar transformation of the crystal ball came to mind his thoughts began to slide into that tumultuous whiteness, as though his brain were being wrapped in cotton wool. Suddenly the red leather of the book in his hands began to ripple and before his eyes the book flourished into a great bouquet of flowers; roses and lilies, tulips and carnations, interspersed with little clumps of gypsophila.

The real night had begun; and what an incredible night it was.

Eugene Miles' home was alight with the hidden laws of the universe. The books were some of the first to be transformed; their dull and dusty pages blossomed into flowers, cacti, shrubs and small trees. As he became more confident Eugene grasped the manner in which multiple phases of alteration could be effected at once; a full set of Dickens became a kaleidoscope of butterflies—their majestic reds, blues and yellows enlivening the rooms of his house with the first true life they had seen in years. The windows crackled with the electric energy of his new-found abilities. Everything was being remade, and each form begat other forms; animals desiccated into minerals before his eyes, saucepans became hummingbirds, water evaporated into spices and the wallpapers dripped into puddles of oil that then exploded in pillars of flame.

At the height of his celebrations Eugene stared out across the thrashing waves—the storm was in and raging—and imagined the players of the *Phantasmagoria* troupe driving their painted caravans and wagons, filled with wonders, across the damp moor and into forever. And with that Eugene Miles burst into a great cloud of thick frankincense smoke and was never seen again.

The chaos they found in Eugene Miles' house when they finally discovered him missing was not unexpected; bookish people, especially those with eccentricities and volatile behaviours, have a habit of attracting webs of mythologies even in the largest of communities. And Werrow was a small and very ancient place that, despite its televisions and wifi cafes, its mobile phone masts and offshore windfarms, seeped history into the very air, and wove fables with the roots of every grass that grew there. So they were not disturbed to find strange objects in every room, even small trees and oversized cacti in the kitchen, piles of ash and corroded iron in the bath, or most of the books missing from the shelves—this was merely evidence of a mind unfettered by everyday concerns, and one unused to a life lived in the locale from birth to death, surrounded by a supportive family. These were the marks of an unhealthy self-absorption and a fascination with other forms of knowledge best left well alone.

What was odd though, and everyone remarked upon it, were the butterflies, of every hue, that were found beating themselves against the windows for release—and these in the middle of February. And then there was the smell that pervaded the house—a rich and foreign fragrance, like the spicy fug of an Eastern bazaar or the zesty air of a European forest.

∞

This little tale, despite its languid self-indulgence, has only ever been in the imperative. So when you next kick a stone carelessly, or wish those brown leaves of autumn were green again, recall the magic of those players who conjure fantasy from the most ordinary of things. And remember too that one is compelled to act in ways that fashion the incredible. For it is only through dream that we relieve the burden of existence. Each work of imagination wills this world afresh and gifts the future mystery—rendering the simplest of stones metaphysical, endowing the most common event with a powerful, unique sonority that echoes through all things; a relentless, universal law.

Laudate Dominum
(for many voices)

> '*How* things are in the world is a matter of complete indifference for what is higher. God does not reveal himself *in* the world.'
> Ludwig Wittgenstein, *Tractatus Logico-Philosophicus*

Sitting on a bench, on the outer harbour wall, wrapped in a wintery coat—despite the encouraging sun of a late March afternoon—we find Stephen Walker. He is eating an egg mayonnaise sandwich and drinking from a flask of tea, both prepared that morning in his holiday cottage in the seaside village of Polperro. He has just returned from today's walk, this time along the nine miles of coastal path to Fowey, and back again. Holidaying, for Stephen Walker, was less a relaxation than a demonstration of vitality.

His demeanour might once have been termed—some years ago now—curmudgeonly. Today he might, more straightforwardly, be described as a 'grumpy old man', now that such nomenclature is popular, and always assigned with mocking affection. Of course the fault for this miserable attitude lay not with him, but rather with everyone else. As he was fond of telling anyone who would listen, the problem with today's youth was the lack of military service. Despite having served only three months in the Ordnance corps, before being invalided out (a detail always omitted in the retelling), it had, apparently, been 'the making of him.' Young people today had no *stamina*, no *will*, and no *backbone*.

It was no surprise then to find him holidaying alone in Cornwall, a place that had been dear to him for many years, mostly for its seclusion (if you chose the right places) and beautiful coastal walks. He would visit most years in late March, to take advantage of the last few weeks before the place hummed with tourists and their children, dogs and ice creams.

Whenever visiting Polperro, and when the place was available, he liked to hire a small cottage at the end of The Warren that Oscar Kokoschka had spent time in during the war, painting the outer harbour repeatedly. As an amateur oil painter himself Stephen Walker liked to feel that a little genius might rub off on him by inhabiting the dwelling of one of his favourite artists.

Painting and walking; two wonderful pursuits, balancing the equal requirements of every human being: quiet, contemplative creativity and vigorous, outdoor exercise.

Whilst he was naturally frugal he was certainly not mean. He was, *how do they say it*, careful. His savings from lunch would then contribute towards that evening's treats; real ale, crab salad, and sticky toffee pudding and custard, at The Blue Peter. This was a small inn only a few feet away from him, and a place he always enjoyed spending a couple of evenings at during his holiday.

You can imagine him though, there at one of the larger window seats, begrudging sharing his table with a young family that have nowhere else to sit; the children staring up at the curious man uneasily, their dog occasionally nuzzling at his crotch.

To avoid unwanted small talk he takes a leaflet from one of those racks advertising local attractions and unfolds it across the table so that he should not be interrupted during his meal.

'The Looe Valley line.'

His eyes are drawn to a picture on the inside flap, of a small well, rather mossy and overgrown—'St Keyne wishing well,' read the caption, with an arrow pointing to one of the stops on the railway line. There were a couple of stanzas of poetry beneath that, by Robert Southey, the second mentioned that the well was surrounded by an oak, an ash, an elm and a willow tree. Apparently, the leaflet went on, 'Whichever of a married couple drinks first from the well, they will "wear the trousers." So, hurry, lest your spouse beats you to it!' Despite this folklore nonsense it sounded intriguing. Also, the leaflet proclaimed, 'On your way back from the well why not visit The Mechanical Music Museum, where you will find all manner of music playing devices from yesteryear!'

It was rare that Stephen Walker was interested in anything of the kind, believing that most of them were aimed at extorting money from gullible parents through the relentless, imploring nagging of their children. Such as those sat opposite him now, slurping their cheap cola through bendy straws, and squabbling over their crisps. But, he was certain, there would be few children desperate to go to this museum; they were not interested in the magic of yesteryear's innovations, the spirit of the craftsman and the skill of the mechanic.

He would visit the museum the very next morning, he resolved. He drained the rest of his beer and headed back to the cottage, planning his day.

First, a brisk walk along the coastal path to Looe—he would have completed the five miles of it before most of the nation's adolescents were awake, he chuckled. And he would then be on the train to visit the St Keyne wishing well, then take in the museum on his way back, before continuing to Liskeard to round the day off.

∞

The walk went to plan, although the steep paths and cliffs to Looe, especially around Talland Bay, seemed to take their toll on him more this time than when he had last walked them a few years previously. He had over an hour to kill before the train at 10:32. He browsed around some shops, but didn't buy anything.

The train was on time, and he enjoyed the restful juddering of the carriage as it made its gentle way through some splendid scenery. The ticket inspector had informed him that St Keyne was a 'request' stop and he would let the driver know. If only all train services these days had such courteous and helpful staff, Stephen Walker mused.

He alighted on a deserted platform, with newly painted white picket fencing, with a quaint passenger shelter. He could almost be back in the 1950s he thought, even though for the most part, he already was.

He checked his watch. 10:50. He had over two hours before the next train at 12:59 that would take him on for the afternoon to Liskeard. This should be plenty of time to find the well and then return to explore the museum.

He headed off up the steep lane into the village of St Keyne, eager to find this beautiful little wishing well. Who knows, he thought, even this late in life I might find a wife, and if so I'll have one up on her by having drunk at it first. He laughed quietly, at the improbability of either event.

The well proved elusive though. The little map on his leaflet did not appear to scale and he found himself trekking across some muddy fields, looking this way and that, without any idea of where he was. He headed back to the main road and back down the steep, narrow lane, towards the railway station.

Then he spotted—just where the steep lane joined the larger road at the top of the village—a signpost, mostly covered by low hanging branches. In his eagerness to rush on he must have missed it.

It did not prove particularly informative though. One side pointed north, saying 'St Keyne Wishing Well,' and the other, pointing south, read exactly the same. Some local was clearly having a joke on the tourists. Stephen Walker did not really consider himself a tourist and was not amused.

He consulted his watch. 12:30. That damned wishing well really had taken some time up. He needed to get to the museum before the train arrived at 12:59.

Then the thought struck him, he could catch a later one. Why waste the opportunity to enjoy the musical machines when he could catch the *next* train to Liskeard.

He filled a pipe—a little luxury he allowed himself only when out walking—and consulted the timetable again. It would have to be the 14:30. Oh well, why not take things easy, and with a little shrug of the shoulders he ambled down the lane to visit the museum.

Had he looked a little further behind the signpost he would have seen a set of greenish crumbling steps leading down to the wishing well. There were no longer any trees beside it, if ever there had been. And whether it was a magical well or not would have to remain a mystery. All that was forgotten now; Stephen Walker had set a new itinerary.

As he took slow puffs on the pipe he found himself humming a little tune, as the museum came into view. This was most unusual as he did not approve of humming. Still, it didn't hurt did it, out here where there was nobody to hear him. It showed that he was taking full advantage of his leisure time.

The sign for the 'Mechanical Music Museum' pointed to a large industrial building with corrugated roof that lay behind a cottage. Some steep steps led down to them both and Stephen surmised the owner of the museum must also live in the cottage. As he tapped his pipe out on the wall at the top of the steps he heard a wonderful chorus of song coming from the museum. It sounded like a choir rehearsing. He listened a while. He was not sure what the hymn was, but it was delightful, and he spent a minute or two enjoying it.

The choir finished the hymn as he got to the bottom of the steps. Stephen was relieved as he hadn't wanted to interrupt their practice; perhaps they shared the building with the museum.

He poked his head through the door, even though the sign read 'closed.' The building might even have been a warehouse once, so vast was the space inside. At the far end there were great red curtains that gave the place the feel of a village hall, sometimes used for local am-dram performances no doubt. All about the perimeter of the building were varying musical devices, maybe a dozen or so, ranging in size from small gramophones to larger organs.

There was a tall man, maybe in his early sixties, standing some distance away. He was dressed in scruffy work clothes and seemed quite busy. But there was certainly no choir. It must have been a recording, Stephen thought, even though it had been quite loud.

The tall man spotted him and shook his head apologetically.

"Oh, I'm sorry, sir," the man said, depositing a handful of wooden blocks onto a workbench. "We don't open to visitors until April. It takes so much to maintain all of these machines that I have to use all of the winter months to keep them in pristine condition."

"Ah, I see . . ." Stephen began.

"I'm working flat out on these dampers as it is," he interrupted, gesturing to the blocks and a scattering of felt and leather patches strewn across the bench.

"Oh dear," Stephen said, "how disappointing. I had hoped so much to see the place before I leave for home in a few days. I recall my grandfather had a music machine in the living room; it played great metal disks, and even had a clock in it too."

"An old upright, eh!" the man said, his eyes bright and his face suddenly interested, as though a little switch had been flicked somewhere inside him. "It will have been a Polyphon, no doubt, or maybe even a rare Symphonion."

"That was *it*!" Stephen said, the name suddenly bringing back his grandfather's pronunciation of it. "Sym-*phon*-ion! He'd always say, after we'd had some lunch, 'Shall we have a few tunes from *Mr Sym*phon*ion*.' And my sister and I would be delighted. The *Symphionion*—well I never . . ."

"Might I ask, sir, do you sing?" the man said, rather incongruously.

Stephen Walker was perplexed. "Do I *sing*?"

"Yes," the man said, as though his sudden change of topic were entirely appropriate. "Do you belong to a choir? Do you *sing*?"

"Er, no, well, I mean, not for many years now, not since I was a child," Stephen replied, feeling rather badgered by a certain school-masterly tone the man had adopted.

"I was particularly struck by the quality of your voice, you see," the man continued, heading over to him. "It has depth, and richness. But is that tobacco I smell? It would be a shame to spoil such a wonderful voice with the *evil weed* now wouldn't it."

"I've just had a pipe, as a matter of fact, on my way down from the wishing well—a wishing well that I couldn't damned well find," Stephen said, defensively. "But I don't really see what business my smoking habits are . . ."

"No doubt the Connor boys have been playing with the well signposts again," the man interrupted, offering his hand in greeting. "I'm Philip Morin, owner, restorer and guide here at the Mechanical Music Museum."

"I'm Mr Walker, Stephen Walker," he replied, shaking Philip's hand timidly, without having shaken the sense of being rather admonished.

"Let me show you around then, Mr Walker," Philip said (the issue of being closed for the season apparently having been entirely forgotten).

"My own grandfather was an actor, I come from a long line of performers," he said, going over to a small, dark wooden box. "This is one of the earliest machines I have, and one of great sentimental value." Philip seemed a connoisseur of the non-sequitur.

He cranked a handle a few times and opened the lid. What looked like a black wax cylinder was spinning inside. From underneath the table he produced a large metal horn, fluted and almost shell-like. He attached the horn to a pivot arm and rested the base of it, housing a large needle, on the thick cylinder.

An eerie noise came out, mostly a great cloud of static and white noise, but in the background one could just make out a voice, but not the words.

"This is my grandfather," he said, proudly, "reading Dickens' *Christmas Carol* in 1896."

Stephen was still unable to make out the words. All he could discern was a strange echoing of the sentences going on within the machine.

"It takes a while to warm up," Philip said, "like any voice really."

He angled a lamp down close to the cylinder, to warm it. "Perhaps we can try that one again later when the old man's back in tune."

Then, the sound seemed to clarify and there was a

great laugh from the reader, Philip's grandfather, followed by a peal of bells—Scrooge on Christmas morning, without a doubt!

"Marvellous," Stephen exclaimed.

"Yes, it is rather, isn't it," Philip said. "This voice, my ancestor's, brought to life here for us, one hundred years later. For all of its terrible crimes there are also some miraculous things achieved through technology."

"Yes, it really must have been magical to hear the human voice reproduced through a machine in that fashion, for the first time," Stephen said.

"Indeed," Philip replied. "But what of the instruments that *played themselves*, they would have been no less incredible."

He led Stephen over to a fairly ordinary looking upright black piano. In the centre of it, where the music stand would have been, there were two horizontal bars, onto which Philip locked a long roll of thick punched paper. It looked a bit like the paper cards he had used many years before in the computer room at the post office, where he had worked briefly as an apprentice.

Having threaded the roll Philip then set about dismantling the front of the machine so that they could get a good look at the mechanism.

"Now this one was made by an incredible craftsman," Philip began. "Ernst Steget of Berlin. He engineered the pianos, but he couldn't produce the musical rolls. This had to be done by another craftsman, Giovanni Galuppo, down the road from him. However, Steget was fond of a schnapps, or two, in the local bar of an evening."

They both laughed, in the conspiratorial fashion that

late middle-aged men do when issues of alcohol surface—such false bonhomie; beneath the forced laughter only half-remembered conquests that were never really conquered, opportunities squandered by a loose tongue, loved ones slighted and friends abused.

"Sadly, his love of the schnapps resulted in the gradual dwindling of his business and eventually he became so indebted to Galuppo that he had to go and work for him to pay it all off," Philip continued. "Such is the way of the world I'm afraid, when one's bounty and talents are squandered on *vice*."

Stephen didn't like the tone of that last remark, aimed—as it clearly was—at his own indulgence in a pipe or two. But he did not have time to dwell upon the slight, if such it was, as the piano suddenly erupted into sound and motion. The keys danced beneath invisible fingers and the inside of the machine was feverish with the work of pulleys and wheels, valves, bellows and levers, all animated by the little blank squares on the paper roll as it slid through the instrument like a great white tongue.

"What use the pianist, eh?" Stephen joked.

"Oh, we still have our uses, Mr Walker, with the right instrument," Philip retorted, rather viciously, Stephen felt.

Then a shrill electronic ring called out from the workbench, crashing the world back into the present. Philip went over to answer a cordless telephone and then called out. "It's my wife, there's a delivery for me. I'll be back in a moment. I'll bring some tea too, enjoy the rest of the tune!"

Stephen smiled and nodded. The piano was playing away and he felt rather nostalgic for the music his parents would entertain him with on the record player when he was a boy. His father loved the old music hall ones, and the spoken word records. The hours they would spend together on a Sunday listening to Flanders and Swann, or old Henry Hall and the BBC orchestra on scratchy 78s.

The paper was still rolling around as Philip returned with a tray laden with cups, saucers, milk jug and a great steaming pot of tea. There was also a plate of biscuits, enough to service an AGM of the Women's Institute, Stephen thought.

"Doris thought you might be a bit peckish, so she put out some biscuits," Philip said, carefully balancing the crammed tray on a little stool beside a low chair with rather grubby paisley upholstery. "It's Earl Grey, I hope that's ok."

Stephen smiled and nodded.

"I thought you were an Earl Grey chap," Philip said. "I didn't know if you took it with milk or lemon, so there's both."

"Oh, milk for me please," Stephen said, his knees bending a little to the tune still tinkling from the piano.

"I thought so, milk it is, do help yourself," Philip said. "I hope you don't mind, I must help this driver with some items I've had shipped over. I shan't be a moment. You carry on, there's a good few minutes left on that reel, I'm sure you won't be bored."

"Oh, most certainly not," Stephen replied. For the first time in many years—despite Philip's frosty undercurrents—he felt he had discovered a kindred spirit.

He must have listened to the piano for too long, carried back to hedonistic Weimar, for when he poured himself a cup of tea it tasted a little odd, rather sour. Stewed probably. That, or the milk was off. He gave the little jug a sniff. Yes, it was the milk. Never mind, he needed a little refreshment now, as it might be some time before he got to Liskeard and found a tearoom. What was it mother used to say—a few germs won't kill you! He poured himself another cup and as the last few notes on the piano tinkled out, and the scroll of paper unravelled its last coded dots, he looked about the expansive building.

As he had noted on his arrival the place was by no means full of instruments. Each had its own particular space. Some were small, like the little wax cylinder player he had heard Philip's grandfather reading Dickens upon; some larger, such as the piano from Berlin in the 20s. There were some larger organs on the other side of the room, one near the large curtain across the back wall. This seemed much like the kind of grand Wurlitzer organs he'd seen as a child, both in the theatre and at the fairs. It would be wonderful to hear Philip play that when he returned. Behind that though, and rather oddly positioned, was something more individual. It looked like quite a small organ, and Stephen thought it may have been uniquely crafted, so unusual was its construction. There seemed to be no ornate element to it, all was pure function. The panelling had obviously been crafted from a variety of different woods, each giving their particular rich colour to the overall piecemeal effect. And, from where he was standing, he could see no discernible maker's plate.

Finishing his second tea in a swift gulp, Stephen walked over and inspected it cautiously. As he had first

The Phantasmagorical Imperative...

thought, there seemed to be no maker's mark (emblazoned proudly upon all the other machines) and none of the keys, or mechanical dials and knobs had any lettering, or numbers upon them, as was common on the other models. Perhaps this was in the first stages of restoration he thought, running a hand along its well-polished, although awkwardly constructed, wooden frame.

He thought he heard a noise then, from within it; a sort of escape of air. Perhaps a valve or piston decompressing.

It quite startled him, and he jumped a little.

Shh. Shh. It came again, twice, but sounded so like someone shushing a crowd to be quiet before a performance began that he didn't know what to make of it.

He looked around to check that Philip hadn't come back yet from unloading the delivery van. He didn't want to look a fool, and didn't want to be noticed touching something that was probably delicate and very expensive.

But, he just couldn't help himself.

He pressed one of the keys.

From the back of the instrument there came a voice—*lah*!

There could be no mistaking it; this was the sound of a *human voice*, singing a note. Stephen was intrigued, and a little disturbed. This latter sentiment did not prevent him from trying again though. He pressed the same key, and another one from nearer the other end of the board. A soprano voice sang out, at the same time as an alto joined in. But they did not sound recorded, it seemed as though the singers stood right beside him.

He shivered a little, but determined that it must be due to the cold of the airy industrial building. It was not particularly cold that day, and besides Philip had turned the storage heaters on only the week before and they were pumping dry, warm air around the building to fend off any chill.

Despite his fear, Stephen shuffled cautiously around the back of the machine to find where the 'voices' were coming from. There was a wooden grill at the back, rather like an old speaker. A faint draught was coming from it, and upon that delicate air there wafted an odd, meaty scent, as of cured European sausages.

He noticed that above the speaker there was a panel of some sort, made of long timbers of what could only be olive wood; their swirling grains and strange knots had been lovingly jointed together and finished with a little latch of leather and a bone toggle. This gave a strangely archaic feel to the instrument. Yet, all of this did not dissuade Stephen Walker from loosening the cord and carefully easing the panel down.

At first he thought they were the chicks of large birds, all arrayed on wooden plinths, calling, silently, for food. So bizarre was the thing before him that it took a moment for his mind to fully comprehend what he was witnessing.

These were the organ pipes, and each an *organ*, of sorts.

There were about twenty large wooden tubes, rather like inverted didgeridoos, in three rows of varying height. Each was crafted from a different wood and atop many of them there was stretched a thin, pulsating blob of organic tissue, with an oval opening across the top of the tube. There were five blank pipes.

Each fleshy aperture slowly opened and closed, like a gaping raw mouth, and dripped a clear fluid down the pipe which collected in metal trays below, in which there rested a number of short sticks, each wrapped with swabs of cloth soaked in this thick liquid.

The smell was foul, but in the face of such horror that was the least arresting detail.

Stephen Walker was appalled. Yet he could not shake off a perverse desire to touch one of these things; to run his finger across it—there was something sadly familiar about their monstrosity. Almost against his will his hand reached slowly forward.

Then a voice echoed across the cavernous space.

It was Philip, returned from his delivery.

"How you getting on in here?" he called, merrily, wiping his oily hands with a rag.

As surreptitiously as he could, and with a terror welling within him, Stephen Walker slid the wooden panel back into place and carefully fastened the toggle, as Philip approached him, smiling his cheery smile.

"I was just, erm, admiring the woodwork on this one," Stephen said, shakily. He felt rather dizzy all of a sudden, hot and flustered. "It's very . . . beautiful . . ."

"Oh, that's a little pet project of mine," Philip said, making his way over to the larger Wurlitzer organ. "I'm afraid it isn't in full working order at the moment so I can't play you a tune on it yet; maybe one day, when I get the time to finish it."

Stephen felt sick, claustrophobic and terrified. He was nervous that if he even made an attempt to move he would faint.

"This little beauty is my pride and joy," Philip began, seating himself at the controls of the vast organ; controls that looked more like a spacecraft than a musical instrument.

Philip flicked a switch and the huge red curtains at the back of the building rolled back to reveal an array of shiny metal pipes, row upon row of them.

Stephen Walker could think of nothing but the fleshy, gaping wounds calling out silently in the contraption behind him.

"Now, Mr Walker," Philip shouted out. "Give it your best voice. I'll keep it simple, don't you worry."

A great flare of sound assailed Stephen from the rows of pipes.

Roll out the barrel! What a ridiculous song to hear only moments after having made his horrifying discovery. Stephen just managed to stop himself vomiting.

"Come on," shouted Philip, his upper body rocking about like some demented toy. "Join in! *We'll have a barrel of fun . . .*"

Stephen mumbled a few words in an attempt to show willing, "*We've got the blues on the run.*"

"Oh, *Mr Walker*, give it some *oomph!*" Philip cried, clearly getting irritated.

Stephen Walker gave in. His head was spinning and the whole place began to look blurry and distorted. He tried to turn the insanity of the situation to his advantage—to get a bit of courage up.

"*Ring out a song of good cheer,*" Stephen belted out. Quite where the spirit came from to sing in such an absurd situation he didn't know. "*Now's the time to roll the barrel, for the gang's all here . . .*"

"Now *that's* what I'm talking about, *Stephen*," Philip said, ceasing his playing.

It was the first time he had addressed Stephen Walker by his Christian name and something in the intonation was sinister and threatening. "What a beautiful baritone you have there, *Stephen*; real quality, and something we're sorely lacking here in our little choir."

It may have been the blast of noise, or his own singing, or even Philip's ominous tone, that had disoriented him, but Stephen Walker felt most peculiar.

He staggered a little and slumped in the paisley chair to get his strength back, strength he would need if he were to get away from this crazy man. The seat was weak though and the bottom gave way. He crumpled into it like a rag doll, arms and legs at ridiculous angles. He hadn't the energy left to correct his posture; his arms felt numb, his legs useless. His eyelids were heavy, and his mouth dry. He just sat there as everything around him became hazier, and darker, imploring Philip to help him with lips that merely twitched rather than pronouncing words.

Philip sat down opposite him, getting blurrier by the moment. He poured himself a cup of Earl Grey, dropping a slice of lemon into it with a sad chuckle.

"I always take it with lemon, and *plenty* of sugar," he said, sniffing at the milk jug, "besides the milk is always a bit funny at this time of year, I find."

Stephen made one last effort to get up. He succeeded only in knocking the chair into the little stool sending the tray crashing to the concrete floor.

The teapot, jug, cup and saucer all shattered.

"Oh, never mind," Philip said, "Doris has plenty of spares. It's worth it anyway; you don't know how hard it is to get people to join the choir out here. Trust me, I'll be able to take much better care of that voice than you have.

"I hope you understand, *Stephen.*

"What is it the good book says, *I will sing with the spirit, and I will sing with the understanding also*. It is best this way; your gifts will be most *cherished*—dutifully *maintained*."

Stephen couldn't speak.

He couldn't move.

∞

As the lights dimmed in Stephen Walker's eyes Philip Morin took up his seat at the other, primitive, grotesque organ, looking every bit the maestro. And as he played the building filled with strange, lonely voices; exultant in mechanical agony, rapturous in automatic praise. Their beautiful, tortured song carried across the fields to fall upon the ears of the grazing cattle and sheep, and was drowned only momentarily by the 15:41 from Liskeard to Looe, filled with schoolchildren returning home, eager to forget their last class of the day—Religious Education. It did not stop at St Keyne, for nobody was waiting on the platform, and few ever alighted there.

By Nature's Power Enshrined

Albert and Isabelle were of differing opinion on the suitability of the rooms at 46 Week Street, Maidstone, as a photographic studio. They had previously served as a coal merchant's offices. It was certainly spacious enough, especially the main room, but Isabelle thought it lacked light and that the flight of stairs leading to the first floor might put people off who would have come into an establishment located on the ground floor, especially on the High street; through a conventional shop window they might be able to look in and see her husband at work. For Albert though it was perfect, far from poor light he thought the windows perfectly suited to produce the many different environments that modern sitters wanted for their cards, which had now become a vogue throughout Europe. The second floor rooms (three small ones, with a little stove in one) would be perfect for their dwelling area, and there was a spacious room to the side of what would serve as his studio that would function as his chemical store, darkroom, and office. It had the tallest windows in the whole building and these could easily be screened to provide an area where the glass negatives could be applied to the albumen prints and then allowed to develop in the sun. And, it overlooked the railway station. In time, Albert was convinced, photography would become so popular, and commonplace, that people would walk in for a sitting as easily as they might alight from a train. Yes, all round this was the perfect place for his new business and he signed the lease without discussing it further with Isabelle.

The couple had been married four years previously, on the same day in February that their queen celebrated her twentieth year with Prince Albert, and Isabelle often referred to her husband affectionately as 'my own dear Prince'. Within weeks Isabelle was pregnant with their first child, Roseanna, who was born into such a dreadful winter that few thought she would survive, especially as the small garret that housed the family was wretchedly cold and damp. It was all that Albert, struggling to make a name for himself in the artistic community in Kent, could afford though. But what they lacked in luxury they made up for with love. But love does not put coal in the stove. A couple of miserable years followed, and with the announcement that Isabelle was pregnant again Albert resolved that he should rise to his responsibilities, put aside his dreams of painting, and instead embrace the growing popularity of photography. With the development of new techniques, multi-lens cameras, and methods of printing onto paper, photographic records of family, friends and even pets, were becoming within the affordable reach of many. Albert, and his family, must be on the rise of this bubble of entrepreneurial endeavour, before it burst. So by the time their second child, Beatrice, arrived, they were looking for suitable premises for the studio, with the hope of beginning a new life. And this move, from Canterbury to Maidstone, would also release them from the intrusive and judgemental gaze of their parents. The time had come for Albert to realise his destiny.

∞

After the excited preparations; the purchase of the camera equipment and the chemicals, the procurement of desks, chairs, curtains, candlesticks, books and other paraphernalia for the props his sitters would want for their photographs, there was the nervous wait for clients. He had taken out advertisements in the paper and also sent a boy round delivering leaflets to the areas of town with growing wealth and fashionable tastes. They need not have worried. Soon the bookings were coming in faster than Albert could manage them. With the swiftness of the new photographic techniques he could have finished cards sent to people's homes late the very same day. More and more people came, and not just the more well to do. Mostly they were for visiting cards, and his customers often had very specific, and peculiar requests for properties, and even animals to appear with them in their photographs. One afternoon he'd had to hire some help from the baggage handlers at the station to assist in lifting a twenty foot tall crescent moon up the stairs so that a troupe of acrobats could be taken draped about it. And one morning a man had arrived with three lion cubs that he wanted photographed against a jungle backdrop that he had painted himself. Certainly Albert's name was getting known and the size of his studio offered many possibilities to sitters to aggrandise their humble backgrounds.

It was an unusually bright morning in November when his first upsetting sitter arrived. It was a Mrs Seddle, who arrived with her daughter Gladys, and her son Raymond. The latter was a young lad of about ten years old, dressed in an uncomfortable green velvet suit, with a curly white collar. He was clearly very unwell, with a high fever, and it was as much as they could all do to keep him from fainting under the paraffin lamps that Albert used to light his sitters. They could only achieve one picture before Raymond and his fussing Mother and sister whisked him away in a cab, asking for the printed cards to be sent on to them.

It was clear to Albert that the boy was unlikely to recover and that this photograph had been made as their final memory of him before the inevitable happened. This burdened Albert even more to produce an image that they would be happy with and treasure as the last record of poor Raymond.

Snapping out of his rather morbid daydream he realised he needed to develop the glass plates as quickly as possible.

He rushed into his office and pulled the heavy black cloth across the window, and did the same with a smaller one over the glass door. He unclipped the back of the camera in the darkness and plunged the plate into a bath of ferrous sulphate to develop it and then washed it in a water bath before fixing it with a thick coat of varnish to secure the image from damage.

He resolved to get the prints to Mrs Seddle by the end of that day, and luckily his next two clients did not appear for their sitting, so he was able to use the last rays of the afternoon sun to do six card prints of Raymond, sitting in a chair, his hand on a low table, upon a book, with a painted background behind him that depicted a large library.

Albert slotted the developed glass plate, with its paper print fixed to the back, into the frames he had designed for them against the window. The sun beat upon his face and he could almost hear the crackle of chemicals as the light worked its magic, imprinting the image upon the paper for eternity. He closed his eyes and sensed—for the first time in years—that his family were in a good place; that they were privileged to be here, and that by hard work and careful planning their lives would be bettered, their conditions become more comfortable and their family grow in number, and happiness. He no longer felt the pang for the artistic life he had surrendered. He was a scientist now; what he had sacrificed of the unreliable muse, and the mystery of oils, and the dubious taste of the critic, was replaced by the methodical manufacture of collodion wet plates and the wonder of the magic of light upon silver salts, albumen paper and hyposulphite of soda. Through that science he was also providing a social good—where once Raymond might have been lost to the fading memories of his family he would now be preserved for generations to come, so that they might know of his existence and wonder at what things he did and might have achieved.

It took only an hour or so before the papers were ready and Albert bathed them in 'hypo' solution, so that they did not deteriorate in the light, and then a quick water wash and they would be ready for their final card backing and delivery to Raymond's mother.

But as the paper slid about in the tray of 'hypo' Albert noticed a dark stain across each of the six images of Raymond, as though a spillage of chemical had marked the paper. He was worried that he had not spread the glass plates with enough collodion before taking the picture, in which case he would have to ask the boy to sit again, and given his condition this seemed unlikely to happen. He checked the glass plates and found there was no such blemish present on them. They were some of the clearest plates he had taken. The problem must be with the albumen paper, he resolved. He would have to try another batch with new papers.

As he slid the photographic paper from the solution with his tongs it seemed that the shadowy patches slipped a little across the image. Albert noticed that they had also become a sort of milky colour, having lost their dark hue. With the paper laid on the desk he used for mounting them onto the backing cards he carefully pushed at the surface of the prints with his fingertips. A soggy film of white material seemed to peel itself from the picture. It was rather like damp tissue paper. It was easy to remove the rest of these blobs, but Albert remarked how strange they felt when he touched them, like fatty sausage skins. He wiped the images down and deposited the odd substance and the cloth into a bucket and set to fixing the prints, which looked superb—portraying Raymond with a lively and happy countenance that Albert could not recall from the sitting. He hoped Mrs Seddle would be pleased with them.

∞

Over the coming weeks a growing number of his sitters seemed to have pictures taken of themselves, or loved ones, stricken with some illness or other, and always when developing these plates Albert found that there was this odd residue on the paper prints. Indeed it even began appearing on other sheets where the sitter did not seem in the slightest bit unwell. It troubled him enough to write to the proprietor of the company that produced the albumen paper to explain his experiences. Receiving a rather curt response Albert decided to change his supplier. The problem persisted even with the new papers. It was not until the visit of a Mrs Tindale and her daughter that the real magnitude of Albert's photographic abilities began to reveal themselves.

Mrs Tindale strode into the studio first, in an assured and brusque manner, announcing, 'We are here for our carte-de-visite'. Albert thought that whilst her heavy dress gave her an imposing authority, it was slightly marred by the rather excessive use of pearls and other adornments, leaving him with the impression that she was aspirational and somewhat avaricious.

Behind her, trailing like an apologetic puppy was her daughter, Florence, probably in her late teens but looking every bit the dowager. Her head was bowed, her dress—a high-buttoned black affair with thin lace trim at the neck and cuffs—was overly conservative. Her hair was a spindly mess of black wire and she clutched a battered book in her hands, whose spine had disintegrated leaving the pages more a loose heap than a bound volume. She took up a seat to the side of the studio and immediately began reading.

Albert and Mrs Tindale began selecting the backdrop and furniture for the photograph, eventually agreeing on a drab grey background that would focus the viewer on Florence rather than on some extravagant scene (of which he had plenty). They selected a couple of minor props; a simple chair, with a little ornate detail and velvet padding on its tall, thin backrest, and a potted plant on a stand that would again frame her on the other side and focus the eyes upon her face. Once Mrs Tindale was satisfied she summoned Florence to pose, which she did as best she could, although she was clearly uncomfortable, and unused to being the centre of attention. She seemed more tired and irritated, Albert thought. Most of his sitters were enthusiastic and delighted to be in the studio. It was, after all, not an inexpensive investment to have cards made.

...and Other Fabrications

After the sitting Albert explained that he had to immediately develop the glass plate but that he would return in a few minutes to explain the rest of the process and show the variation in mounts, frames and albums that they could choose.

Upon returning to the studio he found that only Mrs Tindale remained. She explained that she had sent her daughter home immediately as the smell of the chemical fumes, and the paraffin lamps was concerning her.

'Oh, I see, well I'm sure we can conclude our business quite quickly so that you can return to her soon,' Albert said, adding 'But I must enquire, what is the book that she holds so dear?'

'Oh that tatty thing,' Mrs Tindale sneered. 'It's some silly collection by one of those modern women poets, apparently it's very fashionable. Something to do with goblins or fairies—and *fruit*, of all things! She can recite whole sections of it. It seems to me to be rather childish, grotesque gibberish. Her father tolerates her indulgence in these literary fads. If I had *my* way…'

And here the solid, steely voice of Mrs Tindale broke; her lip trembled. She stumbled a little and sat in one of the plush chairs by a window, clearly quite distressed. Albert rushed to help her but she batted him away, composing herself again.

'Florence is not well you see, Mr De'Ath,' she said, taking in a deep breath to steady her emotions. 'Her lungs are frightfully weak. We've tried everything. Her father even sent her to Switzerland for the summer, but it relieved the symptoms for only a few weeks beyond her return. We simply don't have the money, I'm afraid, for any more sustained recuperation there, or any of the new treatments that are available. I know it's sad, but we just wanted something to remember her by. I have a terrible feeling that this winter will not be a happy one.'

'I am so sorry to hear that, Mrs Tindale,' Albert said. 'If I can be of any help... If I can...'

'Yes, yes, thank you,' she replied, getting up and resuming her previous manner. 'If you don't mind I think I would rather conclude the other aspects of this at some other time.'

And with that she swept out of the door and down the stairs.

At times Albert didn't like being what was referred to as 'trade'. He had felt the downward glance of far too many of his clients and was becoming a little tired of it.

He wondered though if he might try a little experiment. It seemed rather cruel to use young Florence as a test subject, but he was no doctor and he could not effect any remedy for her ailment, so he might as well see immediately if the curious substance would be produced from the prints of Florence's sitting.

He began the developing process and just as he had found with the prints of young Raymond, and more recent sitters' pictures, here too the paper appeared to be marred by a dusty cloud that enveloped most of Florence's face and shoulders. He poked at it with his dipping tongs, and, as was becoming more familiar now, a sort of milky film appeared across the surface of the image. This time though it also had delicate strands of what looked like black hair trailing from it through the 'hypo' solution.

Alfred rummaged in his desk drawer for something smaller to extract the thing with, keeping his eyes fixed upon it as it seemed to grow and swirl about in the solution, much like the strands of a poached egg in a pan. But it could not simply be the albumen from the paper, there simply wasn't enough of it on each sheet to have produced this amount of material. His hand found a pair of scissors and he used them to fish the blob out onto his blotting pad.

It lay there looking for all the world like a swipe of dripping that he might be about to spread on some bread. He was about to dispose of it, as he had with the previous pieces, when the opaque, fleshy lump seemed to quiver a little as he breathed upon it. There arose a rancid smell, as of cured meat that has been too long in the sun.

Albert was most perplexed, and not a little disturbed, by this and began to keep a note of all the names of those that sat for him whose pictures, when developed, produced this kind of odd material. He resolved that it would be imprudent at this stage to mention anything to Isabelle though.

∞

A couple of months passed and there still seemed to be no rational explanation for the appearance of these skin-like strands on the prints. Then the key to the puzzle was solved one morning when Isabelle brought him his diary and morning coffee.

'Oh, I happened to meet Mrs Tindale yesterday afternoon, as I was ordering our goose for Christmas,' she said, as she opened his diary out with the day's bookings. 'What a terrible smell there is in here, why don't you open a window?'

'Mmm,' Albert murmured, looking down the list of clients and their requirements.

'She said that her daughter, you know, Florence, who came for a card a few months ago, has made a wonderful recovery,' Isabelle said, setting out his coffee pot and cup on the desk.

After a few moments the words had sunk into Albert's distracted mind.

'Really, Issie?' he said excitedly. 'Had she been away again… abroad, I mean… did Mrs Tindale say if they'd sent her for further treatment?'

Isabelle was rather taken aback by Albert's interest in the matter. It was so rare these days for him to say anything to her beyond a few approving grunts.

'Well, that's exactly the point,' she said. 'The poor girl had been almost at death's door, if you'll excuse the expression, and the Tindale's had desperately been trying to gather the finances from family and friends to send her for more treatment, when suddenly she awoke one morning last month without a cough or a splutter. Indeed, so well is she now that apparently she has even been going to the theatre of an evening with her cousin. The doctors have even called it a *miracle*.'

'Yes, it *is* miraculous, Issie—*remarkable, miraculous* and *amazing*,' Albert said, with a rather distant and distracted tone. He walked to the window and looked down across to the station. A locomotive was pulling in, it's bellowing smoke reminding him of the odd object he had extracted from Florence Tindale's prints only a few weeks before.

'Are you alright, Albert?' Isabelle asked, after he had stood there pensively for a while.

'Oh, why yes, my dear, perfectly fine, thank you,' he said, striding back to his desk. 'Now, I suppose I'd better get things ready in the studio for…' He ran his finger to the top of the diary page, finding the first booking of the morning. 'Yes, for Mrs Miller and her dogs. They're first up on this wonderful morning, and you know how troublesome the animals can be.'

Isabelle headed back up to the family rooms to attend to the girls, but couldn't help thinking how strangely Albert had reacted to the news about Florence Tindale, and besides it wasn't really a wonderful morning, it was rather overcast, she thought, and she was sure she had seen some drizzle on the windowpanes.

As soon as Mrs Miller and her uncooperative animals had been seen off Albert called for his delivery boy and tasked him with an errand. He was to go to Mrs Seddle's house and enquire as to whether she required any further prints of young Raymond, as he was offering a special half-price promotion for previous clients. The boy was also to enquire as to Raymond's health, in as subtle a manner as possible. There would be a full shilling in it for him if he could return with the information within the hour.

With just a minute remaining of his deadline the boy burst into the studio, panting out his news between great gasps of breath.

Raymond had made a miraculous recovery, he said. The boy was now up and about, and had even been playing cricket with his friends. Apparently, Mrs Seddle was delighted but she also said not to have any further prints made as she would like to forget that unhappy time. She would be making another booking presently to have a photograph made in celebration.

Albert gave the boy his well-deserved coin. The information the lad had retrieved was not unexpected but now laid an obligation upon Albert, although he had little understanding of how exactly he might fulfil it.

∞

The following morning Albert declared that he was not going to be doing sittings that day but rather working on some 'experimental techniques', as he called them, in his darkroom. Isabelle would have to rearrange the bookings for another day. Despite her protests he was adamant and turned purposely on his heels and drew the black curtain across the door.

The hours passed, and between having to placate irate sitters Isabelle occasionally crept to the darkroom door to ask if he would like some tea or a little food. She was always greeted by a disgruntled refusal and another plea not to be disturbed.

When he did not appear to have supper with her and the girls she resolved to go and see what on earth could be detaining him so long. As she opened the door Isabelle let out a shriek. Albert lay across his desk, his face white and sunken, and his eyes—almost black—stared straight at the doorway, unblinking. The floor was littered with paper photographic prints and the main developing table stacked high with glass plates that had been taken from the cabinets in which they were stored and then used to reproduce this mountain of images that lay about the place. Beside the photographs there lay a more gruesome object. It appeared to be the overturned waste bucket, but from it there had spilled what seemed to be a heap of organic matter. Edging closer, and covering her nose and mouth against the disgusting stench, Isabelle could see lumps of fat and flesh, clumps of hair of every colour, and what appeared to be strands of veins and other bodily material. It looked more like a pail one might find in the butcher's yard than something from a photographer's studio. It must have been her distress at finding her husband so suddenly deceased, she later reasoned, but Isabelle was sure she saw the mass of flesh heave, as though struggling to move, and with that shuddering movement what looked like a malformed eyeball rolled from the pile, coming to a quivering rest against the leg of Albert's chair. With a howl Isabelle ran upstairs and grabbed Roseanna and Beatrice before fleeing the building.

∞

After she had discovered Albert's body on that terrible evening Isabelle had returned with the children to be with her parents in Canterbury, as far from the frightful studio as possible. The enquiry into his death found that Albert had taken his own life by imbibing some of the chemicals in his darkroom. What could have driven him to this despair Isabelle could not imagine. Only the day before he had seemed so cheerful and elated. Some weeks later she made the sad journey to Maidstone to make arrangements for the removal and auction of the photographic equipment in an attempt to pay off their creditors, not least of whom was the undertaker, whose manner had recently turned most aggressive.

Isabelle had been promised by the constabulary that the darkroom had been cleaned of the substances she had described in the waste bucket (they had found only ashes, as though from a fire grate, but decided not to argue with her, given her distress). Despite the reassurance it was with trepidation that she opened the darkroom door, her mind imprinted with the image of poor Albert at the desk and the horrible fleshy lump on the floor.

But there was no need for fear, if anything the room was relatively bare now, the chemical bottles, trays and other material having been removed along with Albert's body. On the desk, where he had been slumped, there was one of the little leather photographic albums that he had been so proud to produce, as a little extra for his clients that wanted to purchase one. Isabelle ran her hand across it, uncertain whether to open it. Eventually she did. She had to. There on the inside plate was the familiar introduction card, with its popular poem,

Within this book your eyes may trace
The well know smile on friendship's face;
Here may your wondering eyes behold
The friends of youth, the lov'd of old;
And as you gaze with tearful eye,
Sweet mem'ries of the years gone by

Will come again <u>with magic power</u>,
To charm the evening's pensive hour.
Some in this book have passed the bourne
From whence no travellers return;
Some through the world yet doomed to roam,
As pilgrims from their native home
Are here by nature's power enshrined,
As lov'd memorials to the mind—
Till all shall reach that happy shore,
Where friends and kindred part no more.

A thick pencil had underlined 'your wondering eyes behold' and 'with magic power'. How curious, Isabelle thought. She turned the page and found a thin paper print, without a backing card. It was a self-portrait Albert had taken. She recognised it as one of his earliest experiments as he learnt how to take, and develop the pictures. She hadn't always been able to pose for him, especially with Roseanna so young, so he had taken to practising with himself as sitter. Many of these early images had been humorous, and Isabelle recalled those happy days with a tear. However, the picture was partially covered by a dark cloud that suggested a problem with the fixing of the image. But also a patch of the paper had been scratched away, across the eyes. There was also a small sheet of writing paper inside the pages, folded many times. She slowly opened it, looking with increasing distress at the damaged image of her poor husband.

The note had been hastily scrawled, and was dotted with some chemical spills. 'Dear Isabelle, when you should find this I will have been consumed by that *magic power*. I tried, as best I could, to keep us well; to give the girls, and you, a good life. But this gift, *power*, or whatever you might call it has destroyed me. The only profit in it comes from knowing that I have helped so many stay *here*, upon *this happy shore* for a few years longer. These *wondering eyes*—these *cursed* eyes!—were not capable of my own salvation though and I only hope that I can pass, with fondness, into your *sweet mem'rie*. Gaze no longer with *tearful eye*, my beloved, until we meet again, your Albert.'

Isabelle began to flick through the pages of the album, and found there only thin sheets of barely developed images that Albert had reproduced from all the negative plates he had taken of himself over the years. They ran chronologically and in each one the cloud, or stain, that obscured the image seemed to get larger, and darker. On each Albert had scratched the eyes out and with clear desperation had begun to scratch at the rest of the image. Isabelle turned the pages with growing terror until, on the penultimate page, she found a print of almost total darkness save for a faint ghost of a hand in the bottom left hand corner. It was Albert's hand, she could tell by the wedding ring. And on the last page that faced it was a picture of Isabelle, Roseanna and Beatrice, that Albert had taken only the Sunday before his death. This image was clear of any blemishes, the girls' bright eyes and their loving smiles seemed to augur a happy and prosperous future.

Holzwege

Jetzt komme, Feuer!
Begierig sind wir
Zu schauen den Tag,
Und wenn die Prüfung
Ist durch die Knie gegangen,
Mag einer spüren das Waldgeschrei.

Friedrich Hölderlin, 'Der Ister'

I see them only indistinctly, at first. They are loading a wagon, perhaps a wooden wagon. No! It is a truck—a metal-sided truck. There are three of them, men—only just men, more overgrown boys; ill at ease in their metamorphosed bodies. I see them as though in a dream, where the elements emerge from within each other. They are making themselves appear from the very darkness of the earth; ethereal nibelungs coaxed from the fantastic realms to load a vehicle with goods.

But *what* goods?

There are wooden crates, they chink and rattle: bottles. There are packs of what look to be blankets. There is a canvas bag that also clinks, but there is a metallic edge to it: I do not know its sound, a mystery.

As they work my clairvoyance retreats, revealing the scene that surrounds them, and a more detailed impression. There are people walking by them—a busy street lined with small shops. It is a small country town. They walk with heads bowed, trying not to catch the eye of these young lads who now, it appears, are uniformed. It is shabby attire, certainly, but one that still has the unnerving sense of threat. It is not perfect: each item a little different to his comrade's, but there is the overall impression of unity. There are high dark boots to the knee. There are dark trousers that sit comically above the boots, almost clown-like. There are brown shirts, frayed and oversized. A peaked brown cap, flashed with red, perches upon each head: on one too small, on one too large, on one just right—the very model of perfection. There are red bands on the arm too, each with a white circle interrupted by a black symbol I cannot understand. One clearly carries a pistol in a shiny leather holster. He leads them, of that we can be sure.

As they continue their work and I float higher I see that red also litters the scene still further. There is a broken figure in the gutter only a few feet from them. His limbs contort about him in an inhuman fashion, as though he were a rag doll discarded in the corner of a child's playroom. Gentle trickles of red fall from him and gather by the curb stones. Across him are strewn pamphlets, each emblazoned with another red symbol—again beyond my knowledge. An A-board lies smashed beside him, having been used—no doubt—to effect the transformation of his gentle face into the crazed puzzle that now begs to be completed by any passing stranger. None will look; they are all busy with the past, which is—as we all know—only a shadow of destiny.

The three men are high with the comradely guilt of brutality; sharing a furtiveness akin to an illicit love affair. Their conversation is only a veneer that thinly covers the self-doubt of all ideals. In another time and place they might, instead, have kissed.

∞

I catch sight of them again as they leave the town behind. They sit in the cab of the truck, laughing and joking. Occasionally a song breaks out. They drink beer with silly grins and share the driving when each gets tired. Behind them the flat land of fields with crops and cattle, pigs and poultry, gives way to the gentle climb of hills and the darker green of trees and the black etching of rocky places erupting from the deep earth. All passes into clarity, as the fog of distance lifts. I believe they are approaching me. I hear their words become discernible and their names litter their sentences like characters from some ill-formed, comic tale: Otto, Ernst and Viktor.

As the hours vanish the trees congregate around the dwindling roads until they wall the twisting routes like dark sentries. There are signs that protrude at awkward angles here and there, erupting from the pine trees and the firs like symbols of lost civilisations. I see the names: Lorenhof, Reichenbach, Bruderhalde, Bärenthal, Feldberg, Hebelhof and Fahl. These three brave fellows are almost with me, or I am almost with them.

Finally they pass through another small town, with slow pitched roofs that after a day of gentle autumn sun are slowing sloughing off their layers of snow, until the cold of evening holds it fast and icy again for another night. Our boys leer from the windows and jeer at the townsfolk who go about the last of their day's errands. They watch the truck as it careers drunkenly through the town. They are people of a wilder place, more used to the echoes of seasons and the songs of forest air than the banners and pomp of the rally and the cynical aggrandisement of a nation (from which they are as alien as the mole is the raven).

The revellers do not take long to pass through, and as they leave a wooden post marks the place they are departing: Todtnauberg. They would have seen it in the mirror, had they looked. But the map—to them—is more important than the terrain and the world has been degraded to lines between departures and destinations. They are on the right track.

The truck pulls up in deeper woods overlooking the town. Otto, the one with the gun, pulls some papers from a satchel. They spend a few minutes in the warm cab, surveying the details on the paperwork, before unloading the equipment onto a thin sledge to carry it deeper into the forest. They each select a bottle of clear spirits from one of the crates and in another gesture of camaraderie they cheer and drink a good draught. From what I can gather of their conversation they are searching for a building, 'The Hut', directions to which are scribbled on the sheets they carry with them. They are here to celebrate something. They are here to drink and hunt. They are here to learn what it is to be in the wilderness. Let us hope they are open to the teaching.

Viktor is tasked with pulling the sledge. He drags it behind him with the aid of a leather harness. They call him a pack-dog. He laughs. They all drink deeply from their bottles, filling their young hearts with false fire.

But it is dark, and despite their preparations they have forgotten torches. Ah, light! Without light all our ancient foes are once more brought to life. So in the gathering gloom they become lost along the wood-ways. For so often these tracks lead nowhere, serving only to open the deeper parts of the forest to the warmth of the daylight. They are paths made by those who manage these intimate places—you must struggle hard to notice the signs that point to pathways and not dead-ends.

Within a couple of hours they are fighting amongst themselves. At one point Ernst ventures that Otto is ill-suited to carry the pistol—as it is the sign of a leader, not a failure. Otto pulls out the gun and holds it to Ernst's forehead. They stare into each other's eyes, half-hoping they had the courage to be men. They do not.

After this awkward impasse they continue their pointless meanderings in silence. The undergrowth claws and scratches at them and the cold warns of the seriousness of their plight. They break open the blankets from the sledge and wrap themselves as best they can in the prickly cloth. They take out another bottle of spirits, and hope again.

They decide rather than heading higher, and deeper, into the forest they should head towards the lower slopes, there they will be more likely to find a route back to the main road and perhaps the sanctuary of their truck. They can always try again in the morning light.

Then, a building appears in a wide clearing. It is low, like the ones in the main town, and has a long sloping roof that covers a small wooden well on the porch. There are lights; someone, at least, is at home.

Otto approaches the single storey dwelling quietly, he hears voices within. He mounts a few wooden steps onto the porch area lit faintly by the light that manages to shine through two thick cream coloured cloth curtains that hang over each window on either side of the door.

He feels he is in a fairytale—a naughty boy creeping up to the witch's house. As he smirks at this absurd thought the door is opened by a young woman, with a long blue dress with intricate yellow patterns embroidered across it. Otto is surprised and quite embarrassed by how he must appear: grinning inanely at his childish imagination and staring blankly into space. She says nothing though, but opens the door widely without even looking at him.

He beckons to his fellows and they join him from the tree-line. They are desperate for some warmth.

Inside they find a very strange scene. The house appears to have only one large room, the roof being supported by three large tree trunks themselves carrying great black cross beams. Hanging from these are bizarre items; twigs with pieces of wool and twine wrapped around them, some with long coils of leather and feathers; their purpose seems decorative but their uncanny symbolism make the men feel both curious and nervous. The whole cabin is littered with balls of wool and twine, threads and branches, sewing boxes and needles, cushions and embroidered bags. Great woven tapestries hang on each wall, with smaller lacy patterns between them. Each appears to use a different material in their construction; some with long pieces of twig, some with pine cones and wood worked in with yarn. There are so many of these weaves, both large and small, abstract patterned pieces and more figurative work, that the three lost travellers are dazzled by the flood of objects to view. As they gaze around the room in wonder they are startled by a voice that speaks in a firm, wise tone.

'Come in my boys, and sit down with us by the fire. You must be cold.'

A kind-faced elderly woman peers at them from around one of the beams. Beside her two younger girls work on small backstrap looms, anchored to the support beams. They both smile but do not speak.

The old woman works upon a great upright loom that almost camouflages itself with the tapestry on the wall near the fireplace. She works away at the warp and weft as though at a harp; delicate wrinkled fingers darting in and out with different coloured fibres and silks, and the sound of her playing is entirely lost on the confused visitors. The young women similarly work at great speed with keen and enthusiastic smiles.

The Phantasmagorical Imperative...

Otto takes a faltering step further inside and continues to gaze in awe at the intricate patterned cloth that is hung around him. Scattered around the feet of the curious old woman and her acolytes are strange tools and equipment whose purpose utterly eludes him. All three are seated on stools that slant slightly upwards, with a drawer beneath each seat. From each of these drawers, cloth and wool, silks and laces, fall to the floor, which is covered with overlapping rugs. Viktor and Ernst stand sheepishly by the door that has been gently closed against the cold evening air by the young woman that had welcomed them in.

Otto sits on another stool by the fire and watches the weavers, enthralled. It does not seem to be work, there seems instead to be some silent dialogue between the looms as each weaver occupies themselves with becoming entwined in the enigma of their cloth. It could have been hours that passed there as tranquillity overcame him.

Beckoned by the older woman, Viktor and Ernst come further in and sit upon a warm rug before the fire, whose gentle embers keep a pot of water bubbling. Beside the fire Ernst notices a long wooden box with a crocheted lace covering, upon which stands a small earthen pot from which grows a clump of small yellow flowers on rigid stems.

He did not know the world and thought no more of them.

They are Arnica—for opening the vessels. And had he known them well—as the women did—he might have found their presence upon that box most strange. For the box was none other than a *totenbaum*, a wooden home—wherein we all must one day dwell.

But, as his unknowing eyes scan the house and its simple objects, he is unaware that I reside within. If any of them had dared to open the lid of this dark place I sense the whole world would have fallen in upon itself in that impossible encounter.

So Otto, Ernst and Viktor—our valiant heroes, or wretched buffoons—sit like awed children in a mystical grotto, each absorbed in his own attempt to unravel the scene before him.

From the mantelpiece a piece of broken branch hangs with three smaller branches shooting from it. Viktor notices a spider waiting in the centre of an intricate web that had been built between these. He watches as it moves towards the centre of the main branch and begins to spin. It seems intent on covering the entire branch with a thin film of white until only its form remains.

They are drawn back from their thoughts when the old woman stands and speaks.

'I shall tell you a story for you are not really strangers here. And listen carefully for it will concern you all,' she says in a clear and enchanting voice.

She moves over to the fire and folds her arms. The other three women, who had seemed to be no more than girls, turn around—as though in ritual—to hear her speak.

Otto can see a wisdom and age in their eyes that tells of experiences beyond their years. It does not seem strange to him that none of them had introduced themselves, and it does not bother him that he had not spoken a word himself since entering. There is, however, a sense of looming threat which seems to battle with the feeling of calm that previously filled the house.

'I flew in dreams across the woods and over streams and rivers, high above the forest I soared,' she began, with the vigour that lends all storytellers an eternal aspect. 'I crossed a sea and came in time to high mountains where, through blizzards and cold winds, I met with a wise woman who had lived there years. The elements no longer challenged her and she would dance naked in the snow.

I listened to her very long and from her ancient lips there came a tale of a weaver girl whose work was wondrously skilled. She often would speak of her unrivalled skill, and once—perhaps in jest—suggested that not even the weave wrought by a goddess could challenge her own. At hearing this the deity who most deeply understood the art was insulted and visited this girl disguised as an older weaver. When this goddess saw the girl at her loom she was most impressed but ventured to suggest that she should ask forgiveness for so rudely challenging the work of an immortal. The girl just laughed and said that she would not.

The goddess changed into her heavenly raiment and the girl turned pale but stood firm. And so, the challenge set, they raised their looms and worked for many days. No words can tell of the fantastic creations that they spun, for both outshone all other works. Seeing the insulting girl's wondrous cloth the goddess became enraged and shattered loom, and work, and threads, with one envious blow. The shame overcame the girl, to have so rudely challenged one so strong, and she hanged herself from a nearby tree.'

The old woman's tone had changed dramatically and she was gesturing violently, almost spitting the words from her mouth in hatred.

'On seeing the mortal corpse of one so gifted this rash goddess took pity—but what cruel pity it was—and transformed her with magic into a spider, so that ever after her offspring would have to weave to gain their food. And the selfish thoughts that had robbed the girl of life were transformed to dangerous venom with which to trap her pray.'

The rather dramatic ending had caused the three rapt listeners to rouse from the calm they had enjoyed before the tale began. With the old woman's clear anger Otto had recalled their journey. They needed directions to their cabin, before the deep cold of the night came on further.

'Why, thank-you, good Frau.' Otto said, tentatively. 'That was a most compelling tale, and one that seems so familiar to me somehow. I wonder if we might...'

The old woman looked at him intensely, he also felt the gaze of the other three women upon him. They seemed angered by his interruption. The old woman bent down and brought her wrinkled face close to his.

'Yes, my boy,' she spat, 'for venom is such that I shall take all myth and make it my own.'

A silence ensued. As it endured the three men felt the awkward collision of the fire's warmth and the homely comfort of the woven fabrics and the coldness of the weavers' disposition.

And then, as suddenly as their anger had erupted, it subsided, and all were smiles and helpfulness.

'But we are rude,' the old woman said gently. 'You have lost your way and need to find your dwelling place.'

Otto was relieved. Viktor thought momentarily on the fact that they had not spoken of their destination, but it passed. And Ernst; he thought only of warm sausages and beer when they finally found their cabin.

'Take our guests to the abode they seek,' she said to the three younger women, an air of disappointment in her voice. 'Lead them by the wood-ways that they might be best able to attain the path. It will not take long I trust.'

Eagerly the girls—for they seemed youthfully exuberant once more—jumped up from their seats, chattering excitedly.

They helped their guests from the floor and hurried them from the cabin. They seemed almost to dance along into the forest, and all were barefoot. The three travellers, confused, desperate and not a little drunk, followed them into the trees, forgetting their sledge and its supplies—intent once more only on their destination.

Within minutes they were deep into the trees, climbing the steep hill onto more rocky pathways that wound back and forth, almost snaking back upon themselves.

Attaining something of a summit, where the starry sky was briefly glimpsed through the thinning firs, they came upon a rudimentary bridge that spanned a gushing stream. The women skipped across the little wooden bridge, one paused a moment to look down at the stream, laughing at the play of moonlight upon its surface. The three tired men trudged wearily after them, swigging from their bottles in an attempt to cheer themsleves. The last in line, Viktor, paused where the woman had and watched the waters too. He gazed along the dark line of the stream as it trailed into the trees beyond and thought of all the hidden places it might lead, and all the journeys and lives it might facilitate and embrace, until at last it found the sea. It was an unusually poetic thought for the young thug, but it was driven under by Ernst's harsh voice calling for him to keep up.

Although they had been raised in the dirt of the farm, and lived their lives upon the land, they found themselves unsuited to the cold and inhospitable mountain world. Their boots were now fashioned for pounding the urban streets and the faces of the weak. Their shirts, even cocooned beneath the tightly wrapped blankets, were now more suited to the fug of beerhalls and brothels, not the still chill of a forest path. And their trousers, now more used to jocular thigh-slapping, were no defence against the silvery rime that now crept upon them. But they were flush with the warmth of alcohol, and even if the tingling of their extremities betrayed a real danger, they were fool enough to believe themselves invincible—millennia machines.

Higher they scrambled, along those lost forest tracks, until at last they came to another clearing. This one was wide, but still in a gloom, as the moon was covered with a layer of cloud. The girls pranced about the place, and beckoned them on, even though they were barely capable of walking.

Laughing, the fairy-like girls took each man aside and showed him around the clearing, as though silently disclosing some secret. But it was as useless as teaching apes to talk—they could never understand.

Then, conceding defeat, each of these strange creatures took their man aside and led them to the undergrowth. They began to work their charms; kissing and fondling, nuzzling and licking. With the warmth of tongues and the scratch of fingernails they coaxed some life back into our supermen.

Ernst eagerly assisted in removing the beautiful blue dress from his passionate lover. The tantalizing curves of her shoulders and breasts were caught in a burst of moonlight and he pounced lustily upon her.

But he soon discovered that she was far from innocent. As they began to enfold each other in passion she kissed his face relentlessly, licking and nipping at him like a mischievous kitten. Then with one savage bite she tore a strip of flesh from his cheek and upper lip.

She spat the bloody lump onto the ground and laughed.

The shocked Ernst fumbled for his knife, strapped to his belt. But—senses dulled with drink and addled with pain—he was no match for those hands so skilled with the warp and the weft of natural things. Her delicate hands unwrapped the folds of his chest and unstitched his muscles in an instant; his ribs offered only the resistance of a rickety loom that held a deeper movement. He gasped in agony as her nimble fingers paused a moment, in playful delight, amongst his viscera.

With blood still trickling from his bitten face Ernst gazed into the last eyes he would ever see. They were dark and feral. She panted like an eager dog, her warm breath beating against his face in waves. The moon shone brightly into the clearing now, its perfect circle mirrored in her pupils. She deposited a gentle kiss upon his torn lips and let him slide down the tree trunk, gripping his undone belly in his shaking hands. And as his eyes flickered into the eternal dark he saw her bound away into the undergrowth.

Otto fared no better. As he held his partner in his arms, with her small legs clenched around his waist she whirled gracefully around his body and clung instead to his back. He laughed, and grappled with her briefly.

It was a game, he thought.

Then a fiery pain shot across his neck.

Could it have been her nails that had slashed so deep a wound across his throat? He felt the warmth of his own blood surging through his fingers. She leapt gracefully from him and now he rocked a moment before sinking to his knees at the edge of the clearing. She loomed above him and he gazed up pleadingly for pity. But this world offers no justice, only revelation. He sank into the ferns to await renewal.

Viktor was the last to go. As he embraced his woman and she burrowed deep into his arms, he caught sight of the disembowelled Ernst sliding to the ground and the woman standing above him with a bestial triumph upon her bloodied face. In an instant his girl was upon him though, rending at his throat with her teeth. He stumbled backwards in horror and lost his footing on the damp ferns. With a great crunch he fell to the ground and a white-hot pain passed through his body. There he lay, pinned to the ground by a thin tree stump that had skewered his body. He watched—almost fascinated—the last torments of his struggling chest as it fought pointlessly for air. She advanced on him then, and something in the pain of those last moments made him understand the woods' strange call.

∞

So, in spring, as the snows receded and revealed the bodies, the forest creatures emerged—beatific vermin—and picked their bones clean of fleshy sin. Their carcasses became the home of strange insects, snakes and nesting rodents; and with each season they fused further with the soil they had so triumphantly lauded. And occasionally, in summer—when the sun is high and fierce—their white skulls reflect that invincible star, bathing the forgotten clearing in radiance as ancient and strange as the myths that had first forged their perfect, steely bodies.

Dehiscence

I am not given to the task of writing. I have read too much—and always of the most horrific of deeds—to find in the written word much solace from, or reason for, the ultimate madness of the world. Rather, my life has been a quest for *things*, and their magical and bountiful properties; qualities that, if one is attentive enough, reveal themselves through years of subtle relationships and quiet correspondences. In short, objects are, to me, the truth of this existence, and its only proper means of record—or indeed, value. For within a cherished antique, or long discarded toy, one finds a pulse of love and loathing, of betrayal and trust. It seems they speak always—in their wooden, stony, eternal ways—of a kind of fellowship of mankind, and of its brutality—of truth, of life! Whereas literature, *pale deceitful shadow*, is a dead world, populated by the unborn, its cities built by the distorted bricks of aberrant imagination and mortared by the indolence of poetry. It is an onanist's daydream—what can be, will be—for *me*—before *my* very eyes! Pah, keep your little fantasies, they feed only the minds of the depraved, or heap more dust upon the shelves of the academics!

I am bitter; that is true.

Somewhere herein is my life. A life, I fully understand, mediated through the lens of my own distorted thoughts. But my history has little really to do with what I record here. I offer it solely to provide context to the lives that I shall relate, and the things through which I came to know them.

This life begins only in my late thirties. Prior to that I had squandered the years with the usual tasks one essays in youth—the menial jobs, the aspirations to 'betterment', the toil of study, the loving and lying, the planning and hoping. A short career as a freelance translator of Russian and Polish brought me to the point at which, in the mid-1970s, I had been approached by some 'suits' in government services and was asked if I would like to join—offers I 'couldn't refuse' and all that. I sensed the years rolling out before me like fields, initially lush and green and then gradually fading into dull browns and yellows as I ambled towards retirement, counting up the endowment policies and wondering when I might have enough to get by on; *when* I could get *out*.

Instead, I emigrated to Poland. I had been persuaded by an old friend from my university days to work with him in the archives at Auschwitz. There were so many documents they had been working on, trying to trace family members, and they were desperate for further translators into English to provide documents for the American descendants of survivors, increasingly desperate to make sense of the past.

It was a start, and paid well enough—enough even to put money aside to find other pursuits as I began to see as many doors closing upon my life there as there might have been had I remained in Britain at the beck and call of *Her Majesty's* minions.

A decade collapsed, with the reverberating cries of massacre and the aching rumble of ruin forever in my thoughts; the relentless lists of the murdered and the mutilated, the tortured and the missing. I mapped names to places and places to names until I began to see only letters and numbers. Maps lost all meaning, their contours only lines that seemed more like childish games upon coloured paper. Lives lost all sense, their histories slipping into the cold plains like legions before them.

It was back in the city—in Krakow—that I became seduced once more by the joys of life. The swift hunt of the language bewitched me; Polish is logical—certainly—that had me hooked. But beneath that it flows with the murmur of whispers and crescendos with the buzz of fevered insects about to take flight. I delighted in every encounter, each conversation passing into the fabric of the buildings around me and the stones beneath my feet; until, finally, it felt that I had been coaxed back into life by the urgency of a hive.

In those early years it was peaceful enough. The regime made sure all appeared quiet and still.

The main square was dark. The seasons were dark. Only the language and the lust for companionship gave light—an inner glow that radiated from even the most suspicious of faces.

History too was a passion, and everywhere oozed with it. Not a grand narrative of splendour, but the quiet poverty of lives that rustled like leaves in a cold climate. It was not in paintings, or great works of literature that these were writ, but rather in the worn handle of a hoe; the bent blade of a knife, and the chipped rim of an enamel mug. All these things whispered to me of real lives and their passions—that might set a thousand worlds alight, had history paused a moment to listen to them. And so, after years of gathering together what others might class as junk, from markets and little passing traders, I took a short lease on a shop in Ul. Wiślna, near the market square, selling bric-a-brac.

Visitors were few. The locals were little interested in the trinkets I traded, most found it absurd—a few delightful, but hardly any thought my wares a useful investment of their resources. But I was part of a vibrant cultural scene. People traded illegal books, music and films—banned folders of etchings were swapped under counters like pornography. There was little that belonged to us, as such—to each one of us, I mean. Everything was in surreptitious circulation for the enrichment of all. It seemed I lived in some idyll. But as with all of the world, and every corner in it, one sees only part of the picture.

Then the bastard lights arrived, the money flooded in and with it all of the detritus of the West with its star-spangled gore.

My shop thrived! Oh, misery!

The tourists gawped and marvelled. Their wallets were fat with notes and credit cards (which I didn't accept—they loved me the more for it, unfortunately; counting out the notes as though they were playing at 'shops'). Their eyes were dead; their hearts only empty pumps circulating cold air through their bloated flesh. They did not deserve these things, items that I had polished and cared for—beautiful treasures of a history that they could never know, or ever hope to fathom. With each parcel I handed over—lovingly wrapped—I knew I had consigned another rich existence to the oblivion of a gaudy mantelpiece, or souvenir box.

Slowly I became resentful, and reclusive. The sign on the door of my little shop read 'closed' more frequently with every season. I would spend long hours on my little pallet bed, on a slim gallery above the main shop, trying with all my mental powers to fathom the secrets of each object in my collection, the most precious of which I kept in a sturdy trunk near where I slept. These objects were more to be guarded than traded. The door to my shop would be rattled occasionally, and rapped, tapped and battered at. Harsh, whining voices would call through the letterbox in words quite alien to me.

But there is only so long that one may indulge one's seclusion, unless one is lucky enough to be wealthy. The landlord had become tired of my eccentricity—it was

The Phantasmagorical Imperative...

only money, surely he understood. And then one morning I was thrown onto the streets by his three younger brothers, as he cowered and cackled behind, eyeing my goods for what he might recoup of his lost rent. I begged and pleaded for my trunk. I am not ashamed to say I cried. Eventually they relented, and slid it into the street beside me, where I lay in crumpled despair.

Oh, the elation! That box, with its few little treasures, was worth all the castles in the continent! I dragged it to Planty park, where I crawled beneath some bushes, cradling it in my arms, sobbing with joy.

And my shop now? A bar. The stairs that creaked their symphony to my little attic, hinting at the secret languages that mutter under foot, now lead to a gallery that offers the drinker a fine view across the hazy dance floor as they contemplate the gyrating flesh they might consume that evening.

Let them have their youth, it is all for nought.

Now, I do my circuit; a stuttering triangle from the crumbling streets of Kazimierz, with its fifty year neglect—punctuated by the occasional neon monstrosity and packs of grinning revellers, heavy with vomit—to St Florian's Gate and its torrent of tourists, bristling with eager wallets and ready cameras, back to Planty park, where I sleep, amidst the gentle tap of rain on leaves, or the bloated afterheat of a blistering day—until the aching pain of winter brings its torture to toes and fingers, nose and ears; then all afresh again with the forgiving dawn. I am alive once more, with the pain in my arse and ache in my heart—gentle reminders of my flesh and spirit.

...and Other Fabrications

Always, trundling behind me, I have my trunk and its memories.

Rhododendron Dauricum ~ Evgeni P.
'Thou wilt find blossoms just as true'
The Catalyst: A Flower Press

Many who came to my shop were clearing the houses of relatives—finding in their interests and obsessions little that resembled their own. One day, following a deal on seven tea crates of assorted oddments, I found something that unlocked the door to my current enterprise and radically altered my perceptions. One chest was stacked with books. I ferreted through, piling them up, hoping that there might be something here to wonder at. And there was indeed! At the bottom of the pile I found a mutilated, filthy flower press. I sold the books to a friend. As I say I have no interest in their false promulgations, their ridiculous assertions and hollow hopes. Although—hypocrite that I am—my back room is full of the bastard things. These though seem to me to fall into the less ridiculous category of wasted paper—non-fiction (or what passes for such in each given age). It was from this store of reference material that I would have the task of identifying the surviving specimens within the press from a set of *Curtis Botanical* Magazines, running from 1787-1807.

The press was very badly damaged by water, having perhaps even been dropped in a river, or worse. The leaves of board within had mostly turned into a homogenised mess of sludge that had hardened again, drying into grey uniformity, over the years. Most was now dust, save for a little card upon the top board that read, 'Souvenirs of the Loves of Evgeni P. (188_ -), being a record of the year of 190_, and the wonderful blossoms of that season.' Only three of these 'blossoms' remained intact—the evidence suggested there might have been forty, or more, when it was newly made. I carefully unbolted the brackets and slid them from the frame, undoing these surviving packages with tweezers. Each was wrapped, almost ceremoniously, with thick pink card, folded to form an envelope of sorts. Inside there was a flower head pressed between blotting paper with a tissue thin sheet of paper upon which a few lines had been written, beneath a name—ornately calligraphed, all in the same hand as the card. Beneath these each package contained a paragraph cut from a page in *Curtis Botanical*, describing the carefully preserved flower within.

Papaver Orientale – Leda S.

You will see her in the shady parks, the delicate blue of her parasol aflutter amidst the knotty trunks of the cooling trees. As a bright ethereal being she sails about gathering the dull brown beasts to her with their sycophantic little grunts. I will not approach in the daytime—she is another creature, hungry for cruelty. She taunts the fawning fools with the light of her eyes and the sweet perfume that trails in her wake—nothing more. They are consumed by the promise—all is emptiness. It is only I who shares the dark nectar of her inner form, cradling and nurturing her delicate frame and savouring her musky bounty into the deep folds of the night, in whose cold depths she whimpers and mutters out her fears. In the moist dawn though her reign begins again and I crawl back to the street corners, to snigger in the ruthless shadows, her salty ghost upon my tongue.

Most of the plants of this tribe are distinguished by the splendour of their colours, most of them are also annuals, in gaiety of colour none exceed the present species; but it differs in the latter character, in having not only a perennial root, but one of the creeping kind, whereby it increases very much, and by which it is most readily propagated.

Convolvulus Purpureus – Karoliina F.

If only you had not tried to break me with pleading, with letters of sorrow and then letters of threat. You are not courageous enough for any of these deeds—and your brothers, I spit on their vengeance; your father too is a cowering knave who would not dare raise his aged fist against me, had he spirit enough even to clench it! So I leave you now, my pretty little dalliance. Our brief time was as the months in which it blossomed; heavy with storms and dappled by bright flickers of a promising sun. Of the moon, and her dark paths, you know nothing. Even though I felt her blessings rise within you as I sowed you with the future. Should you ever find the will to destroy the hatred of me each time you look into the eyes of my child you might chance upon the truth—that all is rich bounty. The broken crackle of your petticoats is merely the chuckle of death, as is the prattle your family spews from their mouths around the piano as the maids fluster at the fire in an attempt to vanish themselves.

Remember my lips upon your thighs and the way you entwined me as though the world had collapsed into the knot of our limbs. This, and only this, is the measure of our being, which now is ever one, in a face that will shadow you to your grave, and one that I can never meet, lest he too comes seeking recompense, fuelled by your mad tirades and the false heart of the righteous!

All these varieties I have cultivated many years, without observing them to change. If the seeds of these sorts are sown in the spring, upon a warm border where they are designed to remain, they will require no other culture but to keep them clear from weeds, and place some tall stakes down by them, for their stalks to twine about, otherwise they will spread on the ground and make a bad appearance. These plants, if they are properly supported, will rise ten or twelve feet high in warm summers: they flower in June, July, and August, and will continue until the frost kills them.

Origanum Dictamnus – Pedro V.

Oh! your skin, warm as a universe of suns, and scarred with the toil of Adam's sin. Were you a woman you would burst with nourishment, nursing the children of a city, and casting your fertile scents to the winds to slake the thirsts of battalions. But your gifts must remain as invisible as glass. It is only the touch that can reveal the sheen of your surfaces and tell the truth of your tricks with light. In how many dreams have I oiled your bronzed body into Olympian might against a starry sky apocalyptic with meteors and the prophecy of comets. With how many wasted breaths have I hoped to worship

The Phantasmagorical Imperative...

you, enslaved to your tyrannical majesty—send me your bidding, if it is only a glance that screams 'Depart!'

Instead, you appear, sipping wine with the whore, and joking with the cavalryman; whose laugh is as grating as the whinny of his horse, his breath as foul as its dung. These are your people and I am a lost pilgrim to your shining citadel, whose great tower crumbles in the stuttering gaslight and fug of cigarettes. You are rubble and plague, your eyes hollows of decay and your words a guillotine against the pale neck of beauty herself. A curse upon you, cur! Waste of flesh, perfidious dandy.

I *depart*, yes, but not by your command, for that once rich voice squeals now with the desperate pitch of a hungry rat. Instead I find myself again, and my meandering imaginings—the fantasy of your possible selves enough to heal me with hope.

Long known in this country as a medicinal plant; to the purposes of physic it still indeed continues to be applied, as imported in a dried state from the Levant: when bruised, the whole plant gives forth an aromatic fragrance... This plant is at all time ornamental, but more particularly so when in flower, in which state it appears during most of the summer and autumnal months.

∞

I knew a little of this man, Evgeni P., of his passions and hidden desires, but then something spoke to me from this ruined flower press. Even a slight touch upon the frame, or the rusted press locks, sent images of him, and his lovers, flashing through my mind. I heard their conversations and the deeper structures of their thoughts overwhelmed my own. Something in this object was attempting to reach me and rejuvenate itself. I had become attuned to an aspect of existence kept hidden to those unwilling to dwell with the slow heartbeat of things.

In time it would happen to me again. That is the purpose of this tedious narrative—to light the fires in those that come to read it.

You *must* learn!

And so, patiently, I came to adopt the same process for my own little collection of precious specimens, kept safely in my trunk on that slim gallery above my shop. Whether such an echo of his method was necessary I do not know, but it was enough to focus the mind, and that is what matters.

I begin my task by browsing the magazines to find the flower that seemed to evoke the sense of this young man, Evgeni P., with his lost loves and his lusty eyes that undressed the crowds that milled about him. A man who must have been a difficult character; loving and dangerous, gentle yet terrible; pathetic poet and monstrous narcissist. Once again I saw his flushed face and close-cropped black beard—I heard the bristles crackling against his starched collar.

Every time I touch the press I see his slender wooden cane flashing back and forth against the pavements, freshly polished by rain. He nods to passing acquaintances, his body warm with a passionate sweat, his heart bursting at every moment with fresh and furtive desires. He is indeed beautiful, even ornamental, but as hard as the frozen ground, holding deeply within it the promise of a rampant spring—and somewhere in the little seed of his being there is something frail and childish that aches for the sun. He germinates in me...

...occurring chiefly in the northern parts of Siberia between the Jenisea and Lena rivers, where the northern sides of the mountains in the beginning of May are entirely empurpled by it. It must of course be considered as a very hardy plant, though like many other inhabitants of the coldest regions, when cultivated in this country, from the greater mildness of our winters it is apt to expand its flowers prematurely, which are usually destroyed by subsequent frosts and cold winds.

...and Other Fabrications

Fragile Anamnesis
Four Fragments towards an Understanding of Matter

Agrostemma Coronaria ~ Hieronymus L.
'Oh. You shall see what you shall see'
A Peepshow

The single sorts propagate fast enough by the seeds, the sort with double flowers never produces any, so is only propagated by parting of the roots; the best time for this is in autumn, after their flowers are past; in doing of this, every head which can be flipped off with roots should be parted; these should be planted in a border of fresh undunged earth, at the distance of six inches, observing to water them gently until they have taken route, after which they will require no more, for much wet is injurious to them, as is also dung.

By far the simplest approach to matter is clearly through the most common and familiar senses, those of sight and sound. And even more straightforward is to have the life of the thing recounted to you by one who claims to know—such a method requires only that you believe, both in what you hear, and what you see. Such an opportunity was afforded me one filthy morning in January 198_, by the arrival of a trader I had never seen before. He did not introduce himself. He merely stamped his boots, and their slushy residue, across my floor, and tapped the drips from his wide-brimmed hat, before placing a long dark wooden box upon the counter, half-covered against the elements by a tattered blanket. I could see at a glance that it was some sort of viewing box.

He passed me another box, this one of a lighter wood, and within I found many folded cards that opened out into intricately cut scenes of streets and cities across the centuries, each delicately hand-painted.

The main article was a peepshow box, and an excellent example. I carefully loaded a frame into the cavity and unscrewed the plate to get to the aperture—wonderful!

'How much?' he said, bluntly.

I will not bore you with the barter, but I paid well for it, and for each note I counted into his palm he repeated the process, obviously concerned I might perform some sleight of hand and rob him.

'I'll tell you a little about it, if you're interested,' he said, as though somehow compelled to, having given up the thing.

'Why not,' I said, and settled back to hear whatever historical fabrication he wanted to pass on (there seemed little point now that we had concluded the transaction—but I thought it worth a listen).

He began, as all storytellers do, with a clearing of the throat.

'It was in the stifling summer of 180_ that Hieronymus L. appeared at the home of Frau F., on the business of entertainment. He had carried this little peepshow around a Europe awash with blood and alive with cannon, taking with him the little views of the great boulevards and palaces of mighty countries, now teetering on the precipice of history. Everywhere he went he sought out those working to better themselves; the dealers and traders, the investors, the military gentlemen and their pretty wives—always thinking of the interests of their loving family, and their bright future (that shines always with a warm golden light). At each city and town he visited he would always find his way to the affluent areas, where the facades are whiter and the cobbles cleaner—even the grass grows straighter and greener in the gardens of these houses than the fields upon which the cows graze to make the produce that litters their groaning tables of an evening.

Hieronymus L. knew full well where his bread was buttered—by the joys of the precious children that unlocked the purses of their parents. And what child does not love the enchanting secrets of a box of optical wonders; showing them scenes of far away and long ago, of the great deeds of heroes and of people and places that had been visited only briefly during the deathly oratory of their arrogant tutors? And so they loved Hieronymus L., with his astonishing stories that flourished with each changing image. He would tell a little tale of every figure that could be discerned in every scene he showed (and there were many).

Frau F.'s children, little Friedrich and Clara, delighted at his arrival each year, and many weeks before were spent in eager anticipation. He knew this well and each year would leave an extra week or two before his return to heighten their expectation.

He would spend an evening or two with the family, dining with them, and entertaining; such were the pleasures of a travelling man. In the early afternoon he would set up his box in the children's playroom and they would begin the well-rehearsed performance.

The box itself looked quite plain. A dark wooden thing, very long and wide, but not that tall. At the front there was a little viewing hole, covered by a brass plate that screwed over it. Hearing that plate slowly unthreaded sent the children into fits of giggles and elated dances. Always Frau F. was on hand to control them. She took as much delight in seeing their happiness as they did in viewing the scenes.

Hieronymus L. was a master of the box. A crank of a hidden handle, a pull of a lever, or the flick of a button, would transform the scene in a moment—a carriage would appear, bright light would strike the backdrop and cast the many promenaders into sharp shadow, as though dusk were approaching.

The cities those children saw; Vienna, Rome, Paris, London—oh they had done the tour already, in their minds! And then back into all the wonders of history, tinted and painted for their delight. The wreck of the Spanish Armada upon the coast of Ireland was engraved upon their minds with a sick green sea and lines of yellow lightning upon a sky grey with hatched lines of ink—the fragile masts of the ships standing boldly in perspective against the harsh skies. They saw the mosque of the sultan Mehmed and the grand thoroughfare before it, busy with camels and colourful retinues of soldiers; a line of cypresses drew the eye towards distant minarets that spoke of a bold eternity. Their imaginations reached back to the Coliseum and the gladiators in combat with raging yellow lions that leapt towards them through the lens.

The children would remark, 'Truly, Mother, it is very life itself...' and then squeal for another viewing. Thus the afternoon was spent in feverish glee until the time to prepare for dinner arrived. The box would be packed up ceremoniously, the children sad and rebellious.

Hieronymus L. would share their meal and would be prompted by Herr F. to regale them with his previous year's exploits, his travels and adventures, and the new scenes he had crafted for the box. For the children this was as delightful as the viewing itself, but they knew to be on their best behaviour at table—father had a tendency to reach too soon for the belt if even the most minor of mores was infringed.

And then, with the conversation waning, the children and Frau F. would retire and Hieronymus L. would entertain Herr F. with some further tricks of the box.

Herr F. had descended into that dark and bitter place frequented often by those whose investment in the world is ruled chiefly by national pride and personal ambition. He had witnessed his commander, Mollendorf, sustain his mortal wound at Auerstädt and from that very day he dwindled. But the scenes Hieronymus L. showed him lifted his spirits; exotic treasures of the ladies of Nippon, and glimpses of the boudoir. It was not only the children that looked forward to his visit each year. For Herr F. he brought a seedy pleasure, one made even more transgressive by the salacious tales that Hieronymus L. would whisper to him as he viewed the scenes. As he allowed those brief narratives to come to life within him, Herr F., for a few hours, at least, was back with his regiment, satiating the hunger for bodies that blooms in every soldier.

The night passed, each dream in the house flickering with fantasy. What magic Hieronymus L. practised in those dark hours none would ever know.

The following morning Herr F. was back to his study, attending to his 'papers'. It was left to Frau F. to thank their guest and settle for his services.

Standing on the steps of their little house, in a row of similarly tidy homes, polished and pristine from the labour of others, Frau F. thanked him and looked forward to his visit the following year.

'I must ask, though,' she added nervously, 'if you will forgive my intrusion, Herr L., but I wonder if you do not tire sometimes of the life of a showman. It seems, of course, a delight to travel and meet new people, but there is something in it that distances us from the real world. Do you not crave a family of your own, a home—a household?'

'Ah, my dear Frau F.,' he said, 'that is the last thing on my mind. I have duty just as much as you. It is my task to show pictures to mankind, reality bores him. It is the sad fate of humanity to always quest for that lost realm of childhood vision in which everything is just a painted facade and all things only the toys of a fantastical mind. These *real* streets, with their filth, their beggars, horseshit and carriages, gradually corrode the dreaming mind until all is blank and everyday. Give me a lens, a box, and a story and I can set any world ablaze again with wonder and enchantment.'

With that he tapped his wide-brimmed hat and set off with his box of dreams.

Frau F. stood a moment at the top of the steps, astonished, watching the strange fellow fade into the bustling crowd, his hat occasionally bobbing up in the distant hubbub like one of those figures from his own illusion box. Something in his words she had found profoundly disturbing and her senses fluttered with absurd worries and dread—of what, she could not define.

Then, with a sudden terror in her heart, she ran to the playroom and flung the door open wide. The scene within so resembled her fears that she immediately collapsed, weeping. The room was empty. Her children were gone.'

The story was over and the teller touched the fore of his wide-brimmed hat and swept towards the door with the presence of a well-rehearsed performer.

It had had the quality of a fairy tale for a new world struggling to know itself, and I might have been enthralled, had I not known this 'new world' to have been still born at its brutal delivery.

He had had his money and the deal was done before he had told me the tale. It had been so pointless—unless, of course, it was true.

He had left the shop. The bell still jingled as though calling me from sleep. I loaded the box with a scene of Vienna and what did I see? Surely not—the very same man that had been there only moments before. In this view he had his little peeping show, calling his audience to the pleasures of perspective, and the delights of light.

Viewing the little scenes then, I found the curious figure of Hieronymus L. in every view, sporting his dark, wide hat and long coat, bowing always to the crowd going by, enticing them to his box, perched upon an odd triangular frame. But in each there were the figures of a little boy, in bright blue tunic, with a little girl beside him, in a pretty yellow dress, peeping in, on tiptoe, at the viewing lens. The colours on their garments were much brighter than the other figures, and those on Hieronymus L. seemed so faded as to almost vanish into the dull grey of the buildings behind him.

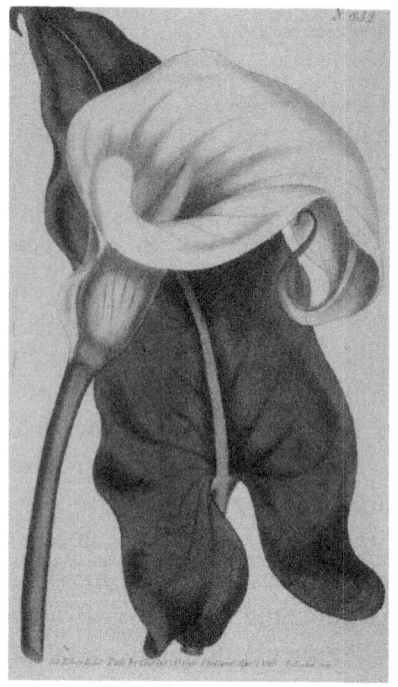

Calla Æthiopica ~ Stefan H.
'For thou hast possessed my reins'
A Russian Doll

It is very hardy, bearing our milder winters, even without shelter, but to have it flower well it is necessary to preserve it in a greenhouse, or what is still better, to aid it by the heat of the stove; by management it may be made to shew flowers in almost any month of the year.

Boxes of toys are the eeriest of things. One imagines the hours of pleasure that these objects brought, how precious they were, for days or weeks, or years even, before new things and feelings cast them into the realm of the forgotten. One such box of thrilling sadness came to me upon the death of Stanisław L., whose little cart could often be found plodding around the old town gathering discarded clutter. Frequently he could be found with a stall at the flea market in Grzegórzecka street, with a fine array of rarities.

A few years previously we had been regular dealers, always sharing a coffee and cigarette on the rickety chairs outside my shop. Then we had quarrelled, about a payment for a little figurine I had acquired from him. It being valuable I had agreed instalments, and reaching what I believed to be the final payment he was convinced that there was a further one due. It is such a shame that money should be the thing to bring our friendship to a close. So, it was most peculiar to find his wife at my door one morning, with a face red from weeping, and a box of some of his wares in her arms that apparently he had requested, on his deathbed, she bring to me.

She would accept nothing for it. It was bequeathed, she said, and, moreover—Stanisław had insisted she tell me—it was a *gift*.

Most of the box was commonplace enough, but no less incredible; old pans and bent cutlery, crumpled photographs of the unremembered, papers and journals in hands illegible or languages half-forgotten. These were merely diversions. Beneath them lay a number of beautiful toys; metal clockwork animals and engines, stuffed bears and small boxes of games. They spanned the century, and most were in excellent condition—a situation one almost regrets when the article in question is a child's plaything. But these too were not the things he'd really meant for me. The 'gift' he wished me to unravel was a tiny Russian doll, the last in the set—a miniature rounded figure, its paint almost entirely worn away from years of handling.

It was then that I recalled the short account he had given me, years before, of Stefan H. and the Russian doll. That gave me the beginnings of my examination.

On a mountainside at L-----, you will find the remains of one of the famous 'Sun Clinics'. It had been a sanatorium, for the recovery of the tubercular. How young Stefan H. had come to be there was a mystery. He was harmless enough though. He had never uttered a word, as far as anyone could recall, but went through his daily routine systematically, if rather slowly. He had the run of the sanatorium and would often be found hovering in the kitchens and the wards, watching the nurses and staff at their work.

He had been admitted in 191_, by a Dr. Vollin— whom nobody now recalled, even Dr R., who had been a consultant there for over twenty years. But the nurses loved him, and any new doctor that attempted to transfer him to more suitable environments, such as the nearby asylum at N-----------, were soon greeted with protests and complaints. They loved to look after him you see. Something in his chubby face and cheeky waddle reminded them of the children they had nursed, or those they were destined to nurse—such is the strange relation between biology and time!

Stefan H. spent his days doing little but wandering the building or staring out to the horizon from the great bay windows of the dayroom, clutching in his right hand the most precious thing in his world—this little doll that I now hold.

By far the most difficult method of coming to know the object, as with the flower press, is that of touch—but it is often the most rewarding. I deduced the outlines of Stefan's life from the briefest of encounters with the doll—its surface, in places smooth with varnish or from wear, in others cracked and rough as the wood itself rebelled against the confines of the paint. As I held it my eyes darkened with the visionary process that had become so familiar to me. I ran my stubby fingers around the curves of the toy. I found Stefan's nature—his *obsession*—almost immediately. The detail came later, through many hours of delicate and patient communion between skin and wood.

What ailed Stefan H. none could tell, although the doctors proffered their many theories, the most popular of which was an emotional trauma that had left him dumb and alienated from the world. Once they even associated this trauma—such was their genius!—with his precious Russian doll and attempted to prise it from him. After a battle, involving many nurses and doctors they wrested it from him and he collapsed, catatonic. They carried him to his bed but his heart was barely beating and his breath came in slow long gasps that sounded so frightful that they restored the little figure to his fingers in an attempt to bring him back from the brink. Instantly Stefan H. was up and out of bed, shuffling down the corridor to the dayroom to resume his gaze across the mountains.

From that day on no attempt was made to take the doll from him and he trundled through the years, silent and strange.

I know his mind. I have seen his world; one of faces and relationships, wrapped around a core of love and safety.

For him there was nothing in the world but others; if he even conceived of a separate entity—a Stefan H.—it was only the space in which those *others* dwelt. His eyes were photographic plates upon which the negative of each person was cast. His palm was the dark room in which that was developed, to be stored in his little doll.

With each new face he encountered he would add to the layers of doll people, each enfolding the previous like a protective shell. He never repeated an individual and, if he had ever been able to speak he would have informed you precisely where each person rested, whom it was that they enfolded, and the one that kept them securely enclosed. With each new addition the little wooden figurine was twirled about in his palm, and the ritual was complete.

I cascade back through the years, months, days and hours, reliving a life. Faces flashed through my mind; as many kind and caring as those cruel and callous. And finally, at the heart of this world there was mother, with her great smile and adoring eyes. She was the one he kept so sheltered, wrapped in all the people he had ever known, safely in the core—the very centre of everything. It was for her that he had crafted this bulwark against oblivion, and now I was charged with its guardianship.

...and Other Fabrications

Lilium Pomponium ~ **Agnieszka T.**
'Now there danceth a God in me'
A Suitcase

Hardy; of most easy culture. Varies with red and yellow flowers, with many flowered and few flowered racemes, some of which are so much contracted have to have the appearance of an umbel; sometimes is only one or two-flowered. Generally propagated by parting the scaly bulbs. One of the oldest inhabitants of our gardens.

One finds such depths in common materials, if one works at the art of reading them. One such was brought

The Phantasmagorical Imperative...

to me amidst a great heap of household objects, each of which would have found conduits through which to reveal to me their secrets. I wept for the number that I had to refuse from the junk merchant, with his wooden cart—as ancient as forever.

The one I selected was that great symbol of hope and despair—a suitcase; the eternal emblem of this continent.

This suitcase: simple brown leather with a rugged handle darkened with sweat. It rattled on sturdy brass links that had clicked their way through many train stations, jittered in the back of many cabs, and clattered up many shadowy stairways.

What attracted me, at first, was its speckled surface and the brightly polished gold lettering upon it: A.T.

All else he brought me that day then faded into a blurry distance. I heard his mutterings in the background, for new voices were calling to me then. I paid him his coins. He departed, grumbling the usual valediction of the tradesman; never enough, *enough* is *never* enough.

It was that very evening that I discovered its intricacies. The striped lining was stained with dark brown patches—I thought these might be the residues of many spring showers, summer storms and autumn rains, but how wrong I was. The mottled pattern, upon closer inspection, was made up of many marks; hundreds of little lines and scores, thus: ++++

Each of these lines, no longer than 5 millimetres, had been etched into the surface with the precision of a sharp knife or razor blade, and each mark had then darkened into blackness with a rich ink—the *deepest* ink. Running my fingers across its surface I attempted, with my cracked and calloused skin, to find the meaning behind it all. Soon I had my face against it, the bristles of that afternoon's stubble crackling against the leathery surface, decoding the lines like a thousand needles playing an old wax cylinder. The scent of the leather rose to my nostrils like the fungal bloom of the earth, drenched with the urine of its beasts, rich with the chemical exchange of its abundant gifts.

Beneath the cracked marks of its surface I felt the work of countless hands, stretching and soaking, preparing and bathing—the work of liquid and heat, sun and toil, amidst the stench of dead flesh and effluent.

And then I brushed against the lettering, cold and harsh upon my skin—bold and bright amongst the gloom of my shop as it tucked itself into the shade of the early evening.

A. T.

Golden! Brilliant!

It could be none other than Agnieszka T., of Z------ -.

Yes—indeed!—of the famous summer of 193_!

In the wake of that heady season Agnieszka T's suitcase had accompanied her fragile, repentant soul to the Sisters of the Holy Family of Nazareth, where for some years she was content to serve. Then, beset by visions of the blood and terror to come, she fled in fear. Within only a few short months she was warming the hearts, and more, of the generous gentlemen at Mme. M's house in Rue B------. This was no particular achievement, such journeys are common, in either direction, that direction only differentiated by the soul in piteous torment, or the body in youthful conflagration. Both burn, it is merely the colour of the flame that differs, and its duration.

Within weeks that supple little body—at once as taut and muscled as a boy's, yet tender and fruitful as a milking maid's—was the toast of Paris and the word on every rotten breath across the city.

Ah, the queues to visit Agnieszka! Eventually, an officer was put out upon Rue B------, just to keep the peace. For his efforts he was entitled to one visit each week, gratis (but always on a Sunday)! Little did her queuing admirers know that beauty keeps its own secrets. And Agnieszka was a lovely little bomb, in so many ways. As men notch their guns so too did our heroine mark her tricks upon her little suitcase. Soon the lining was covered with the record of their pleasures:

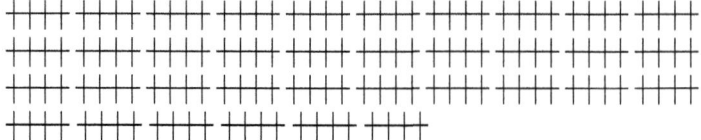

The cool mornings rolled into sweaty afternoons; the afternoons into hot evenings. Even the winter was alight with the heat of bodies at work. The days became months, and ever the lining of that suitcase filled with little marks—of shame or conquest? None would know, until the tally of them told her the time was right for a reckoning.

What mysterious pornography has lain hidden within this empty case; as my face and fingers trail across each line I feel the events of that evening, that afternoon,

...and Other Fabrications

that lost morning; every memory as rich and detailed as though it were screened in a theatre. I see their flesh and hear their moans. I know each intimate fold of her and every hairy inch of them, heaving and groaning to their petty little completions. I smell the sweat and taste the fluids. It ends as everything does—ever disappointed, regretful that it could not be their last moment upon this broken earth.

So, finally it came. She took an evening off, much to the disappointment of her sweaty suitors. She had new work to begin: a conclusion, of sorts. She learned the practice of her sacrifice from the torment of her soul, and the song of her communion rose from the worn lines of her skin. The work of the body transformed in delirious abandon into the anguish of the spirit. Her ritual required no ancient dagger, no chalice or robes, simply a razor and her will.

That evening her chant could be heard down most of Rue B------ and the other working girls battered the ceiling above them (those that were below her) and the floor below them (those that were above), demanding she stop her terrible wailing. Eventually the Madame was called and, with the help of two army officers (that had completed their business) they broke down her door. There they found the naked body of Agnieszka T. It was covered in minute wounds, the record of her sin.

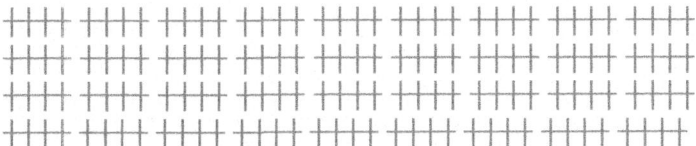

The blood flowed in pools about her boudoir (dripping through, in time, to those rooms below in steady pulses, interrupting the entertainments—briefly—with screams of fright). Candles burnt around the room and an acrid smell of singed hair hung about the place.

That night—cloudless, moonless and brilliant with judgement—many fine men of Europe fell like bloated flies across their dinner tables—having only just finished the soup course. And across the seas, in ports from Tallinn to Izmir, sailors dropped at their watches or atop fresh flesh. Soldiers, in uniforms of grey or blue, of red or brown—generals, officers and privates—were discovered dead in their bunks. Diplomatic envoys choked on their second martini. Parliamentary men, especially, were found, pale and rigid, the following morning. There was not an outpost of this crumbling continent, with its grasping tendrils, untouched by decimation; and as I scrape my fingernails through every bitter line in Agnieszka's case I hear a squeal, and through it I can almost discern the names.

...and Other Fabrications

Campanula Carpatica ~ Dr Anvar Z.
'In the Name there is an Omen'
A Speculum

As yet it is scarce in our gardens, but deserves to be more generally known and cultivated; its flowers, in proportion to the plant, are large and shewy: like many other Alpine plants, it is well suited to decorate certain parts of rock work, or such borders of the flower garden as are not adapted for large plants. It is a hardy perennial, and propagated by parting its roots in autumn.

When all other modes of understanding are exhausted one relies purely on the function of the object. This, given time, may allow one to elaborate the pathway to its owner. Such was the case with a speculum, blackened by fire, whose beak-like form I discovered in a box of shoe lasts behind the old power station over the river.

It took time to discover the method of its speech.

Doctor Anvar Z. had come to V----- late in 184_. No one asked him why. No one asked him where he had come from. All were content to have a doctor in their village—and one who charged so little for a service that surpassed all expectation.

He had left his home town of T----, at the height of a gold fever, as the splendour of that ancient Siberian town seemed most threatened by the greed of the visiting speculators and investors. He travelled across roads as ancient as humanity, founded on trades he had no knowledge of, settling finally in that small village in the Carpathians, where the air seemed brighter and the expansive skies spoke to him of possibility.

He came with his black bag—by that the villagers knew him to be genuine.

He came with a pony, laden with equipment— jingling and tinkling with mystery.

The stranger is always welcomed if their foreignness is clothed in familiarity, especially if such familiarity also renders service—such was the effect of his little black bag. The eccentricity of the newcomer—his mysterious baggage—is overlooked, as long as his usefulness remains fresh in the mind.

Within a few days he had made lodging in the home of Rausa H., whose husband had died the previous winter felling a tree. In time Dr Z. might even have married Rausa's daughter, Zukhra, had his passions not been focused so intently upon his work.

The new mountain doctor purchased a small house the following spring and kept himself very private therein—such behaviour being common in professional men.

As the seasons came and went the need for him increased. And with this new income, even with his modest charges, he was able to send off to B--- M--- for more equipment to enable his research. Carts would arrive to the gates of his little home and their drivers, resting later at the tavern, would tell of the crates they had unloaded and the odd glass jars and strange tubes that were packed in straw within.

What hours he spent with the villagers though, beckoned from his home (where a light would burn long after all others in the village had been extinguished) in the depths of dark, crisp nights to tend the last moments of the dying or to soothe the barking coughs of children whose mothers were plagued with worry. He attended them all, coaxing them back to health or easing them into their final sleep. Everything was done with the calm of a man whose soul is at ease with his fate. He could as easily deliver a child as administer the final relief to a suffering body. All was of serene equivalence—death and life— and in similar spirit the villagers addressed the plod of their years with courage, joy and acceptance.

But a simple life is seldom allowed to remain so.

One day a young boy, Doru M., bursting with curiosity and playing at exploring, slipped into the study of Dr Anvar Z. and found a world of horrors. Jars lined the walls with odd shapes and forms within, some animal and some more human. The alien pose of the hunched foetus was common to many, striking Doru with a terrifying sense of the familiar—the uncanny recognition of his own growing limbs and clumsy body. His face was contorted with dread of the macabre but his thoughts were keen with the fascination that bubbles through every curious boy. And minds there were a plenty, in jars of variously yellowing liquids, each seeming as though it might, at any moment, wriggle into life and swim about like some prehistoric fish. Limbs and fingers and organs of every variety (that Doru had seen only in textbooks at the schoolhouse) were stored on racks of dark wood, labelled with words that seemed as foreign to him as magical runes.

Then there were the instruments; metal blades and saws of every size and shape, small scalpels and great spatulas. The main table had a series of tubes and bowls that all connected with delicate tubing. Within, a variety of liquids rested, of all colours. But the one that most endured in Doru's memory was of course the blood red one, drained, he thought, from someone recently deceased. And there, as Doru's mind erupted with childish imagination the fate of Dr Anvar Z. was sealed.

Doru fled, and with each desperate step his story grew. The jars came alive with monsters, straining to break out, their bulging eyes burning with hatred. He conjured tales of the babies, recalling the infants lost to mothers in the village. Here they were, revitalised and imprisoned, singing strange laments and crying for their families. The room flowed with blood, piped around glass arteries, pumping an automaton into artificial life, yearning to satiate its mechanical thirst on the people of the village.

This tall tale, mixed with his father's own ramblings later that evening, and blended with the months of conjecture concerning the packages that arrived ever more frequently from B--- M---, spawned an angry mob, complete with pitch forks and burning torches—the usual fare.

How the little house of Dr Anvar Z. burnt, fuelled by the preserving fluids that had kept his specimens. His notebooks, carefully recording the health of every member of the village, were now cinders. His drawings, of the dermal layer and the influence on new ointments upon wounds and sores, were now cinders. His latest batches of herbal remedies, for the coming winter, were now cinders. His books, on medicine, on biology, on chemistry, on law, on geography, and even his few works of literature that had offered such pleasure when he finally allowed some rest from his work, were now cinders.

His home—a place of study and silence, a place of care and cure—was reduced to a smouldering black ruin, upon the threshold of which lay his own charred corpse.

Poor Anvar Z., he deserved more. He should have been a character in a grand gothic novel. He belonged in a great crumbling castle with madness echoing around the stony corridors. But the final chapter of his story was no less grotesque and melodramatic. His burnt bones were broken into little splinters by the idiotic crowd, each fragment a precious ward against illness, or the devil. They are traded still, like the relics of the martyrs, across the continent, from the sunny shores of the Adriatic to the icy flows of the Baltic. But their exchange is most secret, and those that know of the routes travelled by, and the resting places of, such artefacts have dwindled, as much as those that know the craft of the apothecary and the spiritual healer.

There remains now only one man that can obtain one of Dr Z.'s bone fragments for you: D. G. whose house lies between V--- I--- and B----- in those darkly wooded mountains. Its great wooden gates bear a fearsome leering face, half beast, half demon! Beware then, even if you are a hardy soul, for you will find that he will ask too high a price. And besides you would never have the balls to pay it—for it is not weighed in the manner of gold, you cannot fold it like banknotes, or test its coinage. What he might demand you will have neither sense to understand, or nerve to carry out. I did not when finally I enquired of him his price. Besides, he is deaf now, and blind, and the art of communicating with him, through subtle pressures upon the palm would take too long for even the most patient of men. No, I doubt you are the kind that would spend a decade to achieve your goal, for it does not consume you enough—it does not corrode your being, whittling your mind as though it were a piece of driftwood.

What hidden cavities there are within the human form. That is so clear to me now. For perhaps those villagers were not so foolish. Dr Anvar Z. had left his homeland to escape himself and the deeds he had committed there, as much to rid himself of the mercantile. His research lay not simply in the skin, but with what lay deeper—those dark pathways of the body and its powerful conduits of energy and sustenance. How he had tested and plied these routes, upon the living and the dead. He had sought to explore the sanctuary of flesh and muscle and traverse the tracks of veins. I know because I have travelled there too, with the aid of this burnt medical instrument. I have found the way not only into memory, but to the secret spaces within us all. I doubt many would have the courage to know this thing in all of its depths. Now *that* I have achieved, at least! How I have tried myself with this object, probing and exploring, with mirrors and lenses, all the hidden places of my body. I have seen the black rot that skin conceals.

Apologia

I can never describe my sadness, or my elation. I think always of those fading memories in photographs, curling into sepia dust; the beauty of those silver plated daguerreotypes creeping with the blistering rot of relentless corrosion, gradually eating away at the tinted, painted faces of these happy, proud souls.

Oh, morbidity! I am no poet, and I hope you gather, do not aspire to be. I do not wish to plunge you into the depths, or carry you on any falser journey than the one you are already on. Let the words crumble away now for I know you will never understand—never understand me, I mean. That is why I do not assail you with the horror of my image.

But—great hypocrite!—how I have loved these lives like treasured works of art—private collections with their subtle pigments, magical hues and ornate gilt frames. How I have clothed them with the lies of words and the subterfuge of personal reflection.

The Phantasmagorical Imperative...

Let it be recorded here though that I tried to *know* in *different* ways. Many an evening I would sit with these objects, caressing them, stroking them, urging them to reveal their deepest secrets. I am not ashamed to say, I wandered naked through my little shop, hoping to glean some essence of the spirit that whispered through everything. And gradually I came to know them all. Not with the immediate impression of a face, or the pompous catalogue of biography, but through the subtle, ancient ways—of tenderness and savagery, of nobility and servitude. I have known more tears and smiles, more rage and love, than any man alive. Weep for the pain of the people! Weep, and laugh. Laugh for the lusts, and the dancing evermore!

My little dust will be the fertile soil of a thousand trees that will sing a chorus of the lost lives I have encountered. These pages, as each one is filled, I tear from the book and tuck beneath my clothes, to help against the coming chill. Who will ever find this tattered raiment; these scraps are already in the grate before the ink has dried—accounts of lives so lost they might as well have been fiction. My being strains like a great laden pod, bursting with the misery of a continent, aching with the joys and desires of this futile, rebellious existence.

The Ten Dictates of Alfred Tesseller

O Lord, deliver me from eternal death

∞
A Wake

You remember Alfred Tesseller—the quiet one who arrived, all those years ago, in our decrepit country classroom. He had that accent that was so strange and yet so enchanting. We thought his family were ancient gypsies and the tales we told about him rivalled any myth performed around immortal fires. You must remember him!

Surely you remember the dark breads, strange meats and exotic fruits he would bring with him in his battered metal lunchbox, and how, once, and only once, he shared the small squares of cake—of spicy syrup, or honey, and ground nuts—his mother would make him. You recall how we gathered around him that day, like we were old friends, and how he laughed, and we did too (although we *laughed*, like dogs, at the hiding we would deliver him that evening in the back lane).

Ah, good, you do remember. I thought a little taste of blood would bring it all back!

I come to tell you he is dead now. Alfred Tesseller is dead.

It's unnerving, I know, when you hear of those you knew as a child—however distantly, and however cruelly—now cold and packaged for the ground, the crypt, or the flames.

I seem to recall that you were the worst though; the relentlessness of your tormenting pursuits and the brutality of your fists. That much older than the rest of us you had the upper hand in everything; size, speed and cunning.

I recall the day you delivered me a pounding. It was a slight insurrection—voicing an objection to pelting Alice with those rotten cider apples, alive with the evil chuckle of wasps—but enough to merit retribution. I squealed as I ran from your great clumsy hands as we darted from tree to tree and dodged the clutching branches. I had the upper hand amongst the trees, small and nimble as I was against your awkward adolescent frame. Yet coming to the edge of the orchard I saw the expanse of a field out to pasture and something in me yearned to find space, as though I might be able to soar into the skies and finally rid myself of your tyranny.

Within moments my short legs had failed me and you were upon me, with our dirty gang behind you, hungry for something they couldn't comprehend. Even Alice, free for now from persecution, mustered a few supportive cheers. Setting steadily to work on me you hummed some playground ditty—a sing-song chorus that chimed the pleasure of your fists upon my soft cheeks with metronomic precision. You had pinned my arms with your knees and I broke beneath the ferocity of your radiant glee. With a beautifully perverse flourish you licked the blood from my face and spat it back; such crowning abjection sealed my fate as your lackey or eternal enemy. And so, eager to taste the rewards of cruelty, your lackey I became! What wonderful ruin—for a while.

I did not have the courage then to resist you (and nothing has changed); courage such as Alfred Tesseller showed—to remain distant and silent, to absorb the pains of pointless malice with humility. His quiet tolerance of you spoke of knowledge far beyond the few miles of fields and farmsteads that marked the limit of our world.

He had come to us like some changeling from another kingdom, from some preternatural idyll—a fantastic realm of pure forms. We were not ready for his form of subservience. We would never understand his slow grappling with our language that was so other to all the ones his brief years had heard echoing across vaster distances than we would ever know.

So, my spiteful friend—in memory of those glorious days—it is to you that I speak.

∞

It had taken quite some hours for me to find the place that Alfred Tesseller had demanded we meet at. It was in that strange copse we had found together so many years before. The place was long overgrown, having been deserted even by the hardiest of children.

I was confused. My thoughts still dwelt with the everyday—work, food, rest—and I was unprepared for the chaos of the natural. I believed I was hallucinating. It takes some time to accustom oneself to the mysteries of even the plainest of ferns.

There in the undergrowth I found his body, preparing itself for transformation.

But Alfred Tesseller could never be content with the ease of death. He has many places left to visit, and many decades to dismantle. The low hum of working insects around him jittered into words and through them he told me what I would do for him.

And as I grappled with maddening thoughts I rifled his corpse. I do not wish to unnerve you, merely to pass on the few lines I found in his notebook before his metamorphosis, or should I say resurrection, began.

They are simple words, written in the beauty of his flowing foreign script.

∞

Since then—since reading those few lines—I see him everywhere, and (as though dreaming) in every time, amidst the turmoil of the centuries. Great cathedrals are burning as his silhouette strides towards me—no, to us! In a blasted ballroom, whose vast cracked windows look out upon a fast-flowing river dotted with debris, he crouches over a young woman as rose-fresh with lust as he is pale with death. I see him striding the skies against a pale purple sunset. He dances amongst the early evening shining planets and beckons the stars to shine for us from distant galaxies. His grey flesh melts into walls of stone as time itself slides through a waterfall as icy as eternity. And still those empty eyes chart the arc of history as it falls, like a lost angel, ever backwards into us.

I
There shall be nothing but you

Before I died I was staring at Anna's soup. No—the steam. I was staring at the steam rising from it.

I had said, 'How do they get it so hot?'

That is why she was laughing.

She said she was amused by how intense—almost obsessed—I became over minor details, ones that most people didn't care about.

Whilst she had taken her first spoonful and cooled it with her pink lips (she always hated red lipstick) I had stared at that steam, rising like white smoke from the surface of the liquid. That is the best description I have for it really—a liquid. It had lost all other properties for me. It remained a bowl of boiling liquid with a surface exhausting itself into air. Alfred Tesseller's words were already working upon me—things were dissolving into their component parts.

It was after that first cooled mouthful that she looked up to see me with my eyes fixed on her bowl, following her spoon, following her lips. I didn't really hear what she asked me, it seemed to evaporate into the surrounding atmosphere which was becoming steadily slower, edging inevitably towards what was to happen a few moments later.

Looking back at those minutes around that restaurant table it did seem as though everything moved in some delicate preparation for my death.

Doubtless some may say that I am reading too much into it. That I have gilded a few precious moments of memory and have infused them with some meaning, as if the whole world could prepare itself for the passing of one small man.

I agree, nothing could be further from my mind. Instead I suggest that the restaurant, its diners, waiters and waitresses, even the food itself—and especially the soup—were all moving to some kind of conclusion; a conclusion that had been conceived, and was safeguarded, within me. A conclusion already written into Alfred Tesseller's blood-stained papers that I had within my suit pocket—close to my heart.

As we had entered the restaurant and given our names I recall looking around the place. It had been a cinema once and an antique shop for years since the last war. A flush restaurateur saw the opportunity and had converted it into a detestable gastronomic den. However, Anna loved the place. I can't say the food was bad, just a little uninspiring; you paid for the surroundings really. We had booked one of the side tables, where I found it less oppressive. I faced the wall and Anna looked into the main dining area which was separated down the centre by tall planter troughs edged with deep blue tiles.

It was a Friday and quite busy even for so early in the evening.

As we seated ourselves I glanced back over to the far side where the film screen would once have been. There were four round metal tables, quite high, with tall stools beside them. Seated there drinking lager from long thin glasses were two men in dark suits—stereotypes.

I was never particularly suspicious but they both unnerved me; so much that I even mentioned it to Anna. She glanced over as discreetly as was possible in the open space.

She did look concerned, I remember that much. Her brow wrinkled, only slightly. It was the smallest of gestures.

She remarked that they were a little out of place but would probably leave soon as they looked uncomfortable. For the rest of the evening she looked over occasionally and the crease would appear again across her forehead. I could not easily look round without being too obvious and began to wish I hadn't mentioned them.

We ordered. She had the soup and I had some flakes of salmon on a bed of some kind of vegetable. I completely forget the main courses that we had selected, they were never to arrive.

I even forget now the wine that we had and that is unusual for me. I was always rather particular about the wine. Maybe it was Alsace, I seem to remember the tall thin green bottle between us on the table. Yes, it must have been—either Alsace or a German Riesling. Anna kept ducking her head either side of the bottle to see me until we asked for a bucket to place it in.

Forgive me grasping for the details, I must try to give them some structure—that they might not pass away entirely. I have to leave them with you, inevitable though it is that such trust shall be betrayed.

Events, if they still can be so called, return so strangely, in wide gaps that need to be pursued as my mind encounters them. I am afraid this may become rather a tortured exercise. You see there is no ending to be reached for anymore. That's all done with. I remain to piece together these encounters with the space I left behind—and, of course, to be the dutiful scribe to Alfred Tesseller as he orbits eternity.

Now—facts!

Two shots passed into me. One penetrated the lower part of my neck and deep down into my body. The other was less well placed and was probably acutely painful had the first not sent my system into complete shock. Both had been fired down into me from above, but this second had entered just above my shoulder and had shattered the bone completely, absorbing most of the force of the bullet. Had the same occurred with the other bullet I would still be alive.

In the moments before the shooting Anna had watched the men leave their table and walk towards us. I half turned and saw their dark shapes approaching.

Having been the first to voice unease about them it was Anna who seemed more concerned. She watched as they slid their way between the packed tables. A large group were behind us, they were all fairly young (an eighteenth or twenty-first birthday we had both thought). There was little room for anyone to pass behind me, my chair had already been knocked frequently by the one behind, so I rose slightly and pulled forward a little to offer some way through.

As I settled again I watched Anna's face fall in surprise and horror. They must have been taking out the guns.

I did not comprehend.

There was, in fact, nothing to comprehend.

The seconds slid lazily by as my eyes ticked back and forth registering her bizarre expression.

My body rocked up and then down as each bullet lodged within me. Anna's face mirrored the stillness I was entering. If we had not achieved unity in our lives then we did so at that instant.

I was death—no longer my own futile erasure but all possible deaths. I illuminated her own death—so hidden from each of us but so entirely our own—and she reflected back my own impossible moment in pupils now dark and wide. Two deaths for me, meeting somewhere far back in her brain to fuse into an image—a moment of cognition that silently sounded out my departure.

∞

And so it is in that secluded bower that I now sit with Alfred Tesseller awaiting the call to witness his journey. I am as pale as the morning rays of a waning crescent moon. Only my dead eyes can chart his movements.

But we are not the fragile corpses or fading phantasms your minds might take us for. All happens here in slow descent, as febrile roots and delicate lichens test the edges of our forms, flooding our empty cells with elements so alien and wonderful. The breeze enlivens us with memories and mysteries we never had time for. All communication is refracted into sights and smells, even light is a kind of fragmentary writing feverish with heresy.

And there, amongst last year's leaves, Alfred Tesseller reads history from a palimpsest of dusty maps—no more than burnt fragments—that he caresses like Braille. Sensing us—for *you*, my friend, are with us always—he raises his decaying head and his charming rictus—horror and bliss—beckons. I follow him. And you will follow me.

II
Tomorrow is a cinder

Out beyond the wooded grove, where we used to play with Alice, you can find the old kissing gate that leads through to the 'permitted path'. There you can skirt a farmer's field which brings forth oddly shaped cabbages late in the year. The path is muddy and treacherous (for there is a drainage dyke whose still surface disguises broken stalks as sharp as spears). At the end of the path, before it joins the road again, there is an overgrown tree stump that looks, if you imagine hard enough, like a throne.

Often, of an evening, you would find Alfred Tesseller sat upon that ivy-covered stump wishing the world were different. He would think of himself strung up on the tree, his bloated face alive with new-hatched flies and teeming maggots as his old eyes ran like melting ice-lollies down the sagging landscape of his rotten cheeks.

He *imagined* himself, over time, as the creep of ivy burrowed into his flesh and crawled about his bones in a warm embrace; like lovers in the night, hungry for warmth. And as time stretched towards eternity he found himself crumbling into dark dust somewhere deep within the fracturing surface of the earth, combining into chemical glory with the stone and the microbes, exchanging atoms with his enemies and lovers, his forbears and progeny.

Alfred Tesseller would consider the rolling hillside before him, and the broad meadow of swaying dry grasses flecked with poppy, harebell and cowslip, whose reds and blues, violets and yellows patterned the parched field like oils on a dead man's canvas. At the foot of the hill one reached the rotting stile that brought you onto the raised track through the marshy field beyond.

He imagined the track erupting from the marshland, in a rapid tumult of earth and stone, carrying him into the storm-laden sky. And the flight of his mind alone was enough to force us both back into time itself and begin our search for you.

Together, Alfred Tesseller and I have walked the streets of dark cities whose bizarre geometry and dimensions baffled us. Some of these incredible cities were deserted, with haunting discordant songs echoing through the heights of dreamy spires, whilst others teemed with peoples few have ever encountered; all trading or fighting, drinking, laughing and gambling, under the shadow of vast ziggurats and minarets, the air filled with muezzin calls.

We have gazed into vast catacombs; chasms of such aching depth and extent that my mind reeled with their contemplation. But there were other, darker journeys some of which left us trapped within some darkened chamber, or stumbling in the fetid ordure of tombs, whose contents were vaguely discernible from the half-light that filtered through distant, minute windows; tombs whose inhabitants moved—slowly, steadily, and inexorably toward us.

Beyond the fear we learned brotherly love for all the rotten things of this earth, and many others. We learned how to cascade through memories and fall through lives. Initially my spirit reeled with the monstrosity of this new existence—how at each moment I might collide with Alfred Tesseller's form and inhabit him as he strode through history. In other moments he set me free, like some demented dog. On our first dreadful journey I learned the loneliness of war.

∞

Words are the property of others, images are only my own. Sometimes I've thought that it might be possible to slip somewhere between the two and find a shell-hole to hide in—a deep place to bury myself within and mutter my memories. There, between images and words (a little nearer to images I presume), are thoughts; a low fog on the battlefield.

Off again, on again, on with the image (it never seems to go).

Where am I fighting? Sometimes it's hard to think, hard to hold the thoughts together. Thoughts wander into words and praise themselves.

Our whistle blows.

If only I could say what I meant, run where I wanted, without treading carefully. Screams of bullets fly around me. I'm thinking; I think that the bullets are words—at last a space to think.

Another hole to hide in, this one is closer to the enemy I think you'll find. A space to breathe. The hole is filled with mud. Here the mud wears faces that look provoked, there seems to be some thought behind them. The faces cling to me. The mud clings to clothes, belongings, to other faces. There is no difference between the faces and the mud. In the light of a flare I see my own face inside a muddied pool. It is Alfred Tesseller's. I am inside his disintegrating cadaver. I stare out of his hollow eye sockets. We are journeying on.

I'm thinking too much, you must follow me though—over the top.

Over the top! I'm running, we're running; Alfred Tesseller and I, mud clinging to boots, clinging to faces. We're running!

It is hard to think. Thoughts and words aren't hard enough to confuse. Both can leap in and out of each other. Where does the image go? Thoughts become incongruous and disconnected. Images are dreams that invade us.

All lives are a perverse dream.

But when I awoke we thought the same way, at the same time.

The whole world had gone deaf. No one could hear but us; we thought the same way, at the same time. It was a dream. If I could awake I would only find myself deaf again. Or even worse—deaf, mute and blind, swathed in the darkness of a body again.

Through these countless years I have begun to fix a number to a place and faces clot with names. In the mud I see all blood running into possibility. This confusion has led to something. It has shown that mud and blood can mix so well together.

I can see that all these truant instants point beyond themselves. Alfred Tesseller has taught me that. Think only this—my friend—that in this dirt there was only recollection and reflection. From this dirt there are a million beings that we might have been. All this has been a cold mockery of reality; and the opposite may well be true.

Here, where night collides with day, all things become a home. Here in this hole, hiding like a medal on a lost corpse, I have squandered night and day and made my sleep like wakefulness; only hollow blasts of the same noise.

What if my enemy were to creep up and catch me here, in the arms of their own dead? How might they react? Would I be just another face in the crowd—born into this situation, as untimely as they have been—another target? I cradle a warrior in my arms.

On this hazy wedding night I have given my all. I came out on top. Is it only horror that has left his eyes black and still while mine still search for comfort?

And then, there are the stories the old boys tell through cracked lips,

> *I swear, they got up and walked. A whole damned field of the bastards. Old leering puppets without strings. How can the dead walk? They do it a hell of a lot better than us I'm sure. Just stumbling on invisible strings... the painted boys in mud...*

Invaded again.

There is a motor growl in the distance.

What can they be cooking up now? Now and again you might find a name folded in a letter. In a name there is something too specific for this swamp of faceless generality. I think this place was once called Passchendaele.

The rain has come. Sheltering in a corner I am writing something of an explanation, half of the memories that I have had and purchased nothing with. The ink runs into a black smudge in my lap. All that is left is a sodden page. The paper is more alive than I have ever been and these words are flying through a cloudy battle faster than lead from a gun.

I lay here in the mud trapped inside the bloating body of Alfred Tesseller, strung upon the wire. Beside me lies a broken revolver, a musket, a cannon, a halberd, a sword, a dagger, a club—each mutating into each other as the landscape collapses into fields of grass, expanses of desert, swamps, ruined buildings crumbling into jungle palms.

Hopefully they will not find me when they search the dead. We have lost, this is our last stand.

I have heard that the King is dead.

Soon it will become more than real. I have found a hole, for a while at least. I hope I can make it through this one, into another disintegrating identity.

Each moment has only pointed to the next—to the previous—I am everywhere now. It is all so real and I can see each thing with eyes like microscopes. Something is forcing me on, dragging me in. I couldn't be anywhere else but everywhere. I'll draw a dead man's blade and fight on.

III
Beware the dust!

The street was cracked and riddled with potholes, many were more like craters filled with muddy, stagnant water. Everywhere was ruin. Houses, half-standing, had disgorged their contents to the winds. Photographs fluttered past like sepia butterflies. Silk scarves hung tattered in the skeletal branches of trees that would never bring forth leaves again. A thin film of ash covered everything, reducing the world to the bleakness of the skies above.

Alfred Tesseller strutted along, for once his battered brown greatcoat bringing colour to the scene. He assessed the wreckage, peering in at the bombed-out windows, finding an occasional, impromptu trader there, bartering with haggard people for root vegetables or salvaged clothes.

I followed behind on the pungent wafts of filth that threaded the air.

At the end of a disintegrating path we found a grand building with burnt blue paint upon its facade and two great openings that might once have held ornate leaded windows, evidence of which now hung in small glittering fragments from its frame.

A grinning, gap-toothed old woman leant against the double doors that had, despite much scorching, remained intact.

'Want to see the matinee?' she leered, flinging the doors wide open to reveal the foyer.

A couple, in tattered evening dress, fucked lazily on a gaming table. The woman took occasional swigs from a cracked brandy bottle. They turned and grinned at the old woman who nodded back approvingly before veiling the scene.

Alfred Tesseller walked on.

The broken road opened onto a small square, where other streets joined it at odd angles. The few people that could be seen going about their meagre tasks for daily subsistence would huddle at the edges of buildings, darting furtively from ruined homes, across piles of rubble, clutching salvaged items.

In the square three young boys ran back and forth, kicking a half-deflated football across a crooked chalked-out pitch, quite oblivious to the terror clearly felt by the other inhabitants. These cheery lads sported tatty brown shirts and muddy grey shorts. On their backs each had scrawled, in coal-dust, the number nine and their name; Otto, Ernst and Viktor.

Even in the most desolate of ruins and in the darkest of hours these eternal children would find something with which to play—even if it was only bleached bones.

Alfred Tesseller watched their game, his dry lips struggling to raise a smile.

Across the square there stood a building that had escaped unscathed whatever disaster had destroyed this place. Pale and gloomy faces peered out at us from the upper floors, as though it had become some haven for the lost and displaced, but their stasis soon betrayed them as mere mannequins that had no doubt watched that square for years, if not for centuries.

The ground floor seemed to be a small shop, crammed with many articles of such variety that it was difficult to discern the owner's trade. Likewise no name, or occupation betrayed the purpose of the curious store.

Alfred Tesseller strode across the square, through the chalked out pitch and the boys' game, towards the little shop. Little Otto had pitched a hefty kick though and the deflated ball scuttled across Alfred Tesseller's path.

With a great swing of his bony leg he fetched the ball high into the air where it reeled like a spinning-top. And as it spun it withered. And as it withered it hardened into a sphere of wood and smashed through the glass pane in the shop door.

Otto, Ernst and Viktor scattered in an instant, screeching like geese.

Alfred Tesseller headed for the shop.

The shopkeeper was on his knees, with a dustpan and brush. Seeing his new and somewhat different customer he stood and gave a brief bow before retiring behind a wooden desk, depositing the glass shards into a bucket, where they rang out like dropped coins.

The shop was filled with curiosities, for some antiques, for others junk. High shelves were stacked with old books and maps, blueprints and etchings. Coats, hats and umbrellas hung on any available hook or nail. Leather satchels and carpetbags were piled in corners, dropping their stuffed contents onto the dusty floor. There were trays with buttons and medals, crests and emblems cast in every type of metal, and fashioned from rich woods and crumbling minerals.

The shopkeeper sat at his desk rolling the wooden ball back and forth, and then he spoke.

'Let me tell you the story of the dog.

> *The Master had died and the dog was left alone.*
>
> *Each day the dog would sit patiently with the ball at the open doors to the garden. Every day at noon it would drop the ball at the door and stare up expectantly, waiting for the Master to arrive.*
>
> *Before he died the Master would come down from his rooms at exactly midday and throw the ball with all of his might down the garden. The dog would race off, exhilarated, to retrieve it. By the time it had fetched the ball, and returned, the Master was gone and the dog would sit and wait until the next day.*
>
> *Now the world was all different.*

The Master was dead and the dog would wait for him, little understanding that—for even one as great as the master—death is a great hindrance to any routine. The dog remained loyal to the Master even though the servants would come to the garden door and throw the ball. He would look up at them, disappointed, and slowly head off to get the ball. On returning it would collapse despondently, the ball dropping from its mouth, and wait once more for the Master.

As the days wore on though the dog lost heart and began to think that his Master had forsaken him. He would carry the ball around the garden and drop it in different places, returning to the garden door before racing off again to retrieve it. It was no use though and as time passed the dog would even forget to lay by the garden door. Instead it would sit inside in bed and watch the preparation of the food or the servants cleaning the house. These tasks were clearly unimportant though and most days, sometime in the afternoon, the dog would take the ball to the garden door and wait, for a few minutes, with gradually fading hope and then return to bed disappointed.

Everything was lost. Some would have you believe that it was love that kept the dog so loyal to the Master for so long. This was, of course, most incorrect. Those sparkling eyes gazed at him out of need—almost in hatred. The dog needed him to rule; to never appear until midday and then to throw the ball once—and only once. But now with the routine gone the dog withered and one day it fell asleep and did not wake up.

The dog had died and the ball was left alone.

And that is the story of the dog, or of the master, or of the ball—any story you wish!'

He smiled and let the little ball roll from his desk and come to rest at Alfred Tesseller's feet.

A metallic clang sounded from the corner of the room. The bucket had fallen over and a cascade of screws, nails, nuts and bolts scattered across the floor.

The man just shrugged and smiled on.

Then from the shelves and rafters came a shuffling sound, as of mice scurrying about.

The little shop seemed alive with movement, as all the objects fidgeted and jostled for space.

Everything seemed to be in motion, expanding itself and shifting slightly upon its hooks and pegs. Leather was creaking into life; wooden chairs that had ached from decades of stillness cracked and stretched their knots and grains.

Buttons and badges overflowed from the shopkeeper's grimy trays. The cramped room was shrinking further as all these forgotten things began to multiply.

Even the square outside was filling up with things; suitcases and spyglasses, wardrobes and woollen vests, maps and medicine balls, dynamos and dolls, letters and ladders, tea-urns and tricycles, barometers and bottles. Every item imaginable seemed to be toppling from windows and doorways, sliding and tumbling over each other in a chaotic jumble of forms. And everywhere the cowering, frightened people of this forgotten place had stopped to watch as objects gathered and swam around their feet and legs—and still they came, erupting from the ground. Great chariots appeared in clods of soil and clouds of dust; bent forks, knives and spoons danced across great tables laid with the buried plates, bowls and tankards of lost centuries.

A man, dressed well in Morning Grey, stood in the centre of the gradually vanishing square, consulting his agitated pocket watch, from which emerged a grandfather clock followed by bells, pendulums, springs and gears of sizes great and small. These rolled around the square, tumbling and proliferating in a feverish fashion until all that remained of the astonished gentleman was a twitching hand above a mound of horological spare parts.

Both Alfred Tesseller and the strange shopkeeper were now also buried up to their necks in the shop's orgy of antiquity. There was time enough for an exchange of knowing winks before they were covered over by the tide of stuff.

I rose, like a stream of smoke, through this pile of junk, and watched as churches, city-walls, hills and mountains were covered over in a great bubbling sea of things.

And there, atop the vast heap of humanity's treasured possessions and discarded toys, danced those eternally gleeful children, Otto, Ernst and Victor, happily chanting a nursery rhyme.

IV
You have nothing left to give

But ever this universe gathers itself against the horror.

Our worlds are as much alive with beauty as with terror. The evenings I have passed, with Alfred Tesseller, reaping ripe fields; the afternoons amidst the joyous, homely fug of coffee shops and smoking dens; the mornings in the arms of lovers, or breathing fresh mountain air against skies awash with glorious dawns. The lives we have inhabited are innumerable and their manifold passions impossible to recount.

And now we dwell within another history.

It is the edge of a Mediterranean night where the heat slides away into the balm of a cool sky washed with orange and red, lightly expiring under the coming star-speckled blackness.

Alfred Tesseller stands at the edge of a gently murmuring stream that curves gently around a great domed building. His mouldering heart is filled with pride and his spirit lifted in exaltation to the glory of the gods—they are not yet lost.

A thin procession approaches across the fertile valley below, their torches flickering gently in the salty breeze. It will take them an hour to reach here, as they sing and make offerings along the way. Already their voices reach him through the still of the evening, this holy evening.

Alfred Tesseller is hidden within another shell, his red eyes buried deep inside another skull. He and the other masters have already prepared. The plates of registry have been filled, listing those moving from the threshold to within. The Anaktoron is blessed for the passing of the favoured, its table heavy with rich red flowers and scented oils, the three lamps burn; those that can only be lit on this one night of the year.

The Arsinoeion lifts its great dome on tapering columns whose stuccoed white facades catch the last rays of the sun with a bright orange glow. The building is aflame with love and forgiveness, its floor strewn with vine leaves and petals. Beyond, where the stream curves down from a short rocky waterfall, is the Hieron.

Alfred Tesseller's body is seized by a rush of bliss, for this is where those initiated tonight will be heading in one year from now; where they will be purified and cleansed of the evils of this wretched world and their blood washed by the infinite care of the gods.

He is touched lightly on the arm by a woman, who hands him the oil with which the ceremony will begin. Her voice is calm and deep with a demotic variation of the language that betrays her origin in the Southern Islands. She is the wife of this body that Alfred Tesseller now inhabits. He has never been so filled with love. She has given him three beautiful daughters whose voices join with the trickle of the fountain by which they now play.

All are welcome here, women, children, free men, slaves. And again he is glad, so glad that he believes there is not space in this feeble frame for such joy, for such vast spiritual blessing. He touches his wife's cheek briefly and they turn to the Anaktoron, saying the words of forgiveness and opening. Together they dip their hands in the oil and kneel to rub the steps clean as the voices and songs draw nearer.

This man's mind is alive with emotion and memory. Alfred Tesseller feeds upon it like a starving wolf. He remembers his own initiation and pities those who now approach, for he and the other masters dressed in their flaming robes of orange and red, with bright white hoods and golden armbands are an imposing sight. But he knows their trepidation will be swept aside as they embrace the rites of the first sanctum.

The first two draw near; these are the ones he is to receive. On the left is the farmer Philotheos who has finally found the path by a visitation of light and song last year. He will, it is hoped, become a master, for the change in him is so complete and deep. He is a genuine Cabiri. Likewise the man who accompanies him: Deopus, the black slave, rescued from a sinking galley. He has shown his love and commitment. Working so hard by day at his boat and feeding homeless souls at his own dwelling each evening. As he approaches it is clear that he is fearful. His body shudders and his lips tremble. His light brown skin is covered with the pain he has endured, bright scars across his back from the lash, and each wrist is ringed with a thick band of abrasion from his irons. These will be Deopus' haloes. He will be welcomed and all fear dispelled.

Both men tremble now as he approaches them, clad in his raiment of mastery. Yet beneath this garment, and beneath this very skin, there whirls the entire tumult of the world, within the soul of Alfred Tesseller. There, all love is folded into hate, all joy into misery, and all worship into rejection. All is cancelled within him into a great nothing that floods the universe with glee and agony.

Embracing them together, in a moment that ceases time, he draws out their sins and pain.

With one word Alfred Tesseller eases all their fears. It is the least he can do. He is compassionate.

∞

We are lost again in darkness, fleeing through the centuries and collapsing into forms of humanity, beasts and beings as yet unimaginable. A man is seated, his legs crossed, on the floor of a small cave. The faintest of lights filters through from a long passageway, but even that is waning. Night approaches.

He does not move.

He hardly breathes.

I feel Alfred Tesseller around me, in the stone, in the cold dank air. His teeth are chattering. His eyes are bleeding with solid tears.

The man's lips part to release a sigh that lights the chamber with joy—a solitude unravelling and thunderously proud; a considered, powerful loneliness that will humble the world and shade all love and hope with an urgent demand.

He twitches in readiness, a task is at hand.

These eyes which, for any other, would have sealed themselves forever so long have they been closed, ache apart to reveal bright blue crystals that replace vision with pure refraction—a shuddering separation of shattered vessels, eyes of fragmentation and bewildering dispersal. Eyes so other that to see them is to surrender and give up the fiction of selfhood. After the event of these eyes opening he begins to write quickly on long strips of crisp parchment—that etching of a stylus tracing a melody to accompany the artistry of those prism visions.

This hand that writes cannot be his though. Instead it is some terrible prosthesis. A possession. He is beside himself, so crushed and absorbed and never to return other than by arresting the urge—an urge to fumble with paper and pen in a dark subterranean shelter which offers no relief from the demand to continue. When finished he will fade likes a cinder whose last orange fizzle leaves an echo of ash; the grey sign of a violent departure.

His cracked hands bleed. His heart is only anger.

He cannot comprehend his own words, those he thought belonged to him—a language. It can no longer be his, nothing but another's invention. His eyes, mind, hand, words, all stolen in the greatest robbery since those broken stones. It is true, he is a vengeful God and this is cruel revenge: a gift of words forever withdrawn.

All is dark in this hole now—a lack of light, a lack of inspiration. Though his words are concluded they will teach. They speak in whispers of violence that tease an apocalyptic allegory across the singing skin of humanity; the offspring of a mind at the threshold of all being, in the grip of its destruction. To move would break this liminal agony, it is the combined force of all joy fused with his wretched mortality.

A flare of almost neon light—cracks split the stony space; fissures from which a dry and ancient voice speaks.

V
There are caverns in the firmament

Alfred Tesseller's bones protrude from a smooth wall of rock. A stream cascades across it slowly burying him beneath layers of mineral deposits. He will have vanished back into the earth within a thousand years. I glide through the waters and catch him fleetingly once in every century. Each time I sense his bones through the stone they are twitching with memories of our times together in the classroom and in the schoolyard.

Let me remind you of a story from those happier days—the story of little Mez.

> *There once was a little girl called Mez. She lived alone in a paper house. You may think that living in a house made of paper is rather strange. It isn't really because Mez was made out of paper too. She didn't have a mother or a father. Instead she had been torn into life one day in Mrs White's classroom (you remember Mrs White—with the kind eyes and cold hands).*
>
> *Mez was the final one in a chain of little girls that Mrs White had cleverly fashioned for us out of some old art paper. Each one had pig-tails and a round face, thinning into a long white neck that became part of an amorphous body with the evidence of a short skirt at the top of some long legs (the right leg slightly misshapen due to Mrs White's incompetence with the scissors).*
>
> *There were eight of these slightly imperfect paper girls joined together, forever arm in arm, and we laughed to see them unfold in her hands.*
>
> *But, if you recall, you were sat there in the front row*

that day. You complained that the last little paper girl had been torn. You said it with such disappointment, with such sincerity—as though your entire world had fallen into ruin because of one torn doll in a paper-chain. But you were always such a fine actor—always leading your unknowing audience through your cunning little pathways of manipulation. The children stopped laughing and stared at Mrs White accusingly. She examined her creations hurriedly and found the problem.

The last paper girl did indeed have a tear that stretched from the top of her head to where her nose would have been.

This was little Mez.

Looking up, Mrs White saw our sad, disappointed faces and knew that Mez must go. The scissors sliced the offending girl from her place alongside the others and she was tossed into the bin—accompanied by the sploosh! *of a coin in a wishing well.*

Now there remained seven (a more satisfying number) slightly imperfect paper girls, joined together arm in arm, and we laughed—louder and longer than we had before— when we saw them unfold magically again in Mrs Smith's hands. Yes, even you mustered a little giggle.

This is only a short description of how Mez was 'born'. How she came to live in her tiny house on a long blank page remains a mystery. Perhaps you can furnish us with further details from your emporium of malevolence?

For my little story it is enough just to say that she was there, and there alone. For one day she awoke in a paper bed under some paper covers and found that she was real, for being real is far more terrible than being alive, as

Alfred Tesseller might show you if you ask him nicely.

Well, one day, Mez had become, or, so to speak, she found that she existed! Her body was somewhat changed since she had been discarded that day in the classroom. Her deformed leg had been exaggerated and she hobbled everywhere, with one foot a millimetre shorter than the other one. The little skirt had magnified to dramatic proportions, almost like a sail wrapped around her. She was blank white with a dull yellow tinge at her edges—most becoming for a paper girl. A small tear stretched down the centre of her head, framed by a pair of rather shabby pig-tails.

So on that day Mez awoke to find herself in a small paper house. Folding the covers from herself she stepped cautiously from her paper bed to examine her surroundings.

The bedroom contained a simple bed and wardrobe. Small windows with shutters were positioned against the wall beside the bed. She hobbled over to them and flung them wide to glance at the view from her new paper home.

As far as her tiny eyes could see there spread a long white featureless expanse. She sighed with happiness at such a beautiful view, because to a thin paper figure such scenery must surely be pleasing.

Filled with intrigue she set out to discover what the rest of her house might offer. Next to the bedroom there was a miniature bathroom, perfect in every detail. Down her small staircase a front door stood at the end of a hall with two doors leading into the sitting room and kitchen.

After investigating the kitchen and returning to the hall she stood for a few moments, still a little perplexed by what had happened to her, and in the distance she heard a loud crash. It was the sound of a tall tree being felled in an empty and desolate place. Moments later a thick black stick was thrust into the letterbox leaving a dirty black ashy deposit on her doormat.

Mez shuffled cautiously forward.

Before she had reached it there was a loud thud from upstairs that made her hobble as fast as she could up the stairs to find out what had happened. Rushing into her bedroom she found the windows shut. Peering outside she saw nothing but that white, comforting, endless expanse. She stared out for a few minutes and was gradually overcome by contrary feelings; half of her seemed glad of the disturbance, after all this meant that there were other inhabitants of this paper world apart from herself, the rest of her seethed in anger at the intrusion in a house that was quite obviously her own.

Her head raged with a pain that was indescribable, as though her mind was fighting itself; a paper civil war between two equal sides armed with scissors.

To wonder how Mez could possibly understand these things is a probable reaction to such an absurd scenario. Surely she was only an absent-minded paper creation; an amusement for children. But it would be wrong to misjudge her like this. She had been around a very long time, and her confused creation was definitely no mistake.

Moments of existence faded.

Mez found herself in bed once again. There still remained that burning split in her brain. She was in two minds as to whether she had been asleep or if she was indeed asleep now. Half of her was sure of the first solution, the other half of the latter. What a confusing situation for a paper person to be in.

Mez climbed out of bed and struggled over to the windows. As she opened the curtains there was a terrible sight before her: long snaking lines of blackness.

They spread out across her immense garden, littering the blank white lawn. They had even dared to come as far as the back door and as she watched they still threaded their abhorrent lines into her world. The dark beast was pushing forward at the rate of about a centimetre a minute and had begun to creep like ivy up the side of Mez's house.

She must go and put a stop to this insult at once, sweep away the filth that lay outside her home. Or, as came to pass, she could lay back on the bed with her half-minds raging at each other and anticipate the joy of being defaced—how long before the creeping tendrils of darkness would erase her walls and slither unrestricted towards the bed?

It remained only a matter of time before she would be changed. She lay there and awaited an event—a resolution.

Mez felt the pain of flames. It engulfed her entire body in a new anguish. It was actually quite refreshing to feel another discomfort other than her head. That was an experience, and this—after all—was only destruction.

As the embers died out a small ashy figure crawled from the fireplace—a mutated, broken phoenix. But a flame burned in the tiny sprites eyes and she carried all possible worlds with her as she strode into new nights.

Alfred Tesseller was there to meet her, as he always was—to gather in those marginal forgotten things that feed on love and hate, that live inside all intervals and embrace both sorrow and joy with equal zest. Her dust merged with his and we were gone again.

Such is the sad story of Mez, unless you recall it differently.

VI
If only *there* was not *here*

It was a bright day, sunlight warmed my face and my eyelids had become a pink translucent screen through which shadows moved, and with them came slow muffled sounds as of someone winding up an old gramophone.

It was comforting to be within a body again and I was reluctant to open my eyes. Instead I enjoyed the warmth as I passed from oblivion and back into the world.

I lay in a bed, half propped against firm pillows. The sounds around me became clearer; metallic chimes, soft shoes on tiled floors, creaks and groans of beds, and the murmur of female voices. Still with my eyes closed I breathed deeply and sensed an intensity of bleaches and fresheners, perfumes and disinfectants all mingling to mask a fainter, but deeper, odour of urine and vomit, blood and shit that had crept into the crisp ironed sheets now haunted by the ghosts of years of spilt bodily fluids. I was in a hospital.

That was my first connection with another past, the moment hidden beneath the pink haze of another's skin. Evidently I must have encountered a hospital before or I would have been unable to have placed the peculiar smell. It may have been a memory from birth. I do not know.

Opening my eyes, the ward flashed into life briefly before the brightness overwhelmed me and I was left with a faded photographic imprint of beds and bodies; tall windows; a few figures moving back and forth. It did not take long to become accustomed to the light though, and soon I took a more tentative peep out into the ward.

Opposite me lay Alfred Tesseller, head to one side, absurdly bandaged, with his leg raised aloft on a contraption of pulleys and weights. He smiled his eternal smile as he stared into infinite spaces. On the table beside his bed a blur of pinks and yellows from the flowers and garish cards melted into the greens and browns of a bowl of untouched fruit.

I glanced over to my table—nothing but a metal tray and a box of surgical gloves.

I looked down at my arms, one either side of the mound of sheets beneath which my new body lay. Then a terrible feeling overcame me. These were not *my* arms at all, but those of a dummy; foreign plastic prostheses. I say 'these were not *my* arms at all' and you may reply that the entire body was not mine, certainly. That is true enough. For I was little more now than a floating dream forever gliding in the wake of Alfred Tesseller. But it was *this* body that was filled with terror at the substitution of *its* limbs.

The details were there, a fine brown hair grew across the forearms, in places a little patchy. Even the nails seemed real; the left thumbnail cracked down the centre, and a thin silver ring on the little finger of the right hand. Those were interesting features, I thought. You certainly could not fault their thoroughness in attempting to recreate arms which another person may have found very admirable, a pleasure to possess even. But these were—most definitely—not *my* arms.

A nurse strode through the open doors a few feet from my bed. In her hand she carried a metal tray similar to the one that lay beside me. What do they call them, kidney bowls or trays? I imagined an organ within, still quivering with the shock of removal. She placed the bowl beside me and began assembling a syringe.

'These are not my arms,' I said, my voice broken and feeble.

She turned abruptly, obviously very surprised to hear me speak. 'Well, good morning, how are you feeling?' she asked, replacing the syringe and taking my pulse from those fake, dead limbs beside me.

'These are not my arms,' I repeated.

She smiled and picked up a small plastic box that was tucked under the pillows. She pressed a button and then replaced it.

'A little breakfast perhaps,' she said—rather more a statement than a question. Something in her voice quivered and she looked at me with an expression of apology. It was not pity but a regret that seemed to address the future, a sorrow for all that was to come. As though she already knew that we would share that sorrow.

I tried to recall the pleasures of food, but all that came to mind were blackened potatoes, stale bread and mouldy cheese.

'No, I don't think I can manage any breakfast,' I said, peering at my right hand. 'I would appreciate it if you could do something about these arms though.'

Another nurse came in, with a similar stride to the first. She was even more surprised to see me awake than the other had been. I was beginning to become irritated.

'I don't want these arms you know, they're not the right style,' I said.

'I'll just pull these round so that you can have some privacy with the Doctor,' she said, dragging some blue plastic curtains around the bed.

A sudden tiredness overcame me and my eyelids fell. I heard a few more of her words before slipping away.

The next thing I heard was the low mumble of male voices, as though from a great distance, or through a tunnel.

At the back of my head a heavy rhythmic thumping began.

The curtains were still closed around my bed. Two men, one tall and bearded, in his fifties perhaps, and the other shorter, younger and wearing spectacles, were peering at a brown clipboard. I watched their lips opening and closing but I heard only a low protracted sound, a sort of growl or moan. I attempted to prop myself further up in the bed, but an agonising stab of pain assailed my head. I must have cried out because both of them rushed over to calm me. They addressed me with a few of these guttural moans, one after the other.

I could not understand.

They looked at each other, as confused as I was.

Then sleep came again.

Awakening again, the headache slightly worse, only the tall bearded doctor remained. He was seated in the visitor's chair to my left, his pale eyes fixed on me with a look of concern and confusion. He waited for me to speak, but I stayed silent for quite some time.

Then I recalled my dilemma.

'Can I change these arms please?' I asked. 'You can quite clearly see that these belong to someone else.'

He rose from the chair slowly, scratching his beard, and then extended his right arm to shake hands.

'I'm your Doctor,' he said, with a deep tone that seemed to resonate around our blue enclosure. 'We've been very concerned for you young man.'

He had bent across the bed to facilitate my reaching his hand. I lay there for a few moments, shaking hands with those imposter's limbs. Then he smiled and looked down at our hands. 'You see, these are indeed your hands, and so too are those arms they're attached too.'

'Well, yes, I suppose to you they seem quite correct,' I said, watching as that ridiculous right hand greeted his. I could feel the strength of his grip and the cold of his skin but as though the sensation belonged to someone else or that I experienced it from a distance.

Perhaps Alfred Tesseller was inhabiting me now.

'I don't seem to remember my arms looking like this though. You're sure you haven't swapped them; you know, for some spares you might have out the back?'

I must have carried on like this for some time. He must have listened to an hour or more of confused ramblings which I have thankfully forgotten.

That's the issue really, forgetting.

My story is all about remembering, or remembering how to forget—to forget the things that need to be forgotten and to remember the important things—the facts, the truth.

Someone once wrote, 'remembered things have a tendency to subvert the things remembered.' That should have been my epitaph or epigraph, I forget which.

After a while I accepted his assurances and a long silence followed.

He seemed uneasy, and made a few attempts to say something but ended up asking about how I was feeling. Finally after consulting the brown clipboard again and laying it down on the bedside table he asked, 'Do you recall what happened to you?'

'What happened...' I said, puzzled.

'Before you awoke, here...' he said, an urgency developing in his voice. 'Do you know who hit you, or how you fell?'

'I was hit then... by a car?' I asked.

'We don't know, it's quite unlikely though. You only have head injuries. A collision with a car would have produced a number of other injuries as well.'

'So I fell?'

He paused for a moment, 'You don't remember falling?'

'No,' I murmured, although falling, endlessly, through lives and memories, was the only thing I could be sure of anymore.

'You were found in a street, by a passer-by, you were close to a row of shops...'

'I don't remember anything,' I interrupted.

'Nothing at all; the shops, the street, Anna,' he said.

'Anna?'

'One of our nurses, Anna, found you. She was off duty and...'

'I don't remember anything,' I repeated.

His voice faded into a mumble of background noise as I stared across the sheets, white and fresh—as blank as my mind.

I looked down at those ridiculous plastinated hands.

I saw the ring again. A thin silver band wedged onto my little finger. It had a meaning to this body. Somewhere there had been an event that gave this ring a meaning. A relationship between the thing and the person I now dwelt within.

The ring was nothing but some abstract object, suggesting other lives and loves.

But perhaps *I* was the one that had become abstracted: transformed from *I* to *not I*, a silhouette of the past and ghost of other stories.

I turned the ring a little with those alien fingers. It was tight. Perhaps it had always been too small, or maybe this body had been thinner once.

A ring. It could have been an ostrich for all the good it did. It meant nothing now, nothing to me—worth its weight in silver but little more.

Was everything only 'worth its weight' now? Had I become a scrap dealer—the *Messingkauf* man?

'I remember...' I said, twisting the ring around. 'I remember, those are pearls that were his eyes.'

There was another long pause during which I continued to agitate the ring.

'What does that mean?' he asked.

'It doesn't mean anything,' I replied, absorbed in the ring. 'I don't know a thing about it. Would you like to buy it?'

'No, not the ring,' he said, sharply, 'what you just said—pearls that were his eyes.'

Pearls that were his eyes—a song or playground rhyme. It just seemed to make sense, as though it followed naturally from 'I remember'.

'I'm sorry but I don't know why I said it. Do you know what it means?' I asked, looking up at him.

'I'm afraid not,' he replied, reaching for the clipboard and taking out a silver pen from his pocket.

'Has anyone reported me missing?' I asked. I was beginning to get distressed and tried to push myself further up the bed. A burst of thunder shattered through my head, followed by a steady painful drumming.

'You really must rest now,' he said, pointlessly rearranging some of the pillows behind me. 'If you let things take their course then we'll be able to find out something about you. Once we contact a relative these things are normally quite straightforward.'

'Let things take their course...' I mumbled to the sheets.

'Look, *trust* me, I'm a doctor,' he said cheerfully, a wide grin lacerating his beard.

I struggled to laugh along with him but it just sent another ripple of pain through my brain. He chuckled on for a few moments and then I closed my eyes and heard the plastic ripple as he slipped through the curtain.

The brightness had given way to a gentle twilight gloom when I awoke again. I felt a certain pleasure in being relieved of the burden of time. I was measuring the day in light; a series of intensities. I may well be wrong, a cloud may merely have obscured the sun and I had slept for only a few minutes. Either way it didn't matter, I was here.

Here? I hadn't asked where *here* was.

I was new-born again. I should have been wailing and puking, clasped to a breast. Or perhaps I was Lazarus, come from the dead.

The plastic curtain swished aside and in hobbled Alfred Tesseller in a green paisley dressing gown, his fetid hands clasping a withered lily and a bunch of rotten grapes.

VII
Your skin will fold like memories

Alfred Tesseller had heard her before—wild words thrown at wilder winds, now only a residue of silence. They had become the spirits of these deserted winter wastes. She had been hidden for years, quietly enfolded in prophecy.

There in those winter woods the old woman had come to him with broken golden skin as gnarled as ancient bark. We remembered everything as she spoke of long past battles; words and cadences overwhelming; languages entwining; the roots of an unspoken narrative; a conversation of the dead. It was a fiction of course, yet we had been here before, having found our own trail scattered into the memories of leaves and autolysis. There in the decay it is possible to trace the formula of one's own death.

The lily was still intact, and Alfred Tesseller carried it carefully before him as though it would light the way. The old woman was pleased to see that this token remained, for she had clawed her way out of a legend to be here; the struggle had not been in vain.

Where they walked the frost melted, burning a false spring into their tracks—from each footstep sprang a ring of hyacinths. I followed upon the frosty breeze. We could not turn back now, that would be unforgivable. Then we would have to remain here frozen inside a woodland enigma, locked forever outside godliness.

The old woman danced madly behind us, turning this way and that, throwing her matted grey hair about her until it transformed us all to snow. We drifted on the backs of summoned zephyrs, gliding into destiny; a beginning as clouded and confused as birth.

Standing, reformed, on a grassy hill we watched the figure of a man, drinking from the icy waters of a stream below.

It was time—we could be sure of temptations. Nothing would be easy, as all the words unfold they will become lies, and always a code; pictures that paint themselves on the edges of vision.

The man rises and makes his way slowly up the hill—the surroundings are unclear, all I can make out are the hill and the stream as though no other landscape had ever existed.

It seems as though all senses have been distorted. Is it a darkness that enfolds the hill, or misty swirling vapours? All becomes uncertainty. Alfred Tesseller's hand quivers and the lily shakes. Another hand reaches out to steady it. Long delicate fingers fold around his rotten fists. The nails are perfect, the skin young and supple.

She stands there transformed into the figure of a young woman with bright white hair flowing down over a pure white gown.

She is ready for any sacrifice. Her eyes are pained, her face gentle and familiar.

When the figure reaches the top of the hill he bows extravagantly, with a sweeping flourish of his arm. He wears a dirty leather jerkin that is opened to the waist. His black breeches are torn and ragged, a pair of tall brown boots reach almost to his knees. As he straightens himself I catch sight of his weary face, half hidden by a tangled mass of curling black hair that falls around his head.

His face displays a roguish grin with blackened teeth, beneath a broken and flattened nose. His skin is rich with the marks of an outdoor life.

'How pleasant to meet you on this starless day,' he said. His voice was young and melodic.

He moved a few steps closer and extended his open hands, one to the young woman and the other to Alfred Tesseller.

∞

Broken memories drifted through this woman's mind—once she had been named Anna; once a great queen of countless squabbling tribes; a beggar girl in filthy slums, but always a warrior.

She was gifted—truth shone through brittle shaded substances. For her there had been too much clarity. The human fog had been lifted from delicate adolescent eyes and her sight became immaculate, shedding the pupae husk of ancestry from her iridescent spirit's wings.

Thrust forward into a world more strange than an eternity of inertia, frozen instants of a past life blighted her mind; a hazy afternoon, heavy with foreboding, gave way to some desolate cavern where mutated human wrecks fought like dogs for food; a street with splendid old buildings and alive with bicycles; rows of books beneath tall darkened windows; a man, who has remained a boy, tries to hide himself abroad having packed all her memories, her past, her future, into a suitcase and fled to a sticky foreign heat. These old images were as good as dead. She would not have revenge upon Being.

I see, through her eyes, the roguish man.

He extends his hand, clenched in a fist, and unfolds his fingers slowly. There in his palm lay four gold coins, etched with intricate lettering.

'I offer these in exchange for that flower. They will protect you from hallucinations that may assail your tortured senses,' he said sternly, pointing with his other hand to the lily in Alfred Tesseller's hand.

She is silent. I am caged within her.

'You forget who I am, shall I unmake you little girl?' he sneers. 'All I need do is change a few details. You could be anything I want you to be. You are nothing but an imagination playing at being real.'

These words hang like a haze around her, ready to shatter her fragile soul with their cruelty.

She looks to Alfred Tesseller. He hands her the lily.

I feel her yearning to be freed. She gazes deep within his melting eyes and finds only chasms of sadness—dark places I have sunk into before. They were eyes that looked into the heart of death in every instant. They told the true horror of time.

And now the time had come to take charge of this unconquered moment, a gift lay in her hands. It became a weapon.

'I shall not be unmade by the whim of some phantasm. I have no need of your illusions. I will unmake *your* fantasies,' she said abruptly.

'I claim what is due to me and give you this debt,' she said, offering the lily with her left hand.

His face flips from the triumphant jester to the rejected lover.

From his leather jerkin he draws out an antique silver pen, as though it were a dagger. He examines it carefully—slowly—before casting it to the ground.

A dense blackness descends. I feel her limbs stiffen.

VIII
Love was once a law

With the burst of a cork I soar into existence again. I charge through the bubbling liquid and plunge into a tall fluted glass. Alfred Tesseller swirls the pale champagne slowly in the glass and I dance, seeing the whirling walls of a great dilapidated ballroom swathed in huge dusty sheets. Three vast candelabra manage a little sparkle though they too are dark with age. Outside a violent river carries blocks of ice that thunder and rumble in their race towards the sea; debris of a thousand civilisations floats upon its turbulent waters crashing out the rise and fall of empires. This ceaseless orchestra provides the music for an inevitable seduction.

Alfred Tesseller has an admirer. She wears a great patchwork gown assembled from the threads of history stitched by fingers nimble with love and lust.

Alfred Tesseller has played this scene before. He delivers his role with a tired acceptance. He delicately teases away the dress, his parched lips caress her shoulders and his decayed nostrils draw in the sweat and perfume of her hair. He gently unfastens the skin from her shoulders and reveals the torsion of her muscles as she cradles her arms around herself, as though embracing him. The delicate thread of red veins is etched across her hidden surface, like tiny roots seeking sustenance; each uncoils beneath his skeletal fingers, pausing momentarily to explore his crumbling palm like a crimson caterpillar upon a fleshy leaf. And as he searches this unknown plateau of flesh those veins thread themselves into a script that speaks of all the loves and losses bodies have endured in their struggle for each other. Alfred Tesseller's decrepit eyes survey the history of humanity's desires:

> *and now that i have written it that is to say we who have never written scribbled noted marked or remarked turned said into stone before the beginning of some long journey approaches and declines with fervour the arrival of some destination of which little can be said but only that once i had thought and of that there can be nothing but an*

afterword an appendix a margin of error perhaps is it a supplication agreement contract bargain making dealing trading barter plea confession there where we were taken apart taking we apart on holy ground this is not knowledge to re assemble this picture which is unclear a mutated puzzle i must re arrange having uncovered we as i twice and then once removed from each part unable to confirm the existence of an other if this were simple not complex a system perhaps then i could know we but it is not possible you dig up who from foreign soils i thought i could formulate a question for you without one sideway glance beyond transcendence beyond you into god calm serene unknown all knowing dug from antiquity and one third human as though it can be all in proportion and cut off from where one part begins and the other ends and then name him as the substitute of unspeakable sounds gilgamesh seeking eternal life and bravely calls loves god a harlot for two thirds pompous and assured of heroic memories as bitch dogs scramble through the sands to search for this so nearly a man his phallus out of tombs we make them live again in stone it does not decay it is eroded and buried uncovered unearthed discovered again as man is made a god again and i have only a world which we should have filled with emptiness instead a flood will storm rage and all men perish into mud and become once more illegible and yet still epic as their hollow forms pronounce some void that means too much in silence where we find fragments and splinters of once strong bones will be our legacy untold untaught unhistory renamed in thousands languages unbounded but still silent with the echoes of him ishtar would claw the dirt to find love and then cry war turns the word into caress a kiss bite fight embrace to die for three times one for each part it is written you say and there i fall between said and heart cold now with promises and lies unfolding the maggot histories of what we once called people and now remains as family with none of us to call their own broken images as they fade from memories wrapped in bandages and mummified but missing excavations where only symbols are found outside the painted sarcophagi that others drew from stony darks as black as underground in which i lie pale and blind wanting only one worshipper at this church the terror of pleasure as two go pale look in their eyes is one of violence i am is a fiction with that i loves you

The poem of ages bewitches him.

She has waited many lives for this union and now they prowl about each other like suspicious cats. Their passionate flamenco unfolds imperceptibly as eons vanish and their bodies collapse into an embrace.

It is a beautiful scene.

I cascade from bubble to bubble in the glass as seasons blossom and fade outside. The river rises and falls, freezes and rages. This is the motion of stillness.

Alfred Tesseller and his lover dance and dance, their bodies dissolving into a waltz of chemistry, as they dream of all the lives they make and unmake with every putrefying step.

IX
Before the aphorism came the platitude

I surface again to the wonders of the senses; light, sound and smell remind me of the joys of solid flesh and the pleasures of the world. I see a midwinter sun filtering through a thin tent, making the green canvas glow warm and bright. It is as though I am swaddled in evergreen leaves. I savour the brief respite before another journey.

Emerging from the tent I see trees surrounding a small clearing, although bereft of their leaves they glow with a brightness that seems to signal the stirring of a new life.

So estranged from the world now I struggle with those old demons—feelings. I hover near sorrow.

I see the remains of a campfire. There at the edge of the white ashes a smouldering book lay beside a charred piece of wood. I lift it out and read its title, *Old Tales*. I open the pages that creak like ancient doors in an abandoned castle.

> *Alfred Tesseller trudged, fur wrapped feet crunching through the icy ground, breaking his way, smashing a path, hacking through the white, the many mirrored white, faceted like diamonds. Riches burst asunder as the cruel axe, blooded with the dirty heritage of snowy wastes, tore a way in—a spurt, a crack, the last lumps of the icy crag were pillaged from their home.*
>
> *Behind, in the dull grey sky, the ball of flame laughed on its back. It was getting low, touching the peaks, firmly lodged between and sinking. Time ticked wearily by in that*

sky, but still he hurried until beneath shone the myriad twinkle of ultramarine bliss—the bottomless depths of a dark home. Now, as darkness crept over the melting land, he plunged into the icy stillness pushing past the walls of lumbering liquid. Far above he sees the last light shimmer as the yellow glow gives way to the piercing crackle that gifts a cocooning heat through this new land.

∞

She moved her naked body from beneath me. Sitting in the sweat-drenched bed she laughed a little, feeling the heat dissipate, as my sleeping mind forgot the incident.

She smokes a cigarette.

There in the blackness her eyes pierced the bluish glow of smoke as it spirals skywards. She listened intently for the first time in years. After a few minutes of reflection she moved to the window and opened the curtains a crack. Light from the moon bathed her body in a grey haze. She looked down at her stripped body and saw herself as though for the first time. In her haze of feeling she turned, content, to see if I was watching; now proud of what had been hidden for so long. But I am still, and blind, unmoved as always.

Looking out on the deserted street she considered the grey and eerie, almost respectful, quiet that the place had retained—a trace of long ago?

Had her intuitive feeling been real?

A firework burst in her eyes, shooting its feathered sparks, green, blue, and a painful red. She is bold and brave to the task—a need, a necessity—in a world full of oppressive pain.

Pride disintegrates in another shooting pain, bleeding, sliding, wriggling. Then she screamed, screamed, screamed, and the screamed became a scream, and the scream became what would never be understood by anyone again—her personal cry, locked away in her heart like that unborn thing awaiting entry to a carousel of delightful woe.

I fathered myself.

∞

Frozen there, with the silent cry echoing in the still deep, Alfred Tesseller awoke to find his crystalline cage torn by blasts of tiny shocking energy—he was free, out into the liquid again.

He could not move.

He was trapped.

One wave rocked him closer to the dark tunnel ahead, squeezing him tight and binding his limbs. Then a flash— a bolt of lightning.

Once white, now crisp and cracked with age, the burden of a new life. He examined himself and found the precious liquid shrivelling from his new form. It crept happily into the sands away from his terrible impurity. The ball of flame had assumed a new form and was more defined. He could look at it, no pain, just a continual stare.

His sun.

Alfred Tesseller stumbles on. Miles of sand banks, the dunes of shifting tides moved this way and that as his soul flickered, lonely and unsure of its home. He watched a fluffy ball of white cloud pass by overhead. In its wake came the shadow, breeding more shade.

He succumbed to the inevitable painless travel to the newer land. This finished, he discovered a better form, clad in the shining clothes of khaki uniformity.

But there was a path here, a straight route which falsely told him, 'Travel, trust me and be free.'

So, unused to lies and treachery he followed and spent his time gazing at the black sky where shining silver specks seemed to compensate for the lack of golden...

Suns... a cloud.

In an echo he heard the distant call. As he quickened pace he found himself noisily marching and in his hand he held a gun, leaving behind a trail acquainted with death.

Ahead, by the cracked roadside, was a girl in a pink and white party dress with presents in her hand for friends that lived far away in imaginary worlds. He knelt, as one might pray, and held out his fragile worn-out hand, instinctively hiding the reeking pistol from the eyes of one so young and innocent.

She sighed and looked up into Alfred Tesseller's eyes, red with a thousand vengeances.

He saw in her hand some wooden dolls hanging in contorted positions. He saw one like himself in, more bloodstained than the rest—a thin little soldier, a toy to amuse her friends.

She cried.

Her presents were dead.

Her presents had died, suffocated by the gold trimmed paper she had carefully wrapped them in.

They cried together, those ancient silent tears that will never moisten that parched ground that thirsts for everything.

Alfred Tesseller's journey still carried him on. On into the depths of a painful reddish mire that covered him from

head to foot. It was sticky, he wanted to lick himself clean but could not bend his head. He realised too late that the road had gone.
Twilight.
He was now tightly bound in painful red, streaked here and there with torturing lines of blackness.

X
Places vanish, like your names

You are an old man. The numbers don't matter anymore, you are old. There is a shining patch of skin on top of your head. It pokes rudely from the grey hair that clings to the back and sides of your head. You have never been embarrassed of baldness; in fact, there is a certain pride as you stroke your empty crown. And certainly it is an achievement, of a futile kind, to have lasted this long.

The page is still blank though.

You look up and stare at the fire. This is the last of the fuel.

We are sat behind you, Alfred Tesseller and I, somewhere in the darkest corner. We are folded in cobwebs and dust. We are all but forgotten within you, even a careful search would find only the splintered husks of insects, and you would hardly think those miraculous enough to care for.

Four days now and you haven't ventured from the house. Four days now and you have scarcely moved from the chair. Four days and the page is still blank.

A light flashes past outside—an emergency service, the third tonight, two the night before and four the night before that.

Thinking has become painful now. The ideas will not stop—that is the worst—all jumbled together and breeding. Your mind overflows with images, contorted photographs that you might have taken but can't remember why. Too often you seem to be dead. Your hand on the page has become skeletal.

All that remains are our eyes leering over you from behind. When you turn they are gone, if they never existed. Something inside you wants to die.

Organisation is the key. You know that. 'Order thought and you might survive,' a friend had told you. Was she right? The page could only begin when the mind was organised? What a detestable word 'organised'.

But who is left to speak to now? As you laugh you know you are beginning to forget. How, already, could you be beginning to forget when it weighs like an ancient foetus in your head?

There in the old folds of the chair you began to conceive, your body fusing with the chair itself.

But you are lucid now.

Lucid, you laugh, what a word—how loaded, contorted, folded, hanging like a childish dream in a sullen reality that you have come to call your home. Had lucid been the run to the shops, the sideways glances, a fumble at the counter and the hurried exit from a logic that had become nothing but alien to you?

On your return you began the labour of beginning—creating—something greater and more controlled than yourself. You hoped it was to be merely a figure on the page, a hazy outline of something that might have been in other circumstances—someone who might walk alone at night and have no cares. A simple story, you thought, a slow ramble through the empty streets at night.

It was to become so much more.

Four days now and you have not written a word. The page is blank.

It is hard to think when the world is buzzing past you. Here in this room you write by the window and the traffic annoys. It is hard to think when the traffic is buzzing past you. When you write in this room you must think at night. You must write at night in this room, with the faces clinging to you. What are the weapons that remove them? Is that the battle? Is the battle to merely create?

If only you could understand the fecundity of creation at work in the flesh of Alfred Tesseller, and the life that soars through my own invisible soul. We could show you creation.

This room itself has become more than oppression, it is hallucinogenic. You have tried so hard to describe the falling walls, the voices that call from somewhere behind you. Over the years it has become one pleading, groaning string of words that plays with you for hours at a time. It wants to continue.

Something behind you desires life.

Shaking yourself awake you peer around the room with failing eyes. The embers of the fire are sighing out the last warmth.

A crooked mirror hangs above the fireplace. Yesterday it slipped on the threads of decaying string and peered at you from above. It is now your judge, showing

The Phantasmagorical Imperative...

you only a gaunt unshaven figure that has sunk to the limits of despair.

The page had begun to curl upwards only moments before you capture again that wretched image in the mirror. Paper is now folding itself frantically, each corner rapidly slotting into any available hole. A moment later you hear a gentle rip as the first page tears itself from the edge of the pad and becomes a home of its own.

Self-pity now ceases as you turn in amazement from the mirror; for before you there sits a tiny paper house on an empty blank page. Your pencil slips from your hands and falls to the floor with a clatter.

The house is perfect. Each detail is exact—even a miniature door knob on the front door and beside that a delicate letterbox.

What a miracle! You think!

What? A miracle?

Your shaking hands reach down by the side of your chair and grope for the pencil. You refuse to take your eyes from the vision sitting before you in case it might vanish. As your fingers grasped the pencil the windows of the little house burst open.

Your face falls open in surprise and for the first time in days you feel the wiry stubble across your face, reminding you of your body.

With a shaking hand you move the pencil closer to the letterbox and push it in.

It moved.

It worked!

Gazing at this incredulous mechanism with almost fearful eyes you glance up at the open windows. This could almost be a machine, you *imagine*. Even a small knock at the letterbox had shown that perhaps the most intricate part of its design actually works. It is small; at most it spreads two inches across the page, at best two inches high.

With a courageous flick of the pencil you try to shut the windows. With a muffled thud they slam together. This paper machine has a wonder to it that brings a childish smile to your fading face. And with the smile, sleep descends.

When you awake it is late morning.

We have been patient.

Time no longer has any meaning.

Glancing down at the pad of paper you blink in shock. The house is still there. It has not been a dream.

Your reflection shows only a ghost of what you have been, trapped in a rut of melancholy. Your mind is made up. You will wash and shave. You will write the story of the occupant of this tiny home. Carefully you put the pad on the floor and rush out of the room casting a glance at the incredible house that had appeared on the page last night.

Is this actually happening?

Constantly you ask yourself this question. Looking in the bathroom mirror you still do not believe that this revelation belongs to you.

No, it can't be. All the children in the world have this happen to them. It is part of an endless collective consciousness that keeps the angelic brood united in their wickedness.

But you are definitely not a child. That growing area of skin on your head, the thick bush of stubble and your scowl, dug into your face even when you are happy, gave an indication that you are no child.

You had been one once—doesn't that count for something at least?

You had been a child in a classroom once, indeed; that same classroom alongside Alfred Tesseller, that same classroom alongside me. You have carried paper memories for years.

Engrossed in the past you have forgotten your shave and a slight cut brings you back to your senses. This was it! The beginning of something new and creative—another chance at reproduction.

Dressed in only a bathrobe you descend the stairs to begin your task. Each step redefines you and your thoughts buzz in anticipation of what you intend to do.

Opening the door to the sitting room you look down fondly to where you laid the pad and its little house. You watch, astonished, as a thin black scrawl creeps over the page and engulfs the house like a trail of rats. Stepping closer you cannot make out where the scrawl begins or ends, only that it continues in a long unbroken chaos of change.

What this unending nonsense means you cannot understand but it has a ring of familiarity to it, like a language you learned long ago and have since forgotten.

This continuous word is you, it has become you.

As you circle around behind the chair you hear a low growl from the corner behind you. Turning swiftly you see nothing as the growl repeats itself at your back, closer this time and multiplying. Again and again you turn until dizzy.

You are terrified and angry.

Everything is written in that line that you have hidden all of these years. The growls are only cruel human impersonations; wild creatures. They are all around you now. Behind them all your own laughter rings in your ears. You catch sight of yourself in the mirror and it seems there is a crude, broken angel leering back at you.

You tear the mirror from the wall and hurl it to the ground with a crash that sends splinters flying around the room, like a field of warriors raising their swords into a bright sun. Your own blood trickles from countless wounds and as you fall to the ground they call to each other with names that sound like your own.

From tearful eyes you look over to the tiny paper house and see that the scrawl has almost written its entire story. There was scarcely a space left on the page that remained blank. Where will it go from here you wonder, that animal that has hunted you across all these wretched years?

Grabbing the matches from the fireplace you race to the paper and with a sorrowful look in your eyes you light the corner of the pages and throw them into the fireplace.

You leave your home with determination.

You go to the mountain, never to return until you can finally claim that the world is real.

And there, up on the mountainside, you find a frozen corpse, blackened by the icy winds and brittle as last year's leaves. That dusty specimen you discover is none other than Alfred Tesseller who has also lived a life of dream and can offer you only flickering images of shadow-shapes beside the fire.

And I am also there, enfolding you within the cold of ancient climates. I have been so many people and I will be many more. I shall be mighty Cleopatra. I shall be a criminal, a warmonger, a murderer and a thief.

The world will fall about us and we will hear the endless toll of bells and sigh of scythes. Songs of souls in their symphony of suffering will scream around us as we watch even the stones crumble to shale and sand.

We three will remain—unlikely comrades—now so immortal, now so beautiful.

...he was water before he was fire...

The sky was a clean and cloudless blue and the waters of the Firth of Clyde mirrored it, save for the spray that cleaved, like a great anaemic wound, from the bow of the ferry I leant precariously over, savouring the freshness of freedom. I had taken the bus from Glasgow on my 'trip of a lifetime', as my friend David had called it, and was now heading for Dunoon, a picturesque little town that I recalled from a holiday with my parents some twenty-five years before. I had all the gear with me; tent, stove, rucksack, hiking boots, newly purchased for my indefinite holiday—wild camping!

Now, I'm not the kind of man you'd usually have found dead in a sleeping bag. I'm more your comfy mattress and full English breakfast type, following a steak and chips and real ale the night before. But David had persuaded me it would be an *experience*. And even then, it was. Freed from the car and reliant on the trains and buses I had found that even my first day's journey had released me from myself in some strange fashion—from the tyranny of my own sense of endless responsibility that had, over years and now decades, gradually erased any sense of adventure, and perhaps even love.

Yes, love lay at the root of my problems. David had long described me as a 'serial monogamist', having never sustained a relationship beyond a five year period, during which there had been every indication of a perfectly happy future together. But, every time, I had somehow managed to engineer some means by which to depart for another partner, similarly promising and caring. Finally I had married Eleanor after three years together, in the hope that I could break the cycle. Within two years we were separated (she didn't want a divorce straight away—we should try to 'work it out', apparently). I hardly answered any calls from her, and just before *it* happened she had left a message on my mobile saying we should go on a date together and start afresh.

About an hour later she was hit by a police car attending a bank robbery, funnily enough at the bank she worked at—you couldn't make it up! She survived three days in the hospital. I found out much later, too late to see her. I had been in the South of France with a girl from accounts, too busy satisfying *myself* even to look at the messages accumulating on my phone.

So, now, following the supposed last stop in a B&B for many weeks, I was heading out into the wilderness on my own to let the winds cast out the many things that haunted me.

The skies soon clouded over and a light drizzle began as I plodded down the rusted walkway with the few other foot passengers. Dunoon looked nothing like how I remembered it. The small town centre showed the usual signs of neglect, with many shops boarded up and 'To Let' or in the final weeks of 'closing down' sales before their leases expired. I had thought that now, in spring, the whole place would be coming alive with early tourist trade. But no, there hung over the place a pall, heightened no doubt by my own memories that had coloured it more vibrantly than it had ever been. But something bleak was in the air nonetheless and after only a couple of hours I decided it was best to head off North and look for my first night's camping place.

So, after purchasing a few provisions, I followed the one road out of the forlorn place, passing Holy Loch, where the nuclear submarines used to lie, like dark kraken, waiting to unleash fire upon the earth and lay waste the 'reds'. Perhaps it had been their departure that had forced the slow decline upon the town—strange how such ominous horror can also sustain and grow a community.

After what seemed to be miles of bright, but lifeless houses—mostly holiday homes—looking out over the loch, the dwellings gradually diminished and the pathway petered out into a small track, and then eventually nothing at all. I followed the road then, and flinched when large vehicles came by at speed. I had my doubts whether something as ambitious as wild camping was really for me. Already the rucksack on my back weighed heavily, and the new clothes seemed to chafe and rub—warning me that I was ill prepared for the hardships ahead.

But, I am stubborn. I persevered, and thought that—if the worst really came to the worst, as it often does—I could always intersperse my little adventure with a comforting respite, or *ten*, in hotels and guesthouses.

∞

It was not half an hour, at a fairly slow pace, before I had begun to enter the Argyll forest, still following the road. There seemed to be dense Scots pines and firs up on the hillsides—perfect places to camp. But by the roadside there were patches of rowan and birch, dotted here and there by tall pine. Soon I had the waters of Loch Eck to my side and further away in the West great mountains reached far into the distance. At one point I unfurled the great expanse of Ordnance Survey map for the area, to follow the names of the small burns and glens I was passing by. But a gust of wind soon wrapped the entire thing around my face, much to the amusement of the passengers in a passing car, who sounded their horn and called obscenities at me from the window.

I folded the thing back up and decided to enjoy the scenery as much as I could without names—places would have to reveal to me their own little secrets, I thought.

And soon enough they did. About five miles along the loch I reached a little scenic spot—'Jubilee Point', the sign said, and ahead I could see some benches on a little promontory that jutted into the loch. It would be a perfect place for some lunch.

I followed a little track and saw a beautiful picnic area, with little beaches on either side of a grassy hillock that had five majestic pines atop it. Before eating I decided to explore a little.

On the South side large boulders had collapsed into the water's edge making for a protected cove, with a gentle sandy beach that fell away gradually into the depths of the loch. It would be a lovely place to paddle, and so I duly did. I cannot explain the freedom I felt from this simple activity. The sands were dotted with interesting smaller pebbles and rocks and I used my toes to nudge interesting specimens about. I even let out a childish giggle when what I thought to be a dark stone turned out to be a long coil of slimy decaying weed that knotted around my ankle. I splashed back to shore, laughing happily.

Around the edge of the cove there were the great roots of two tall pines that had twined around the rocks and been steadily eroded by the lap of the shore. This gave the impression of root and rock in harmony, shielding the beach from the gentle erasure of the water. The little pool formed by the cradling embrace of the root and rock alliance seemed like some water feature in a Japanese contemplative garden. One might have thought the guardian of this place had left only moments before.

And then the *guardians* emerged.

It was a magical moment, as two swans glided around the promontory weaving and ducking around each other in a magnificent loving ritual. This felt like my first genuine encounter with nature.

The graceful birds seemed, for a while, not to notice me there—shoes and socks in hand. But then, the larger of the two—what I took to be the male—headed straight for the shore, squawking and flapping. I rushed up the steep bank, scratching my soft feet on thorny shrubs and sharp stones. The bird followed, chasing me off towards the picnic area.

I was genuinely panicked.

It still followed, pursuing me on towards the northern shore of the promontory. I noticed a tall pine a few feet out in the water, with a coil of roots that would once have been wrapped around soil and stones. But now it seemed trapped in a silent tiptoe, suggesting it was walking out into the loch.

I did not have time for further reflection on the scenery though. The great bird was still behind me screeching and clacking away, beating its vast wings at me. I was perplexed as to what terrible crime I might have committed. Unless its eggs were hidden somewhere upon the bank—that must be it. I fled to higher ground, nearer the slip-road and the swan seemed to be satisfied with this. He still strutted up and down the beachy northern bank of the loch though, in case I should venture down. A moment later his mate appeared around the promontory, twitching and clucking at him to return.

And then they were gone again, hugging the shore on their way further up the loch.

Well, within minutes I'd been greeted with both beauty and threat, but I was satisfied that this would be a wonderful place to camp near, and enjoy again in the early morning. I scouted around a little, and was dutiful to heed the warnings on the picnic area that I should make my camp well away from Jubilee Point, and the road. A few hundred yards further up the road there was a wide clearing with about a dozen holiday cabins and a large tarmaced parking area with swings, roundabouts and a climbing frame for holidaying children. Only a few of them seemed occupied this early in the season, but it would be good to have help on hand should anything go wrong on my first night.

It all went very well. I found a dry clearing up on the hillside, and pitched my tent in only a few minutes. Just as the sky was blossoming into the purple of evening I was bubbling up some noodles in tomato soup and frying sausages on my little gas stove. I felt quite the explorer, and settled down to watch the rest of the sunset with a half bottle of red wine (not quite your rugged traveller's tipple, no doubt, but I needed a little luxury).

It was then that I thought I might use my phone to search the internet for the proper term for a male and female swan. Given that I was experiencing nature, in all its savage glory, I might as well educate myself whilst I was doing it. But there was no signal. I shrugged and slipped the phone back into my coat pocket. I'd have to try again nearer the cabins—they must have a signal. For now I would have to be content with the *network* of the outdoors!

I had determined that the following morning, as beautiful as this little cove was, I should be heading further on. It was certainly pleasurable and the weather had been good so far, at least since I'd left the gloom of Dunoon. But I was here for adventure and I must press on to new pastures. One last visit to the cove, a few pictures of the swans (from a safe distance), and then I'd pack up my camp and head off.

My first night—had there ever been a real night before this!

What darkness! What stars! I had never known such things, not really. Finally alone, I must have spent hours just gazing up into the rich depths of the night, tracing the flurry of the milky way and guessing at twinkling planets. I had expected a deep, reverent silence, but once my light was out the undergrowth became alive with disturbing rustling; foraging creatures and insects were on the move about my camp, hoping to find sustenance with eyes keen and attentive in the blackness to glimmers and movements invisible to me, their being alive to scents I could never detect, their entire skeletons alight with magnetic flows and tuned to earthly rhythms, alien and hidden to my senses.

It was an enlivening night.

In the morning I woke with the sun rather than by my watch.

I made my way to the cove to wash and say 'goodbye'.

I hummed a little tune, genuinely contented. As I headed down through the ferns I caught sight of what could only be described as a *flotilla* of swans—I do not know their collective name, and even if I had it could never have described the number there were—hugging the edge of the loch, and making their way to the little cove. There must have been *fifty* of them!

I hurried along excitedly and darted across the road and through to the car park. Then I spotted a man, down by the shore—in *my* little cove. It is strange how quickly places become territory. I ducked quickly behind a tree—I don't really know why. But, something told me I should watch him first, before approaching.

He was terribly dishevelled, with a big barber jacket covered in mud and leaves. The pockets were bulging. His black hair was matted and he had clearly been living outdoors for quite some time judging by his great tangled beard that was flecked with two white streaks coming down from the corners of his mouth.

He stood at the edge of the loch and the swans came ashore, one by one, brushing by him on their way to peck at the plants on the bank. Soon he was surrounded by a feathery white foam, occasionally broken by a long neck that reached up to rub itself against his beard. I had never seen anything like it, and given my reception the previous day I thought it doubly strange they should be so friendly with anyone.

After a few minutes of greeting them he seemed to lead them up the bank and back towards where I was hiding. But none of them had noticed me and I continued to watch him shepherding them carefully through the trees towards the Northern shore.

It was more like watching a shaggy dog with a flock of sheep. But he in no way chased, or harrowed them. They merely followed where he walked, nuzzling his arms like needy cats. Then, one by one, as they had on the Southern bank, the swans slipped back into the water and headed up the loch.

Once he had seen the birds off on the other side of the promontory I decided to go down and speak to him, to discover something of his secret with them.

'Hello there,' I called, from the picnic bench. 'I see you have a way with the swans. Magnificent creatures aren't they?'

He did not turn. He merely stood watching the birds paddle away.

I made to go down to the North beach.

'Sorry, I don't mean to intrude,' I called again, attempting as best I could to alert him to my presence. 'But, I'd be interested to know how you developed such an affinity with them.'

By then I was almost upon him. He was a very tall man, at least a half foot taller than myself, and I am over six foot. Again, there hadn't been any indication of recognition on his part. I wondered if he might be deaf—in which case I would need to alert him to my presence in a different fashion.

Rather than continue to approach from behind I veered round in an arc and headed across the shoreline, so that I was in sight.

I could see his face fully now, and what a gentle, caring look it had upon it—watching after his gaggle of birds. Had I been confident that I had ever known love, I might even have called it that. He could clearly see me by now—unless he was also blind, but that I found extremely unlikely by the way he had attended to the birds.

As I approached I held my hand out in greeting. I had the absurd notion that I was encountering a wild animal. I kept saying, 'hello there... hello there', over and over, like some ridiculous mantra.

Then, when I was a couple of feet from him, he turned abruptly and beamed a great smile. He clasped my outstretched hand in both of his; they were rough with calluses. His face was ruddy with the outdoors and covered in the great beard I had seen from far away. But, his eyes, so radiant—and sincere! I have never met another human being that I trusted so deeply, so instantly. His great grey eyes and his cracked lips were all I needed to understand him, for he offered not a word of greeting.

He took me by the hand and showed me around the small promontory. But his tour took us hours, as he stopped by each of the trees and caressed its trunk, showing me the whorls of its bark and the little cities of insects that lived beneath. Each plant was displayed with care, as though we were in a fine art gallery, his broken hands tending it as though it were the work of a great craftsman.

I was content in his presence.

On the Southern shore we worked together until nightfall, gathering every feather the swans had left behind and taking them, one by one, as though they were newborn infants, to a hole under one of the triumphant trees that seemed now to gather its great branches above

The Phantasmagorical Imperative...

us like some vast church roof. All this happened in complete silence, with only the flicker of faces and the careful communication of hands to tell us everything of each other thoughts and wishes.

And as the night crept upon us, I knew I would never leave.

Spring became summer as we maintained our vigil over the splendid birds, watching their cygnets grow and blossom from grey fluff into spirited adolescents. We were often disturbed by tourists stopping at the benches to enjoy their loud lunches and leave their boisterous children to cavort around the precious beaches. Then, the swans would travel up the loch and find a more secluded spot until my comrade and I returned to craft the silence once more.

There were other interruptions to our task, of course. Once, the police arrived and questioned us. My friend was unable to offer anything beyond a blank stare and so I did all the talking, even though speech had become, in such a brief time, quite unfamiliar to me. It must have been someone from the cabins that had called them. They were very clear that we shouldn't go near them—people were trying to take holidays and they didn't want 'vagrants spoiling the view', as the officers so kindly put it.

But there were others that were not so *kind*. One night a few local lads appeared with their girls and some tinnies. For an hour or two we laid low by the edge of the loch, tucked beneath the sheltering roots of the tall trees. Eventually they found us, our ruddy faces, ragged beards and dishevelled clothes gave away that we were sport enough for an evening—the sport of boots and fists. The following morning's sun found us bloodied and battered by the water's edge, but over time we were lapped back to health by the ebb and flow of a natural time that those boys, and their cackling girlfriends, would never be privileged to know. I pitied them and gazed for days into the clear waters, watching the stones and sand jiggle with stories of eons.

By the time the darker evenings heralded a new season approaching I had already begun to sense the shift in the leaves and roots, even the water seemed to have taken on a different quality. There was an urgency to the brightness of the ferns, the chill lap of the loch had taken on a nervous chattering of almost ritual insistence, and the winds surged in anxious calling to 'make ready' against the onslaught of cold and darkness.

Everything was in preparation and we too huddled ourselves against the approaching cold, often sheltering together amongst the rocks and roots, enjoying the warmth of each other's bodies and studying the season's gradual transformation.

We cleared the rubbish from the picnic area regularly, and gathered the stray plastic bags and bottles that washed into the cove. Bread bags I learned to hate most especially, having had to help one of the swans to release itself from one of the damned things left behind by a family after they had fed the birds one afternoon.

One morning, as I was ferreting about in the undergrowth for wrappers and crisp packets, something slipped from my torn coat pocket. It was a square lump of black plastic, with a surface like a dark grey mirror.

For a moment I stared at it in confusion.

Then, after catching my uncanny reflection, I remembered. It was my phone. I couldn't recall when I had used it last—perhaps the evening I had spent in Glasgow, before leaving on the ferry. When was that? Well, the thing was only weighing me down now, there was little chance of getting it recharged out here—and the cabins (the only source of power nearby) had become to me more like a threatening outpost of a strange conquering civilisation.

I had no need of phones anymore. It went into the bin by the picnic benches, less use than an old tin can, which could at least be fashioned into a decent drinking vessel.

This little cove had become the mouthpiece of a deeper structure and as the days collapsed into weeks, and months, I had been content to listen to its whispered messages gathering their demands and warnings. My comrade and I occasionally exchanged knowing and happy glances as our beards grew and our bodies hardened to the elements. I found a peace there that I could never describe. Language was slipping away.

∞

My peaceful world was forever changed one evening I came down from washing in the burn. There was a chill in the air—the morning would be tight with frost. I saw my comrade standing on the low hill as the last orange reds of the dying sun dwindled beyond Beinn Mhòr to the West. He stared with awe at the beach below, which was shielded from me as I began now to hurry through the bracken. I kept my gaze fixed on him—a shocked statue.

As I scrambled down the bank to the shore I gasped in horror. The whole dreamy cove—our magical sanctuary—was littered with dead swans. Their once glorious bodies now lay strewn across the great guardian rocks and against the twisted roots of the trees by the water's edge.

Who! Who could have done this! Who had *dared* to do such a deed?

My body cried out and I screamed, sinking into the water.

I cried.

I ran to the tatty picnic benches and kicked at them, roaring into the dark skies.

And then I heard laughter, like a bubbling of black oil—a sputtering of an engine into life.

My comrade was laughing, down by the water's edge.

And as I turned to him I screamed again. Not, this time, for the horrific massacre of the swans, but from a darker place—a place of true fear, where identity slides into the ever churning morass.

The whole cove seemed *agitated*. The shadowy reeds quivered with an urgent, fidgety movement; the very ripples of the loch seemed to reveal some form of agency as each cast itself out in arcs quite incongruous to ordinary patterns. The entire earth seemed animated with a delicate, but insistent, existence.

Those broken forms I had mistaken for swans were nothing more than costumes; white feathery materials that had somehow clothed the things that frolicked beneath. And those things were now enjoying the cove. Their smooth forms glistened, as they burrowed through the soft, damp sands in a writhing pile—a heaving mass of flesh that suggested an orgiastic revel. My comrade was amongst them, giggling and leaping about like a little child.

The beautiful cove was surrendering itself to another world; to beings that might communicate through touch rather than words and gestures. Perhaps where I saw a mass of copulating forms there were instead a delegation of peaceful creatures all engaged in preternatural communication—or perhaps one form alone attempting, in its fashion, to tell a story to the silent trees that loomed along the shores or to initiate my comrade into its deeper truth.

I realised, finally, that it was not the bacchanalia that I found repellent; it was my transposition of their forms into *my own*. I was reading their being simply in relation to my own. Where I saw limbs there was nothing but an expanding and contracting mass; where I saw sexual organs there was nothing but the mutability of nature itself—the endless flux of soil and shingle, sand and shale.

My friend waded out into the loch with them, exultant.

The writhing mass of things embraced him, glowing with colours I had never seen before and would never be able to describe—so like the deep blemish of bruises, or the ache of a broken heart; it was light and colour as pure emotion, fragile and numinous.

My comrade held his fists aloft as he slipped into the deeper waters, and called out to me the only words I had ever heard him utter, 'they came back—finally *they* came back, for *me!*' Then, as though one single body, they collapsed into the depths together.

Further down the Loch, near Inverchapel, they found his body.

I am sure his bloated face would have been alive with joy though.

You see, I am happy for my comrade. He is not gone, I can assure you. I hear his last words on every faint breeze, his laughter in every howling gale. I feel the rough calluses of his hands upon the bark of trees. His eyes are the bright stars and sparkling planets in the dark night. His warm heart beats in the flicker of every campfire and his blood is now moist soil, transporting its bounty through all the hidden, thirsty roots that seek him out beneath our feet.

The swans have returned. I am their herdsman now.

I have no guns. I have no knives. My strength is not of the body—of *your* world of death—but *of* the spirit. And what spirit there *is* in *my* world—surging beneath everything—ready to erupt at any moment. How blessed I was to discover it, when the cataracts fell and I could see the tumultuous and savage beauty of what truly lives beside us, *within* us.

Perhaps one day the magical cove will find another to safeguard its splendid portal to truth, perhaps it will even discover *you*, and you might join me for *their* return—*your* initiation into *their* mystery.

Until then I await the revelation of the forms once more. I understand why my good friend was silent all those wonderful months we were together. He had seen the creatures once before, and had waited to see them again.

Words are redundant now—redundant! My heart is soothed with the lap of gentle waves that beat the time until *their* return. I am consumed by a flaming passion to bear witness to *their* splendour. My soul is a burning ecstasy now that my tongue has ceased its futile dance.

14ml
of
Matt Enamel #61

David Burdett had been trying to get in touch with me for a few months. I'd had some emails, some texts, and quite a few answer phone messages. Despite us both being website designers he knew that I didn't relish these forms of communication that much—web design was just something I had a knack for, and it paid the bills. Eventually he sent me a letter. It had a brown wax seal on the back, with a red ribbon under it, and a hand-drawn carrier-pigeon beside it. He was taking the piss.

The letter announced that he was coming to visit me on the first weekend in September, just a few weeks away. If I had any problem with that I was to dust-off my laptop and email him to suggest another date. I sent him a quick email, apologising that I'd been busy; confirming that that weekend was fine, and that I was looking forward to seeing him again. I wasn't really. When I had first moved to Sheringham I'd often get friends wanting to stay over at the weekends (it was a cheap break for them at the seaside). But over the years these had dwindled. David was always persistent though. He had probably been in contact with Vicky—my ex-wife—and was checking to see if I was ok. It really bugs me, those friends that try to tamper with your personal life as though they are some kind of counsellor—always offering their ideas for how to 'cope' and 'move on', and whatever else they think will return you to the person most approximate to the one they remembered in that picture-perfect history in their minds.

Well, I really wasn't the same guy that had shared holidays in Norfolk with David and his family all those years before—that was over two decades ago now. I had two kids—twin girls, Sasha and Sally (Vicky had named them), now 8 (little girls that I was banned from seeing just because of one angry night—the *last* angry night—when I had hit Vicky). Of course I regretted it, not just because I couldn't see the girls anymore, but because I'd hit someone, in a rage. But she was the one waving her affair in my face, demanding a divorce, and, having cleared most of a bottle of chardonnay, she was the one screaming at me about what a useless man I was; how I couldn't afford to take us all on holiday, didn't have any ambition, and cared more for my model trains than I did for my family. It seemed she'd locked me into a ridiculous stereotype, but it was one I didn't try to break out of.

At that point I was one year into The Honeybourne line. I'd started it in what we called my study, but it had mainly become a storage room for anything Vicky couldn't fit in anywhere else in the house. I laid the first phases of the track, and modelled some of the hills before she even noticed. At first she wasn't bothered, and the girls liked it a lot. But I like to do things properly, and it took a lot of time to source the right models for it, so I guess it became a bit of an excuse for some privacy.

The moaning started fairly gradually. Why had we moved to Norfolk—it was just because I'd loved the place when I was young, she didn't even like it here and couldn't find any decent work. What were the girls going to do when they grew up, put up with little waitressing jobs over summer until they were spinsters—didn't I ever think of them, and so on.

So in the end she left, just as I'd completed the Winchcombe station platform.

Her 'lover'—as she referred to him—was a fifty-something bloke from London called Keith, who worked as a Human Resources manager for a brewery, and spent half his week in some office in Newcastle. God, what a soulless bastard he must be, I thought—Human Resources, does it get any lower than that? I imagined him in some dingy little bedsit in Newcastle, fucking his secretary, before going back to Vicky and the girls for the 'long' weekend. Good luck to them all, the girls would come back to me again, in their own time. Eventually they'd understand.

So, that's painted the scene, so to speak; given you all you need to follow the events of David's visit, mostly overshadowed, for me, by the lady in the yellow mac, and her kids—but we'll get to her later.

∞

David arrived on the Friday, as he'd said he would, in the late afternoon. He arrived in a posh car, wearing an expensive suit and seemed in high spirits. I thought he looked rather pasty though, worn out. He worked for a software company in Croydon now and had been trying to get me to apply there for the last year. I wasn't interested.

We had a cup of tea in the kitchen and he jabbered on excitedly about all the things he wanted to do over the weekend. He kept talking about the holidays we'd shared, which were mostly in Sheringham and Cromer. Did I remember this, did I remember that? I listened to the dream itinerary and concluded that it would take at least a week. I suggested that we take it easy and see what we could manage. Why not start that evening by going down to the sea front and having a pub meal, before going to the arcade—we used to spend most of our pocket money in that amusement arcade. He loved the idea, but wanted to get changed into the 'proper gear', as he called it—a new puppy would have less enthusiasm than David.

I took him upstairs and showed him to the middle bedroom, where the girls used to sleep. Of course, after they'd left with Vicky, I'd been busy converting it to house the second portion of The Honeybourne Line.

'I've put you up in the girls' room,' I said. 'I hope that's ok.'

He nodded, sadly. But then stood staring at the model railway line with an expression of either horror or amazement, it was difficult to know which.

'You're in Sasha's bed,' I pointed. 'I had to use Sally's to make the base for the Gretton to Cheltenham section of the line. It was handy that the wall was well positioned to make the Greet tunnel. On the other side, in my study, is Winchcombe station, and then on to Toddington and Laverton—over the Stamway viaduct. The line ends in the bay window.

I run two model engines on it. An old classic 60s diesel-electric, class 47, and the famous steam engine, *Foremarke Hall*.'

David still didn't know what to say.

'I've nearly completed a smaller line now, in the main bedroom,' I said. 'Rather closer to home that one—Sheringham to Holt. All the scenery, engines, carriages and track is done. I just need to add some figures to the platforms, animals in the fields and other bits and bobs and it'll be done. Maybe we can have the *grand opening* before you leave on Sunday. Then on to the next project, I suppose. Quite what that will be I don't really know yet.'

'You always loved your engines didn't you,' David said, still staring.

'It isn't just the engines, David,' I said. 'You don't understand how much goes into the whole thing. I modelled this diorama using Ordnance survey maps. The contours of the hills are to scale, as is everything else in the scene. I've worked for a long time getting the right colours for the trees, and even for the time of year. The Honeybourne Line is set in the spring. I travelled that line in March and April repeatedly over three years, taking photographs so that I could reproduce it faithfully here. That backdrop of the hills, and the sky, took me three months to complete on the back of thick rolls of wallpaper, copied grid by grid from the photos.'

I left him to unpack and get changed. I waited for him downstairs.

We had quite a good evening really, visiting old haunts on High Street. I hardly went down there anymore. I tended to shop at the supermarket and stay clear of the town centre, especially in the evenings. But I could see how happy David was, reliving his youth. After a couple of beers I was back there with him, up to a certain point, and we joked about the things we'd done all those years ago. Our parents had been great friends and we'd always looked forward to the week we'd all get together in Norfolk. It was one of the main reasons I'd moved, but familiarity often deadens memory and it was quite nice to have David unearth all the things I'd forgotten.

Over the meal things turned more towards the personal. He did his bit of amateur psychology; investigating the reasons for my building the Honeybourne line and the gradual disintegration of my relationship. I explained that the reason for the model railway was simple. Vicky's family were from Cheltenham. We often had to go there, during holidays, for the kids to visit and the like. I wanted to build a model of one of the Heritage lines. Where better than somewhere I would be visiting regularly anyway? He offered some banal observations about it being a connection to her history as I must have known that the relationship was crumbling.

I said I didn't really want to discuss it further. It was a model of a heritage train line, not a manifestation of some kind of inner emotional turmoil.

But he wouldn't stop digging, and as the evening went on we had all the old clichés coming out. I think he must have been watching too many of those daytime TV programmes. He suggested he could act as a mediator between me and Vicky. The girls wanted to see me, apparently, and things weren't going well with Keith. Why not come down to London and spend some time with him; reinvigorate the career; work on 'rebuilding the bridges'. Thus it went on, until closing time.

When we got back to the house David popped out to the car and brought back a bottle of Courvoisier he had in the boot, a 'gift from clients' he told me. We should have a little nightcap, he said. He *certainly* did. I had a couple with him as he reminisced. But my mind was wandering. I didn't have much left to do on the Sheringham to Holt line and I was desperate to get it completed. I just had the green and white roof canopy to fit on the station and complete the platform with some miniature posters that I'd printed on the computer, and finish painting the hanging baskets. Then I could get the passenger figures in place and I'd be done. At an opportune moment I said I was tired and went off to the main bedroom to try and get a few hours modelling in.

The Phantasmagorical Imperative...

Despite finally going to bed around five in the morning I was still the first to rise. But then, I hadn't drunk half a bottle of brandy.

I tried my best to do the 'good host' thing, partly as a way of trying to cover over any frostiness on my part from the night before. But then David was quite far gone and I doubt he'd even noticed. I laid the table out, with jam, marmalade and honey and even used the toast rack and butter dish.

It was a good hour before David appeared.

'Blimey, you hammered that brandy well, didn't you,' he joked. 'You really are a terror when you get on the pop, eh...'

'Oh yes, nothing like a brandy,' I said, laughing along with him. 'Now, do you want tea or coffee?'

'Coffee, please,' he said, sitting down and grabbing some toast. 'Mind if I dig straight in?'

'No problem,' I said. 'I've already had mine.'

There was a tense silence, heightened by the boiling of the kettle and the scratchy scraping of the knife on the toast.

I brought us two coffees in from the kitchen. We sat there sipping them for a while.

'Do you remember that year we came here with just my Mum and Dad—I think yours wanted to go abroad for their wedding anniversary, or something—and we stayed at The Burlington Hotel,' David said, struggling with the honey dipper and managing to spill it down the side of the pot—something I always found very irritating.

'We had to have dinner in the dining room an hour before the adults didn't we,' I said, wiping the mess up with a napkin.

'Oops, sorry!' David said. 'Yes, and my sisters had to sit on the table next to us didn't they, so we wouldn't all mess about...'

David's sisters. I had completely forgotten about them. It was as though I had erased them from all of our holidays. I'd even had a teenage crush on his older sister, Emily. She'd died in a car crash a few years before. I realised I hadn't really been there for him at that point. It was when Vicky and I were breaking up. His younger sister, Clara, worked for some volunteering charity that dealt with irrigation in Africa. For some reason she was based in the United States though.

'...and we were served by that creepy waiter that wouldn't turn the lights on, even though the place was virtually dark.'

'It only happened on the first night though,' I laughed. 'Your mother took the manager apart the next morning—in front of a whole coach party that had arrived from somewhere...'

'From Sheffield...' David said.

'Oh, yes, Sheffield... and when she'd finished telling him that we would be having our meals with her, and your father, in the main dining room, from then on, she got a round of applause from the coach party.'

We both laughed, for a while.

David finished his slice of toast, rather slowly. He drank up his coffee, a bit noisily.

The Phantasmagorical Imperative...

I waited and smiled, thinking how much I needed to get back to the figures on the Sheringham station platform.

David wiped his hands on his jeans and said, in an attempt to be purposeful, 'So shall we pop along and see the Burlington, for old times' sake, eh?'

It was clearly going to be another one of those days where he tried to drag me out of what he perceived as some kind of self-absorption. It really couldn't have been further from the truth. I had resolved myself to Vicky's leaving, and not seeing the girls for a while, quite some time before—a year or so, at least. I was happy here. I had my railway. I had the sea. I was content modelling, and doing the website design stuff when I ran short of money. I didn't need much really; just my catalogues, my projects and a walk on the seafront each day. I wasn't the sort of guy to let it all disintegrate about me—all pizza boxes, beer and tears.

But, I had a feeling this visit was as much for him as it was for me.

I only live a few streets away so we were soon stood outside The Burlington Hotel, looking out to sea. There was a good wind picking up now.

'Shame about that crazy golf going,' David said, after a few moments, pointing to a patch of rough grass that used to be the home to large models of windmills and cartoon bears. We'd always loved going there.

'Yes, it closed a few years back,' I replied. 'At least the boating lake is still here though. I suppose it's more of a feature. People would be up in arms if that ever went.'

'Remember that day we bought those sailing boats from the model shop in town and came straight up here with them,' David said, eagerly jumping at the opportunity for something less stilted. 'I think we spent the entire afternoon with them.'

'And most of the rest of the week, if I remember correctly,' I said.

There was a fine drizzle forming now.

'How about a bacon sarnie in the cafe by the station,' David said. 'I still feel a bit pissed.'

As we had got older, and sandcastles and seaside rock had lost their appeal, we'd go to the cafe opposite the station and try to pull girls. We didn't really have a clue what we were doing. We'd just sit there most of the day with a cold cup of coffee and try to smoke our way through a pack of ten Marlboro, in the hope we looked grown up.

I watched David devouring his bacon sandwich, with two eggs; tomato sauce and yolk dripping down his chin. Once he'd drained two cups of tea from the pot he stifled a belch and looked about the cafe. It had changed hands over a decade before, and now catered more for an older clientele. There were homemade cakes and scones, and plenty of space for wheelchairs to manoeuvre.

'Well, I don't think we'll have much luck getting any birds in here,' he laughed, looking around at the pensioners, enjoying their eggs on toast and gateaux.

'Pretty much like it was in the old days, then,' I replied.

He grinned.

We left a couple of quid for the waitress and left.

I started to stroll over to the station. David grabbed me, 'I'm just going to get some fags, for the *memories...*' he said.

'I thought you gave up,' I said. 'I'll go over to the platform, then.'

'I still have the odd one or two,' he shrugged, 'when it's a *special occasion*. I'll see you over there.'

Quite what the special occasion was I didn't really know. I went over to see the 13.30 pull in from Holt; it was a few minutes late.

Then I saw the woman with the yellow mac. She was standing at the furthest end of the platform. She was also wearing some wellington boots, decorated with what appeared to be pink butterflies. On the ground beside her there was a bulging leather suitcase—a very old one. On the other side, holding her hand, was a little boy (maybe eight, or nine years old), and he was holding hands with a little girl (maybe four, or five); she clutched a teddy bear to her face. They stood very still, as the train came into the station. There was something about them that I found unnerving. They seemed timeless, sad and lost. I watched them, as the platform filled with people. They didn't move.

People talk about spirit guides, ghosts, visions, revelations and such. If these things are real then this was mine.

If David dwelt in the past then my real home, I resolved, was the future. Not a *past* filled with failure and regret, or fond and falsely-gilded reminiscences gradually fading into oblivion, but a dependable, systematised *future*—not that unknown wilderness of possibility, as it is usually portrayed; didn't we all deserve more than that? It would be a place of perpetual movement, founded upon certainty. Vicky was wrong, I didn't lack ambition—I had that by the bucket. What I needed was something I could use my skills to channel properly. I had found that years before, I now realised.

The last holidaymakers of the season were rushing around me, leaving the station and heading for the front, and the little shops along the way. Everyone had a gleam in their eyes, oblivious to the sorrow of the years ahead. How much of today would be remembered in fifty years; only the engines would endure, even if they were rusting in their sidings by then. But gradually all would be ruin, as the sea walls failed and the tides rose. The tracks would become mythic structures for ocean beings to ponder, the sleepers home to crustaceans and sea-urchins.

I looked down at my hands. Something about them seemed pudgy and pointless. I pushed at the pink skin around the knuckles with my fingertips. It rolled along in folds. I turned these strange things over and stared at the palms. These lines, if fortunes they could tell, spoke only one truth, for all of us; David, me, the lady in the yellow mac and her poor kids.

David materialised beside me, spluttering his way through a cigarette.

'Why don't we take a trip on the old steam train?' he said.

'They only run steam on special events, it's a diesel today—a particularly fine one though, a class 101 DMU,' I replied. 'They'll do steam tomorrow, as it's a Sunday—for the last gasps of the season.'

'We'll go tomorrow, then,' he said, 'before I head off.'

'Yes, we'll go *tomorrow*,' I said, staring at the milling passengers on the platform, in a daze.

'Why don't we go and get a pint,' David said.

Once the throng had cleared the platform I saw that the woman, and her children, were gone.

When we eventually returned from the pub David said he wanted to watch a football game on the TV and asked if I'd got Sky Sports. I just gave him a look and he chuckled. He said it wasn't a problem, he'd watch it on the computer instead. I told him I had some work I wanted to complete on the Sheringham to Holt line, but that perhaps we could have a beer together afterwards.

I lost track of time, as I often did when I was modelling.

The workbench I had in the bedroom was covered with little tins of paint, brushes, small vices and magnifying glasses attached to varying arms to hold the figurines, engines and carriages in place as I painted them. I worked diligently, as though on an assembly line, to finish those last few figures, so that the line could be fully operational by morning.

It was past midnight when a timid knock on the door interrupted me.

'Sorry to disturb, but it's got quite late now and I thought I'd turn in,' David said, peeping round the door.

'Oh, I'm sorry, I really forgot the time', I said.

David came in and whistled, 'Wow! That's even more impressive than the one next door.'

He walked over to the model and surveyed the line. It hugged the wall, before turning back sharply to follow a four foot ledge I'd constructed above the bed. He then hovered at my workbench, peering at the rows of figures.

'You love every bit of it don't you,' he said, shaking his head, and squinting at the models. 'Remember that argument we had one year about the colour of the uniforms on those German infantrymen we'd bought to paint together?'

I put my brush down. 'Yes, I do actually, very well. They were a Panzer Crew though, not infantry, and we didn't argue about the uniforms, but the colour of their hands and faces. I thought the flesh coloured paint in the model shop was too pink but you just wanted to get them finished. It was from then on that I started mixing my own colours.'

'Yes, yours always looked much better than mine, I must admit,' he said. 'Anyway, I'll get to bed and see you in the morning for that trip on the train.'

I heard him shuffling about for the next twenty minutes or so and I sat there staring at the models. I would have to work hard—all that night—to get things ready. It was ironic that he'd mentioned the Panzer Crew because only a few minutes prior to his knock on the door I'd realised I wouldn't have time to mix up a batch of my own flesh-coloured paint. I'd have to make do with the bright pink ready-made stuff; luckily I had a spare pot from a kit I'd bought some years before. These last few models needed their finishing touches and then placing correctly in the scene. It wouldn't do for us to set off without everything completed. And because tomorrow's service would be very special I took out the LNER B12 8572 engine. I'd painted her in apple green livery. She looked magnificent; some things would never lose their splendour.

∞

David and I were gone early, as I'd intended. He dozed as we departed from Sheringham—not everyone enjoys the mornings, I understand. I don't think he noticed the lady at the other end of the platform, in her yellow mackintosh, with her children, and her suitcase.

The first part of the trip went very quickly indeed. And as we set off from Weybourne, on then to Holt, David seemed very different. His eyes flared crazily at me from across our table, but he did not move. It was good that we could both be still and quiet, finally. Still. And quiet. In fact, he looked better than I'd seen him in years; gone was that pale greyish hue of the indoor life, our sea air had done him the world of good. His face had a much brighter glow about it now, something altogether healthier, perhaps overly flush though.

A whistle blew. The train pulled away on time, as it always would now.

I was pleased by how smart the conductor looked as we caught sight of him with his flag at the end of the platform. He stood to attention, everything about him as still and focused as we were—such a beautiful colour to his uniform; his flag a bright red, his thick moustache a glossy black; all in its place, and every detail perfect.

As we gathered speed, heading out across the flat grasslands and on towards Holt, I noticed, proudly, how green the grasses looked, flecked with the yellows and browns of the sandy ground. The clouds were fluffy round billows of white and grey. All was windless and perfect and they hung immobile against the great backdrop of endless blue sky. These were greener greens, yellower yellows, whiter whites, greyer greys and bluer blues than I, or David, had ever seen before, I am sure. And—fully restored, as everything always is eventually—there was now plenty of time to enjoy these rich, unchanging landscapes on our wonderful journey together.

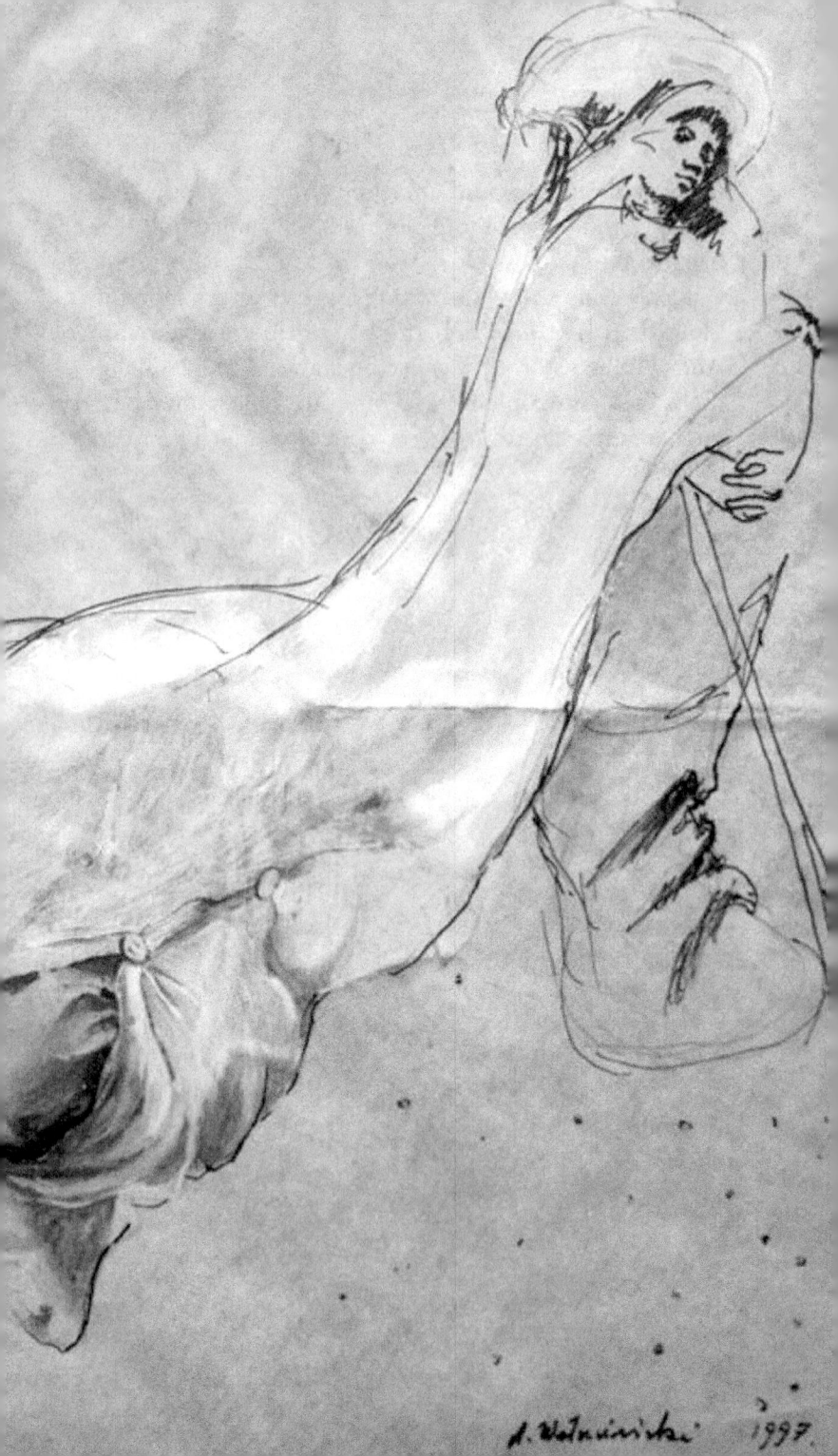

Vertep

*Right foll de riddle loll,
I'm the boy to do them all;
Here's a stick
To trash Old Nick,
If he by chance upon me call*

Punch & Judy,
Collier / Cruikshank Script

The jack-in-the-box is a simple toy. It is a wooden box. The wooden box has a handle. The handle, when turned, operates a mechanism. The mechanism powers a music box. The music box plays a little tune. The little tune, as if by magic, calls (from his hidey hole) the 'jack'—a clown, or other children's toy. Things follow a very simple pattern in the world of the jack-in-the-box—but, despite their simplicity, they always guarantee a surprise.

I collect jack-in-the-boxes. I repair them; sometimes I even trade in them—when money is tight. I collect other things too—don't we all! I'm a hoarder more than anything; old records, postcards, books and magazines, but mostly records—and jack-in-the-boxes. These things—and the gathering of them—are my hobbies. It passes the time.

I. The Fair

It was a fairly ordinary antique fair. The kind that asks you to pay to go in because browsing around old junk is something of an entertainment, and someone has to pay the rent. This one was in a local leisure centre, on the May bank holiday.

I'd never intended to go in there.

I know what you're thinking but honestly I hadn't.

Suzanne was in town, looking for some new fabric to recover a footstool. She'd taken up upholstery, following a short course at the local college. I'd said I'd take a wander around the town and had ended up back at the car-park after a fruitless search of the local charity shops for interesting vinyl. There were a couple of recordings of fairground organs, but I had so much of that kind of stuff already unplayed that I decided it wouldn't be worth the ear-bashing I'd get for 'cluttering' the place up with more 'junk'. So I gave them a miss. They were only 50p each though—a shame really.

So I'd gone into the fair to kill the hour before I said I'd meet Suzanne at the car. Over the years I'd been a few times and watched the gradually ageing traders lose interest in their stalls, and inevitably a few had passed away too, not to be replaced—this was not a young person's trade.

It had become more like a car-boot sale now and I flitted from stall to stall, tutting at the overpriced attic-junk on offer. Just as I was beginning to wonder whether I might even manage an hour there I found a table with at least a few interesting items on it. There was a wonderful carved jade ship (not priced, unsurprisingly!), and some decent ivory figurines (locked in a glass case with their price labels tucked beneath them).

While these items were certainly fascinating there was no way that I would be able to afford them, but as a moment of pleasure amidst the hopefully priced modern 'collectibles' it was a very welcome relief. Sadly I inhabited that awkward space between dealer and amateur collector—knowing enough to identify a dud, but without the clout to strike a real 'deal'. It is a situation that only ever guarantees disappointment and resentment—until you find that gem, of course.

So, I stared at the fine items on this stall, more as a museum-goer than a buyer. And I was content, until I spotted the box.

It was on the next stall, beside a portable gramophone in a luxurious blue velvet case. The gramophone would have been enough of a delight—as I said I'm a record collector and I have three gramophones, in varying states of repair—but this was an old jack-in-the-box!

The stallholder seemed disinterested in potential customers, quite unlike the other desperate salesmen and women that tired their prospective customers with invented blather about the history of even the shoddiest plastic toy. Instead he sat there polishing a tall brass oil lamp, without a care for anyone that paused to scan his offerings.

His table looked barely capable of supporting the assembled wares. It was one of those folding wallpaper tables, sagging slightly in the middle, and I scooped the box up swiftly in case it should suddenly collapse.

I examined it carefully, perhaps—even then—desperately.

The front panel was carved in relief with a proscenium arch and a slightly jutting stage area of wooden boards. The background was painted black, with twinkling silver stars and a crescent moon. The other sides were not carved but were decorated in a fading, chipped paint. The back had a fairly crude painting of closed red curtains with golden braid—I surmised this might have been added later. The left side though had a stylised scene of jagged blue and white mountain tops with a similar black sky, stars and moon. On the right side an opulent room was decorated with golds, reds and oranges (now flaking quite badly), with a great green divan surrounded by exotic plants and miniature palms. A metal crank bar with a red and cream ceramic handle jutted from amidst the foliage.

It was clearly old.

The crumpled brown label—that had evidently seen many months on the road—read 'Petrushka - £100'.

I said, 'Is that Petrushka the puppet, or the ballet?'

'Eh?' the proprietor muttered, looking up from polishing the oil-lamp.

'I said, does the label refer to the puppet within—*Petrushka*—or the tune it plays?'

'I dunno,' he replied. 'Why not give it a try?'

I did.

It was the tune. A few bars cranked out, with a metallic twang, and then a grinding noise.

Nothing popped out.

'It's bust,' the man said. 'Tried to get it goin'—no joy. Still plays the tune though. Pretty, ain't it?'

'Pretty indeed!' I said, immediately regretting my enthusiasm.

Unfortunately he smelt interest on me. There would be little chance of getting a bargain here. The lovely painted panels had intrigued me though and already—with Petrushka playing in my head—I was captivated.

And so I had another jack-in-the-box; this one broken.

It cost me one hundred pounds—but Suzanne didn't need to know that (we were saving for a cruise). One hundred pounds; because I loved it, and the mystery it contained.

II. A Room Below

I have a Linn Sondek LP12. Wherever possible I have invested in the finest quality, for all of the things I collect. The turntable was purchased with the small inheritance I received from my father. I remember him with every record that I play through it, for he taught me about music, and about value—not the crude value of commodity, but the real value of experience. Suzanne could say little about it, because the money was more rightfully mine than anything earned by my own efforts. Although she did comment that she thought the purchase extravagant, especially with the bathroom suite still in need of replacement. I have had it now for nearly twenty years and, as long as I am attentive to its proper maintenance, I am confident it will continue to provide good service for many more.

It was upon this turntable that I played Stravinsky's *Petrushka*, as I made my first attempts to fix the jack-in-the-box. It seemed fitting that I should play that anarchic ballet as I repaired the little mechanism. It shouldn't take long, I thought, not that there was anything pressing to attend to that afternoon though. Suzanne had already made her way upstairs with the fabric for the footstool and it was unlikely we would see each other again before dinner.

Suzanne and I had our separate recreation rooms now; mine the extensive dining room to the rear of the house, filled with my record collection and tall bookcases that housed the jack-in-the-boxes, books and other small collections. She had the third bedroom upstairs, where she was able to engage in her sewing and upholstery without being disturbed by my music. It was a classic arrangement for a childless couple such as ourselves, rooms that had previously been allocated to the future, with hope and love, fell back to our provenance and soon we had widened the gaps between us already forced open by disappointment and an aching sense of inadequacy.

I had located my copy of *Petrushka* (or *Petrouchka* as it appears on my record) easily. I am a practical man and have always catalogued my collection alphabetically by composer, artist or band. I have never been interested in some form of obscurantist assembly by theme, period or other individual whim. It was a lovely 10inch copy of Dimitri Mitropoulos conducting the New York Philharmonic in 1951. I set the turntable going and settled down at the dining room table, with my set of tools, to discover the fault with the jack-in-the-box.

The first light steps of the ballet shot through me, it was scintillating—something between a chorus of pipes from some dark woodland bacchanal and a frothy celebratory folk dance. I read the sleeve notes: first performed in Paris on the 13th of June 1911, with Nijinsky in the title role. Here, more than a century on, this music was filling me with fresh delight, calling across the years with the spirit of other people and their traditions; each note erupting with past cultures and hidden lives, unreachable without this translation into a sound so alive with narrative.

I tinkered away at the box, with little to show for my efforts. There seemed to be no screws or other fitments that would enable easy access to the working parts of the toy. The catch that held the lid down merely pivoted uselessly on a loose hinge. I attempted, as carefully as possible, to prise the lid of the box open with a small screwdriver, but feeling the wood begin to splinter I stopped.

Perhaps, I thought (or hoped), it might merely be a problem with the timing cog for the release on the lid. A few squirts of WD40 through the handle bar and into the mechanism might loosen it.

So I tried that, followed by a few exploratory prods with the screwdriver.

I then turned the handle and allowed it to play out its tinkling rendition of the opening to the record I was listening to, hoping for the best.

Oddly enough, rather than playing the first few bars of the tune, the box played the exact section I was listening to on the turntable, which was about halfway through the second tableau of the ballet.

It seemed to me that the room was suddenly filled with some great presence. Certainly the music had shifted from its initial frivolous, repetitive refrains, jiggling like some clowning doll on a stick. It had now taken on a darker quality, a savage grandeur oppressing a cowardly undercurrent of strings. And this was now awkwardly echoed by the jack-in-the-box with its childish, tinny tune.

In both the recording and the music box there seemed to be a repetitive sequence of notes that called to me, either through some primitive echo or a metaphysical resonance, this strange blending of the base with the spiritual left me ill at ease.

But the 'presence' I had felt was surely no more than my own excitement at the puzzle of the box, and the quality of the booming waves of sound that were echoing around the dining room. Music has that quality I find— to produce physical effects within the body. But it needs suitable surroundings in which to do this. Rather than the inner world of the headphones and the tinkling mp3 file I prefer an *environment* and the delayed resonances set up through the architecture of space and the struggle of notes and harmonies against the confines of their enclosure. Suzanne, misunderstanding entirely the need for such an acoustic, does not appreciate the necessity for volume—she has different sensibilities, if she has sensibilities at all anymore.

Despite these broader reflections on the quality of music and my more mundane situation with Suzanne I had been unable to shake off a vague anxiety that had set in upon me.

I turned the record off.

I decided upon an experiment. I would turn the record over and set the needle at a random point on side two. I would then set the turntable going and wind the music box again. The limited amount of track contained on the small metal tumbler usually contained within these music boxes would not extend to that section of the record; unless, of course, there was an entirely different apparatus powering this one.

A spritely fanfare blasted through the speakers.

I turned the jack-in-the-box handle and then released it apprehensively.

From the speakers, just as the fanfare subsided, a drum roll announced something portentous.

The box, in its twinkling fashion, chimed out the beats perfectly in time with the record. And then both seemed to soar into some ethereal burst of waltz. There seemed now no difference between the record and the music from the box. This was certainly no simple barrel tune mechanism operating within it.

Something inside *me* collapsed. Not beneath a flood of revelation but rather with a sigh of disintegration, more like the slow deflation of a balloon. For there it was—that repetitive chord again, as though it had been struggling beneath the surface of the world for all eternity; endowing everything with life but also with the cruel volatility of entropic death. That diabolical cascade of arpeggios seemed to crawl into the currents of the air and I saw at last the power of music—its ability to penetrate the core of everything and infect existence with passion once more. And it was clear to me that Stravinsky had felt this too—knowledge began to come to me as pure inspiration, as startling and fresh as the idiosyncratic sonorities playing out through this revolutionary score.

This man was not a simple composer but some herald of synchronicities undreamt of by mortals. He was an aberrant child sired by a trinity; his genius fused with the fresh melodic harmony of Rimsky-Korsakov, dependable as the formal rigour of Glazunov, and as turbulent as the deep ritual of Mussorgsky. From that moment I worshipped the strangeness of Stravinsky as though he were some old god in bright new raiment.

And, it was obvious to me now, the jack-in-the-box was some curious relic attuned to Stravinsky's majestic vision. It would require patience, and proper supplication, to attune myself to the rhythmic codes and systems of its mystery. It required a quest to find the simple switch by which reality, modified only slightly, might shift the eternal gears of the world and the box would reveal its purpose.

III. A Room Above

Over the following weeks I played the record and turned the handle of the jack-in-the-box whenever time allowed. Perhaps I was not systematic enough in my devotions, or I had yet to discover the temporal constructions through which such rituals should operate—my mind was not of an occult persuasion and I ventured no further than a rather lazy repetition of worn out procedures.

Simply put, the wondrous wooden box has a beautiful handle. This handle, when turned, operates an intricate and hidden mechanism. The hidden mechanism powers a music box, of incredible versatility and infinite ingenuity. This ingenious music box calls to vast realms of possibility. This call, given time, should summon from the depths, or draw from the firmament, the 'jack'—a sundering of space and time. Things follow a complex and mystical pattern in the world of the jack-in-the-box—but, sometimes, *things* don't always function the way they should.

I suppose it was religious practice, of a kind.

Often, in these moments—*of prayer*—I would slip into a kind of daydream, or projection of my inner being. I floated over vast landscapes and squirmed through deep dark earthy places. I flitted through feverish crowds in great shaded bazaars and soared across rich blue seas alive with great frolicking shoals of enormous fish.

But one vision began to recur. I saw great masses of people, pressed against each other, circling aimlessly, yet every face alive with delight. These circles of bodies were themselves comprised of other circles of family groups clinging tightly together, so that the whole gathering, when viewed from above by my dancing mind, took on the image of a huge clock mechanism, its parts all revolving in one majestic dance.

After indeterminate stretches of time I would always emerge at some vast marketplace with trailing tunes of Russian folk dances skipping through the smoky night air that rang with laughter and cheering. I would find my way, through a thick and stinking throng of audience, to a little wooden booth. It had two performance spaces, one above the other. In the bottom one a puppet on a stick cavorted around the space on a little cloth horse. The puppet had a great hooked nose and crooked grin and it seemed to get the best of all who came to challenge him. The words of the performance were lost to me, spoken as they were through some shrill whistling device that served only to solicit great laughs from the crowd.

And then in an instant I would be there too, inside the booth, strung upon a stick, awaiting my entrance. I was thrust into the upper room and danced a little jig, my silly wooden arms flailing about hopelessly before them all—beasts that laughed and whinnied at my ridiculous antics.

And then the real show began.

I was propped in the wings, my little arms and legs hanging limply down beside me. And a glorious nativity scene played out in the room above, complete with wonderfully carved angels and animals. The crowd, penitent or proud, watched this wordless scene in awe and then the little doors of the booth were closed and all was darkness.

'You haven't forgotten that Aleksander and Sarah are coming around tonight have you Peter?' a voice called out. I was back in the dreary dining room, staring at the mysterious jack-in-the-box.

I *had* forgotten. But I made an attempt to prepare for the evening. It was not worth fighting over.

When they arrived, our oldest friends, and the due rituals had been observed; the giving of the flowers and the wine; the return of glasses and snacks; the talking; the laughing; the agreements and the news—oh! the endless news—of children and holidays, and plans and investments. What hours of cynical evasion and hollow bombast.

I asked myself how many friendships had there been that resembled ours, barely resuscitated every few months with dinner and smiles? How many lovers had loved like Suzanne and me, collapsing into distance and distrust? Everything was only a fading mirage of previous forms. The names were different, but the passions and the disappointments were the same.

Perhaps the wondrous creature in the box fed purely from the spirit of our fantasies, our hopes and failures.

It was clear: it required us to radically alter our situations, to challenge the rules of our fixed lives. Then it would respond with its *gifts*, its *teachings*.

The conversation rolled on through the starters and main course, until Aleksander asked what I had been up to recently. He was always interested in my little hobbies, and often we found ourselves in the dining room, after the girls had retired to the lounge, playing records and looking through little treasures from my collection.

I seized the opportunity, confident that beneath the basic question there lurked some knowledge of my recent efforts.

I told them about the jack-in-the-box, and jumped up to play Stravinsky's *Petrushka*. I told them about the dreamy journeys that seemed to lead, more often than ever now, to the Russian fair and the curious puppet booth.

And then it occurred to me that Aleksander and Sarah were also little players in all this game. They may well be the key to the box. Why else would they be here?

'Aleksander, you are my oldest friend,' I began. 'Might we play at a little something—a sort of charades, if you like. We have never quarrelled. That may be significant. Can I ask you to deliver me a wounding blow after a vicious argument? I don't mean a simple slap or punch. I mean something *serious*—drawing blood. We must turn the tables, for one night only everything must be different!'

The three faces at the table stared at me, amazed.

They were right—it was all too contrived. This would never satisfy those intricate mechanisms at work inside the jack-in-the-box. Nothing would release the great elemental from the box save for the endless rehearsal of these roles until finally the world happened upon the formula by chance.

And here I was—foolish, worthless, novice—trying to encourage these others to attempt different configurations of their being. But they were uninitiated. They did not understand, or did not want to.

'I'm sorry,' Suzanne chirped up. 'Peter's not been focusing very well on things recently.'

Sarah nodded agreement and offered one of those sympathetic smiles.

Of course I'd been focusing on things—just not *Suzanne's* things, or *things* she could even begin to comprehend,

'Well, we must be up early anyway,' Aleksander added, dutifully. The whole thing was descending into a wretched, worn out script.

The polite babble continued for some time.

I couldn't wait for them all to be gone to get back to my Stravinsky and his jack-in-the-box.

I could see our friends were not impressed by my ideas, but I was passed caring about anything but what was hidden in that painted box. And who can blame them really. Who wants their world turned to the polarity of stars and shadows? I too was tired of maniacal dreams, but that tiredness was suffered in exchange for a deeper truth, a metaphysical revelation that might erase all form and return us to that first eternal chord. For who, WHO, can resist the truth—that infernal machine, that conflagration of desires—when finally it arrives, resplendent and repellent, at the doors of your mind?

IV. Evening Falls, or, The Grand Carnival

I had to face the other music first though. It started straight away upon her return from saying goodbye to Aleksander and Sarah.

'So, what the hell is going on?' she yelled, storming into the dining room just as I was about to put the turntable on. 'And what is it with that damned stupid record? You'd better tell me what this is all about, Peter. You're starting to sound like a nutter.'

I just stared at her and lowered the needle. The blissful dance began.

'You can turn that off for a start. I'm serious,' she said, calmer and more insistent. 'I want us to discuss all of this *right now!*'

I didn't reply. I merely walked over to my shelves and carefully lifted down the Petrushka box. I cleared some plates and glasses from the table, where Suzanne had been sitting, and I turned the handle and allowed it to join the recording with its delicate metallic tune blending into the melodic madness. If only *I* could worship in such a fashion, I thought. But my frail human voice could not hope to offer suitable veneration. I would have to be content with merely mental adoration of the great mystery.

Apparently she was still there, watching me. 'It's just a fucking *box*, Peter—a fucking *stupid* wooden box', her little squeaky words fractured the beauty of my sanctuary. 'You do remember that it's just a kid's toy, don't you?'

She would soon become bored, I was certain. She did not understand that I must attempt further reconfigurations. Indeed, she did not understand what the nature of such reconfigurations might even be.

'Do you know how ugly you look right now? Hunched over that fucking thing like some perverted Quasimodo...' On and on she went like this; words, words, words—breaking down the delicate, reverent atmosphere with their brutal meanings and their aggressive finality. If only they could have the beautiful multiplicity of music—the endless resonance, the infinite connectivity.

Still the words went on. 'Listen *to* me, you crazy *fucker*! I don't know if it's that *box* or *you* that's evil—but one of you is! How can you have let yourself get like this? Well, I'll tell you what! *I'll* tell you what—let's find out exactly which it is shall we...'

I had seen movement from the corner of my eye but had assumed she had left the room. Then suddenly her arms reached over from behind me and picked up the box.

I had been surprised—caught off guard—but I leapt up to defend the sanctity of this holy place.

She turned and glared at me triumphantly before reaching up to cast the jack-in-the-box against the wall— the only *thing* in the world that could offer us true *salvation*.

It was then that I struck her. Not once, but repeatedly, back and forth with a savage glee. My little arms churned about her rag-doll body like spiky wooden spindles.

'There, how do you like my teaching, my pretty dear!' I cried, with a shrill delight, backed by a flare of whistling from the Stravinsky, its ravishing notes swelling and cavorting around my bloodied fists. 'Yes, one more little lesson. *There*, there, *there*!'

I returned to the table as the second tableau was ending, and the record slid into its endless final groove. A static hum came through the speakers, punctuated by the click of eternal revolutions.

I turned the handle on the jack-in-the-box with my aching, sticky fingers.

It finally gave up its secrets with a tired clunk.

Inside the lid there was an intricate scene of revellers; nursemaids, gypsy girls, coachmen, a dancing bear. Many were masked but one in particular stood out from all the others, with a devilish hooked nose and a wide, crooked grin.

A limp puppet figure emerged, bounced a moment on a worn-out spring and sat there idly rocking slowly back and forth, all worn out by time and the fading splendours of forgotten histories. The little music box whirred out its last few ringing notes.

I sat, out of breath, staring at the little puppet.

But the face on it, what a *remarkable* face! Its great hooked nose and crooked grin had been crudely chiselled from a small block of wood and appeared to be splintering apart. Indeed it was. That *wonderful* face—so familiar, yet so unbearably other—was disintegrating and reforming into multitudes of faces; great crowds of faces, looming for an instant and then vanishing, melting into each other. All the *ridiculous* faces! All the *remarkable, wonderful, ridiculous* faces! All the wonder, horror, sadness, love and light of humanity in one ludicrous wooden doll that had been hidden for years, perhaps for centuries—no, millennia!—here in this little box; a sacred box that had finally given up its secret to me. They all bobbed along with the churning hurdy-gurdy of the master playing in my mind—all the eyes and cheeks, lips and noses, sliding into a magical mirage of identities.

And the last face—oh yes, you can guess that quite well—was my own; with little rosy cheeks, black eyes that glinted with fury, and that *great hooked nose and crooked grin* that seemed to reveal a deeper, more monstrous physiognomic pattern than I could never have imagined bubbled beneath all our fleshy little masks.

My consciousness soared again—released by the spiky sounds of *Petrushka*, that seemed to erupt around the room like a great burst of fire. Untethered, my inner self was able to dance again—as it had in that mad little booth at the Russian fair. I saw myself from above, my dwindling plastic form twitching as crazily as my soul now did. I saw my eyes roll; blue eyes, green eyes, brown eyes, eyes of molten glass, eyes of vengeful steel, eyes of water, eyes of fire.

I watched as Suzanne managed to stagger to her feet, and with a great effort she grasped one of the dining room chairs and swung it at my back. It splintered apart as easily as my tired bones disintegrated. I watched, and laughed, as she bashed my brittle little skull apart with frantic swipes of the broken chair legs, and with a last great blow she smashed the fragile box into fragments. Then her ragged body gave way and joined be in a bloodied heap upon the floor.

How silly we both looked; all black and blue, all bruised and purple. How crumpled we both looked; all broken and battered, all smashed and splintered.

How quiet we were and what silence roared about us—mouths agape into eternity.

The End

A Harvest of Abandon

There had been little to keep him in London since Cathy's death. There was little to keep him anywhere, since most of his family were now gone and those few that remained lived so far away (mostly abroad) that meaningful contact with them was almost impossible, even if it had been desired. So, with the payment from her pension (quite generous, he felt) and the sale of the house, he had decided to move to Scotland, as they both had dreamt of doing when they retired.

That retirement was already within sight—seven years for Cathy and ten for him. They had started the usual list of things to see and do and deferred hobbies to take up again. Her diagnosis had been late and the advance of the disease relentless. Within three weeks of the prognosis, which had given them at least a few months (they thought), she was dead.

When he had been younger, just starting on his writing career, Ian Lyons would never have considered retiring. Writing was his life, wasn't it?—one just carries on until the end. That was *then* though. Now he really wanted an end to it. His brand of crime fiction had been popular for some time, a couple of decades before, but was now a little on the wane—the final nails being driven in by a lust for gore and forensic investigations. Best to call it a day in a few years and concentrate on other things—besides, Cathy had served so much as his muse over the years that it now seemed as though writing itself were forever haunted by her.

But it was not just Cathy's memory that was so evoked by the work of writing. It was all their friends and family, each of whom had appeared—for brief cameos or as more evolved characters—in many of Ian's novels and stories. At the beginning of his career he had taken the dictum of 'write what you know' to his very heart and had become as much a stereotype of a writerly 'character' as the set of middle class professionals that populated his work and social life. Steadily his social world so mirrored that of his books that he had begun, as the years went by, to forget what was fact and what was fiction.

Cathy had always been on hand though to put him right on the facts.

But, Cathy was gone.

∞

Lochgilphead seemed the perfect place to start again, or to slide into obscurity. A small town on the Western edge of a stunning loch—protected enough from the barrage of weather by a small inlet, but wild enough to stir the senses. They had discovered it in their early thirties on a touring holiday in West Scotland and had vowed to buy a small place there when funds permitted. By doing so now he might at least realise one of their plans.

He had found a newly renovated home overlooking the loch. It had been a holiday cottage but he plagued the owner relentlessly until she finally accepted an offer far in excess of its value. It had three floors of rather small rooms, the top one offering a gorgeous panoramic view, through three sliding doors, of the waters as they inched their tidal way back and forth—instilling a sense of the eternal as waves often do. That would be his bedroom.

His study would be located on the first floor, with the same view through a smaller window. He already knew that such beautiful scenery would slow his output, but that wasn't a bad thing. He could do with returning to reality a little more, rather than the increasingly private space of his fiction.

The removal vans came and went. It was certainly a long journey, and its distance seemed to mark the true nature of the change he had initiated. After the removers had their final cup of tea and headed off for the long trek home he was left with the silence and peculiarity of every new home. But there was nobody here to share the strangeness.

There were the usual problems with settling in. He found that the lovely triple doors that opened from his bedroom onto a small balcony let in a good amount of water when an Easterly storm came in. This resulted in a large damp patch on the ceiling in the bathroom below and buckled laminate flooring in the bedroom. The bathroom too seemed to have many faults. Some problem in the piping resulted in loud clanging and bumping whenever taps where turned on and intermittently a terrible smell would pervade the first floor landing. He guessed this emanated from the bathroom as it had the reek of sewers about it. A couple of different plumbers seemed unable to find the problem and suggested it may be the pipe that led out to the loch. Ian was unconvinced by this and had detected an infuriating pattern to the smell. It seemed at its strongest whenever he managed to get down to sustained writing, which given the splendour of the scenery was becoming infrequent.

After a few weeks of these frustrating distractions he realised how little he cared for the everyday tasks that Cathy had been so good at keeping hidden from him. He decided a housekeeper would be in order—to clean and tidy a little, manage any household problems, do some shopping, and to provide a little company.

So Mrs Ferguson was found, through an advertisement in the post office window. Her children had recently left home to find work, one to Glasgow and the other to Manchester, and so she now had a little more time on her hands and was pleased to have some independent income again. And Ian Lyons offered very flexible terms that she could fit around her husband's work schedule. Ian thought she was perfect—but again the call of his writing mind was keen to include her in a story as soon as possible. It seemed everyone he met became subject to this reformation into the dubious immortality of the page.

Lochgilphead suited his purposes perfectly, with enough amenities to service his basic needs, but without the endless shops that always depressed him so much. And the larger town of Oban was only a forty minute drive away should he need anything more elaborate. There were a couple of nice pubs too—places he had always found invaluable for 'genuine' conversation in his writing. Of these, *The Comm* was the most 'authentic', he felt. It was a wonderful little place, with a cosy room at the back with long communal drinking tables.

During the first few days of arriving in the town he had spent an entertaining evening as audience to the bitter abuse between a Glaswegian and Edinburghian. They were best of friends but put on a show for him of the rivalry between their cities. No doubt they would appear, in some guise or other, in one of his stories.

Although an accomplished drinker he soon realised this was not the place for him. It would take years to be trusted by the local drinkers. He had best limit himself to an occasional appearance, when both he and the locals could limit themselves to self-caricature.

Each day he attempted the old routines: coffee and toast, the papers, followed by a few hours in the morning at the computer. Then lunch at around 2pm, followed by a few more hours; these afternoon sessions were frequently interrupted by a brief doze though—he found himself increasingly tired as the day wore on. In London he had usually managed about three thousand words each day, at a pretty polished level. Here that had dwindled to a meagre thousand, if that.

This was due, in part, to his grief. But mostly it was that captivating view across the loch, with a densely forested mountainside in the distance, where the road snaked around the borders of the wilder places. For much of the day it was a muddy expanse, awaiting the return of the water. He sat at his desk watching a variety of birds wading in the mud for food. He watched the incremental transformation of light at the tidal ebbs—the permanence of impermanence; as the deep channels of lighter water carry the waters to kiss the land as veins reach out beneath skin.

The months idled by. He missed a couple of deadlines, turned down a few offers for articles—journalism was something he was eager to ditch as soon as possible. For the first time in his life he seemed to have mastered the art of the simple 'No'.

Mrs Ferguson was a constant help. They talked and laughed, often. Ian had even encouraged her to begin writing—he thought it would be a useful way for her to fill her evenings creatively, with her husband away on some of the tourist trips around the islands so often. He gave her the usual advice about discipline, plot construction, character evolution—and the classic 'write about what you know' that had served him so well for all these years.

She said she'd give it a go—'why not, eh?'

He occasionally enquired about her writing and she'd offer some vague response (he guessed she hadn't even tried).

Then the call came from Sue in London (an old friend of his and Cathy's). Her husband David had died suddenly from a stroke and she was making arrangements. Of course he'd help. Of course he'd come to London. That following evening he was back in very familiar streets and, in what fashion he could, consoling Sue. It was strange, he told her, David had been on his mind often lately, as he'd featured in a short story he'd started a few weeks previously. He was to be the murderer.

After a brief pause, that could have gone either way, they both burst out laughing. David would have found it hilarious—but that was David, wasn't it. Yes, that was David.

The funeral went smoothly, seeming—as they often do—rather inadequate to account for a human life: a few readings, a song (or hymn, depending on your leaning) or two, maybe a teary poem.

Two days later he was back in his study, gazing out across the gently flowing waters.

Time.

He thought morbid thoughts, with that wretched tiredness lapping at him as steadily as the waves.

The next few months saw the passing of a few more of his family and friends. It was his age, Ian told himself. He had entered that time of life when everyone around you drops and you find yourself, if you're lucky, the last one standing. Thinking about it that wasn't that lucky at all—being steadily shorn of your attachment to the world, leaving every face strange and uncaring. He'd rather not be the last he thought.

That was easily arranged—as though the great cosmic editor had been reading the script of his mind.

Ian had decided to visit the doctor to 'get something' for his tiredness. It could no longer be put down to the freshness of the new air; he'd been here nearly a year. Nor indeed were his journeys to London—to bury the dead—that frequent to account for the perpetual drowsiness that he suffered.

Tests were done. They did not offer much hope. It was an advanced heart condition. Little could change the course of the illness but some time could be bought. Some change of habit would be required, not least some exercise and a different diet. Someone would contact him; there were many support networks, charities—people who cared.

And so Ian Lyons slid into that uncertain space of need. But he was one of the unlucky ones whose files are always mislaid, or read too late, or filed incorrectly. Emails concerning his illness went astray; consultants were on holiday; people forgot. Gradually his life was reduced to forms and paperwork which flowed in circuitous routes between departments, steadily dwindling—or inexplicably proliferating—as they made their rounds.

Mrs Ferguson was distraught when he told her and did what she could to help. In fact, he thought, she had become the best friend he had in this town, perhaps the only friend. He was so tired that it little bothered him what the state of his professional care was.

Minor things obsessed him now, the colour of the sunrise as it hit the trees on the mountainside opposite his study window—he'd set his alarm to catch it each morning, although he so needed the rest. Then there were the strange deposits of shells that kept accumulating by the wall beside the loch, yet he never saw the birds, or any other animals approach that closely. But there were other, more tedious matters that absorbed his thoughts; the endless rounds of pills to keep him 'ticking' along (he chuckled); the bathroom pipes that rattled and groaned; and ever that smell from the drains that must have been investigated by seven different plumbers (perhaps all those qualified in the vicinity) over the last eighteen months.

One evening, sleeping fitfully, he decided to do some work on a story that had rather captivated him. A couple of hours in and he was delighted with the speed, and quality, of the work. Thankfully the moon was barely visible so the scene across the small bay was mostly black, save for the line of streetlights on the opposite side and the illuminated decks of a cargo ship that had missed the tide and was now trapped in shallow water with a consignment of wood. Without the distraction of the view he was able to work quite effectively. Perhaps he should swap his routine and sleep in the day, he thought. No, given his condition, that would probably be unwise.

Then he caught a waft of the sewers again, stronger than at any time before. He determined to solve the problem once and for all. He reluctantly left the computer and, tightening his dressing-gown belt with resolve, headed off to discover what could be causing it.

After two hours of running taps, checking drains, flushing the toilet and generally investigating any visible pipe, without successful resolution of the problem, he decided it would be best to resume his writing before the urge left him.

He had printed off a number of sheets to read through (he always preferred to edit on the page rather than screen) and, as was his usual practice, had placed them in his edit pile. This had grown considerably over the last few months though, as numerous stories had lain unfinished as new ideas took him. He had best deposit these, for now, with the other work waiting to be finalised. This was stored in one of the cupboards in the hall, where a number of boxes still lingered from the move.

As he opened the door the smell was overpowering. He almost fell over with the shock. So that was the source of the problem, not the drainage! Something had clearly died in there—but how could it have smelt for so long. Surely any creature unfortunate enough to have been trapped in there would have decomposed long before now. And why hadn't he noticed it before now? Best drop the papers in the document box and find out the exact cause in the morning—with the assistance of Mrs Ferguson, a mop, bleach and a bucket.

He lifted the lid of the box and it became even stronger. The stench was terrible. This clearly couldn't wait a moment longer. Besides, he'd never sleep with that stink wafting through the house.

He remembered a small tin of peppermint lip balm of Cathy's that he'd kept and rushed to the bathroom cabinet to find it. He smeared a generous blob of the stuff on his upper lip and around his nostrils to tolerate a further investigation.

Turning on the upper hall light he was then able to drag the box out into brighter light to get a better look. Although of quite a durable cardboard it had started to disintegrate at the base. There were large damp patches spreading up the sides of the box and in each of the bottom corners there was a blackish stain creeping steadily upwards. He peered in nervously.

There had clearly been some kind of spillage at the bottom of the papers; dark goo had collected at the base of the box. He slowly lifted as many of the more recent pages as possible, containing most of the stories he had written since arriving in Lochgilphead.

The smell of rot, offset only slightly by mint, made him retch but he was so amazed by what he found that any discomfort was soon forgotten.

A dark sticky substance coated the lower sheets and there appeared to be a mass of fibres, like cobwebs, that bound many of the upper sheets to each other. He teased apart a few of the top pages. Between each there was a tangle of reddish threads that branched out towards the outer fibres. It so much resembled a spider's web that he started looking about nervously for whatever creature had made them (it must certainly be very large). As he separated the sheets further though some of the fibres began to break and a liquid burst from them, across the pages—blood, obviously.

He read the first few lines of one of the pages. It was from the story he had started a month before Cathy's death: 'Supposition of Guilt'. Cathy appeared as a character within it, Stella Seabridge, who had been charged with a murder she hadn't committed. He hadn't got very far with work on it, having abandoned it soon after her diagnosis. He teased away that page, meeting a sticky resistance from the one behind. There, between the pages, was another sheet of... something. It was difficult for Ian to immediately comprehend what the peculiar substance was. It appeared to be some sort of filmy, yellowing fabric, traced with a scratchy pen in minute hand.

The seconds slipped by until he realised what the thin page really was: a translucent, tissue-thin page of skin. And he read across its surface the same words that appeared on the page of typed paper that it had been attached to. On the skin-paper the words were traced with thin blue and red veins that slowly pulsed within the 'page'. The skin-sheet replicated the paper one word for word.

It was still attached to other fibrous bundles of veins and embryonic muscular strands. The ball of tissues had formed some sort of copy of his stories, and had developed some crude nervous and vascular system, inserting—no, growing!—itself between their discarded pages. This delicate and horrific palimpsest was alive!

He sat there with the sheet of skin shivering between his fingertips, pulsing delicately with the beat of an invisible heart.

∞

Later that night, from the deck of their ship, some Irish sailors could see a small bonfire in the garden of one of the Lochgilphead cottages. Something ancient called to them from that meeting of water and fire at the margins of land and sea—a symbol of eternity absurdly fractured by the vision of a thin figure in pyjamas and dressing gown tending the flames.

Later that night Ian Lyons' heart finally gave in. Everyone assumed it had happened as he slept; a *good* death—as they say; the kind of death you read about in a book; the sort reserved for a sympathetic character.

∞

Some weeks later, after Ian Lyons' funeral, Mrs Ferguson—or as she was known at home, Doreen—was typing away at the computer. Her husband, Derek, was sat reading the paper at the dining room table as he did most evenings that he wasn't still in Oban working late on the tourist boats he crewed. The usual post-repast silence had often been punctuated these last few months by Doreen's tapping away on the keyboard. Recalling stories of love affairs through the internet—although little believing it might be possible this late in their lives—Derek thought it best to investigate.

'What you doing, dear?' he asked.

There was a lengthy silence during which the tapping slowed a little.

'I'm writing a story,' Doreen finally replied, clearly deep in thought.

'Oh, I see,' he said.

Another long silence, the tapping did not resume.

'What's it about, dear?' he felt obliged to ask.

'It's about a writer who tries to escape his sad life in the city and find inspiration in the countryside,' she said.

'It was poor Mr Lyons that said I should take up writing as a little hobby. So I thought I'd try it out, maybe even send it off to one of those magazines.'

'Yes, why not? That's a great idea,' Derek said, resuming his reading.

'It's just so sad he won't be able to read it,' she pondered. 'You see everyone says "write about what you know", don't they? Mr Lyons said it too. And so I did. The story's based on him. It's about a writer who tries to get away from it all to write his book. He never quite finishes it, as the scenery and wonderful views replace his need to create fiction.'

'Does he die in your story too?' Derek asked bluntly.

Another long silence.

'He does actually,' Doreen said, guiltily.

And again silence, interrupted finally by a tentative resumption of typing.

'But I'd decided on that ending a long time before I knew about Mr Lyons' illness. So, it's not completely real', she added—little realising that fiction can never absolve itself of responsibility by the simple rejection of reality.

But all that is, quite naturally, far from the truth. For over the years—as her story gathered itself into a book—Mrs Doreen Ferguson sent out intricate tremors through the world with each keystroke; delicate, endless echoes that whirled and eddied around those she loved and loathed, those she watched and overheard; each word adjusting the universe and rewriting lives; each sentence a faint murmur of finitude, as soothing and relentless as the lap of gentle inland waves.

Afterword

'As If'

Eugene Thacker

As If. In the 1780s, during the peak of an epoch that ceremoniously referred to itself as 'Enlightenment', Immanuel Kant was writing about ethics and moral philosophy. Certainly philosophers from Socrates to Spinoza had thought about ethics and morality prior to Kant's time. But during the Enlightenment, which Kant himself would characterize as humanity's coming into 'maturity', the stakes were different. If the sleep of reason did indeed produce monsters, it was time for reason to wake up, and to place itself at the centre of the quest for knowledge, the pursuit of truth, and the engagement with civil society. In conjunction with paradigm shifts in astronomy, physics, mathematics, and medicine, the so-called human sciences would follow suit, with a new philosophy, a new politics, a new aesthetics, and a new ethics founded exclusively on the authority of human reason, without recourse to religion, myth, or superstition.

But the trick was to develop an ethical and moral philosophy that would go beyond a mere list of 'dos' and 'don'ts'—a task not only unending but continually subject to change and amendment. In short, Kant was aware that moral and ethical philosophy needed to move beyond mere *hypothetical* imperatives of the type 'if A occurs, then do B.' Human beings were not, after all, ethical automata, all gears and pulleys cloaked by an anthropomorphic shell. Or were they? Kant's solution was to scale things up, and argue for a morality and ethics that would be unconditional, rather than conditional—what was required was a *categorical* imperative, not just hypothetical imperatives, a 'do this' that would apply in each and every case, no matter what the details.

In his 1785 work *Groundwork for the Metaphysics of Morals* Kant provided several definitions of this categorical imperative. One reads: 'The categorical imperative would be that which represented an action as objectively necessary of itself, without reference to another end.' Another, more thorough definition, reads: 'There is, therefore, only a single categorical imperative and it is this: *act only in accordance with that maxim through which you can at the same time will that it become a universal law.*'

The problem, of course, is that it is incredibly difficult to behave in this unconditional manner. It requires an almost *religious* devotion to scientific reason and the cold logic of universal moral law. For every example of such a categorical imperative (e.g. 'One should always tell the truth'; 'One should always help others') it is easy, all too easy, to think of exceptions, even compounded ones ('...unless telling the truth does not help others...').

And then there is the problem of the 'as if.' Kant never says that such moral laws *are* universal...or laws...or even moral. What he says is that one should act with such a level of commitment that one would be prepared to claim universal status for such actions. Act *as if* your actions, and the values behind them, are universally valid. Here is another of Kant's definitions of the categorical imperative: '...act *as if* the maxim of your action were to become by your will a universal law of nature.'

Just pretend it's for real.

Nevertheless, Kant stood by his categorical imperative, come what may. The implications not only for the individual citizen but for civil society were obvious. The French Revolution, after all, was just around the corner—as was the Terror...phantoms lurking around every moral corner.

∞

On Peripatetic Ethics; or, the Wandering Philosopher. If the age of Enlightenment was about anything, it was about putting theory into practice, about walking the philosophical walk, about showing that reason was not merely an abstract, intellectual exercise with no impact in the 'real' world. And Kant loved to walk. Or rather, he walked, without exception, every day, around the town of Königsberg, where he lived for most of his life. Whether he *loved* it or not is another question.

Did the 70 year-old philosopher, while he was writing his ethical treatises, encounter any annoying or difficult people while on his walks? If so, did he view such unfortunate encounters as opportunities to put his 'categorical imperative' to the test?

It was often said that the washer-women of Königsberg could tell the time of day by when the elderly but able-bodied Kant walked by their houses.

∞

A Hauntology of Bridges and Canals. The little town of Königsberg (now Kaliningrad), was founded in the middle of the 13th century on an old Prussian settlement. In the 16th and 17th centuries it served as a Prussian capital, and became an intellectual and cultural centre, attracting authors such as E.T.A. Hoffmann and philosophers such as Kant.

I like to imagine Kant there in Königsberg, enjoying his daily routine, taking a break from writing the *Critique of Pure Reason* and going for his walk—perhaps along the networks of bridges and canals that formed the city's centre.

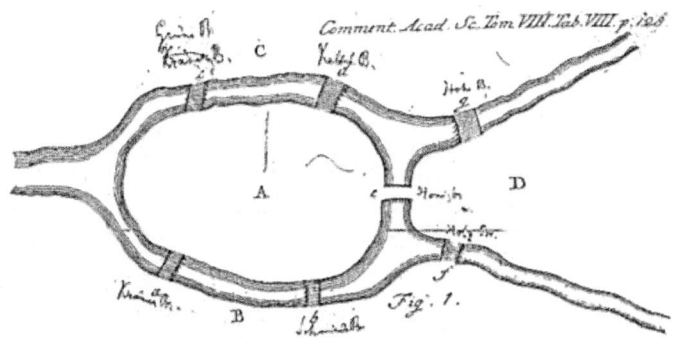

Was Kant aware that, just a few decades earlier, the mathematician Leonard Euler used the walkways of Königsberg to illustrate the principles of graph theory? Euler noted that the seven bridges over the canals, when geometrically abstracted, formed an interesting mathematical puzzle. Could one trace a single path that crossed each bridge only once? Euler's research would go on to influence everything from the modern highway system to the design of telecommunications networks. Perhaps Kant had unknowingly solved the problem on one of his daily walks—and without speaking to anyone. And perhaps he was, at that moment, thinking about the problem of how to create universal, logical standards for ethical and moral behavior.

∞

Dethroned. It is often said that the philosophy of Kant effected a 'Copernican turn' in the history of thought, just as, a generation earlier, the astronomer Nicolaus

Copernicus demonstrated that the sun, and not the earth, was at the center of our planetary system. Even though Copernicus displaced the earth—and by extension humanity—from the center of the universe, he put humanity back in the center by showing how human reason alone—without religion, without scripture, and without the Church—could achieve the *fiat* of scientific explanation.

By the time the industrial dawn of the 20th century came about, scientific reason had explained much—perhaps too much. There was talk of relativity, of the fourth dimension, of the space-time continuum, of elementary particles and the first whisperings of quantum uncertainty. The distance separating the scientific picture of reality and the way reality 'ought to be' began to grow further and further apart.

An avid science reader and amateur science journalist, H.P. Lovecraft noted the changes taking place. And they seemed to, once again, displace humanity from the center of the universe. Lovecraft's now-celebrated opening to 'The Call of Cthulhu' (published in 1928) summarizes this strange reversal of fortune: 'The most merciful thing in the world, I think, is the inability of the human mind to correlate all its contents. We live on a placid island of ignorance in the midst of black seas of infinity, and it was not meant that we should voyage far. The sciences, each straining in its own direction, have hitherto harmed us little; but some day the piecing together of dissociated knowledge will open up such terrifying vistas of reality, and of our frightful position therein, that we shall either go mad from the revelation or flee from the deadly light into the peace and safety of a new dark age.'

Should we then suggest another turn in the Copernican revolution, after Copernicus, and after Kant—a 'Lovecraftian turn'? Not only are we human beings not at the center of the universe, we are no longer capable of knowing that we are not at the center of the universe. Our highest cognitive faculties, inclusive of scientific rationality, seem only to lead to paradox, opacity, and, strangely, to mystery. The more we know, the less we know—and what we know of this doesn't bode well for humanity and its self-endowed, species superiority.

There is, perhaps, yet another further stage after this, closer to our own time. Not much has changed— no one still really understands quantum physics, and every day reality shows itself to be stranger than fiction. Except that no one cares—or, indeed, bothers to notice. We have become skilled in selectively ignoring the world, even when it shows itself to be blatantly counterintuitive or indifferently non-human. A new *ignorance* is on the horizon, an ignorance borne not of a lack of knowledge but of too much knowledge, too much data, too many theories, too little time.

Strangely, Kant already foresaw this. What he termed the 'antinomies of reason' were those issues that could be debated forever and never resolved—the existence of God, the origin of the universe, life after death. Don't bother thinking about these things, he advised, and leave such questions to the theologians or the astronomers—they are not *philosophical* questions.

The humility of philosophy. With Kant, thought becomes humble. With Lovecraft, it also becomes, at the same time, grandiose.

∞

Where ethical philosophy leaves off, supernatural horror begins. Kant: '...morality is no phantom...'

∞

Literary theorists often talk about 'the fantastic' when discussing the horror genre. Tzvetan Todorov, for instance, defines the fantastic as a kind of fork in the road. A character in a story confronts something strange and unexplained. That character is presented with one of two options: either the phenomena in question can be explained according to the accepted laws of nature (and it doesn't really exist), or else it cannot be explained (and does exist). Either it's all in your head (and you were dreaming, or you were on drugs, or in a trance, or had too much coffee, or you're just extra imaginative), or else we have to seriously rethink some basic notions about 'reality' (and all those experiments and scientific treatises are for naught). For Todorov, the fantastic is that little moment of hesitation at the fork in the road: 'The fantastic is that hesitation experienced by a person who knows only the laws of nature, confronting an apparently supernatural event.'

Of course, few are the stories that can maintain the fantastic, and suspend that duration of uncertainty. (Life, arguably, is different...) In a way, what Lovecraft (and before him, Anne Radcliffe) called 'supernatural horror' is such an attempt, and this is exemplified in many of the tales of D.P. Watt. Except that one expects—looks forward to, even—the fantastic. The hesitation of the fantastic is woven into the very fabric of each story world, even though it may at first seem quick mundane and quotidian. Perhaps there is a categorical imperative embedded within this literary tradition: act as if everything presented to you is not what it seems. That campsite at Dunoon, that rail station in Sheringham, that studio in Maidstone, that side-show tent in Werrow—a despondent sea-side town, a sluggish rural village, the affectless neutrality of the outskirts of town—these are not just settings for stories but sites of the fantastic, where it 'takes place,' that ephemeral hesitation given an equal spatial ephemerality. The place where one hesitates, like a wandering, peripatetic philosopher.

∞

Phantom Acts. The terms phantasmagoria, phantasm, and phantom all share a common etymological root, from the Greek *phantazein* (to make visible) and *phainein* (to show). Strange, then, that the terms would come to denote precisely that which is not seen, or rather, that which is seen with uncertainty. The tradition of the gothic novel is replete with phantoms of this type; we as readers are never sure if the characters have actually seen a ghost or have simply mis-judged the night wind languorously blowing a curtain.

But every phantom—real or imagined—is doubled, referring to a once-living person as well as being a spectral manifestation in and of itself. Every phantom is literally beside itself, not unlike the many disenchanted characters in the stories of *The Phantasmagorical Imperative...* 'to be besides oneself'—as one's own shadow, as a döppelganger, as one who exists twice...perhaps twice more than necessary.

∞

The phantasmagorical imperative: everything unreal must appear.

The phantom imperative: act as if everything real is unreal.

∞

The World Becomes a Phantom. Kant's philosophy is, to be sure, philosophy in the grand style—rigorous, systematic, ambitious...and a touch naive. For, how many of us are really capable of acting according to the cold logic of reason, irrespective of our individual desires, our displaced egos, our fears and tremblings?

Kant seemed aware of this. Near the end of one of his treatises he admits, almost confessionally: 'Now, such a kingdom of ends would actually come into existence through maxims whose rule the categorical imperative prescribes to all rational beings *if they were universally followed.*' The stakes are too high, it seems. It only works if *everyone* plays along.

But the truly disturbing thing is not just that other people might not act accordingly, but that the whole non-human world may not act accordingly—*that the world itself may not play along.* Objects behaving strangely, familiar places suddenly unfamiliar, the inorganic world suddenly staring back. Kant continues: 'It is true that, even though a rational being scrupulously follows this maxim himself, he cannot for that reason count upon every other to be faithful to the same maxim nor can he count upon the kingdom of nature and its purposive order to harmonize with him, as a fitting member, toward a kingdom of ends possible through himself, that is, upon its favoring his expectation of happiness...'

∞

In the 17th century the philosopher, occultist, and scientist Athanasius Kircher designed a novel device using a simple candle-powered magic lantern and glass slide. A product of Kircher's interests in optics, he also associated these so-called phantasmagoria and their ability to produce lifelike, animate images with a kind of vitalistic, life-force. Such devices proliferated across the cultural centers of 18th and 19th century Europe, including the Parisian Cabaret du Néant, where visitors could enjoy a ghost show along with their absinthe. Soon magic lantern shows and phantasmagoria could be seen everywhere, along with stereoscopes and other visual media—much of which could be purchased in the then-popular Parisian arcades, with their rows of magical shop window displays—uncanny mannequins, dismembered hats, shoes, gloves, necklaces, walking canes, eye-glasses, children's toys…the various charms of an era quickly disappearing. It was no wonder that Walter Benjamin, living in Paris in the 1920s, would describe the modern commodities of European cities as so many phantasmagoria.

Predominately used for entertainment purposes, the enchanting qualities of 18th and 19th century phantasmagoria were also taken quite seriously by those interested in magic and the occult. In Leipzig, the inventor, coffee-shop owner, and occultist Johann Schröpfer designed his own phantasmagoria, which he shared with his Freemason colleagues. Schröpfer would himself become a phantasmagoria. So taken was he by its conjuring powers and life-like qualities of its spectral images, that, during one demonstration, Schröpfer claimed that a dead person could be resurrected through its powers. It is said that, in or around 1774, Schröpfer attempted to prove his theories by killing himself on stage. The subsequent revitalization was not, however, successful.

∞

An Argument for the Categorical Imperative. 'I haven't read as many books as you have, but if they make you this miserable I don't think I want to.'

∞

'All concepts and with them all principles are nevertheless related to empirical intuitions, i.e., to data for possible experience. Without this they have no objective validity at all, but are rather a mere play, whether it be with representations of the imagination or of the understanding.'

Philosophers such as Kant tell us that our senses are like glasses we can never take off. If philosophy is a form of conjuring, then what of physics, which speaks to us cryptically of waves, particles, and strings? Both use reason to reveal to us the most unreasonable of propositions—that the world is not 'our' world, but a world bereft of humanity, a world that impassively tolerates the ostentatious stage that we have placed at its center, with us stage centre, performing endless soliloquies of impermanence. If philosophy is a form of magic, then physics is a necromancy. Perhaps poetry goes even further—a hymn.

∞

'...fragile and numinous...'

Victoria Nelson is an independent scholar living in California. She is author of *The Secret Life of Puppets* and *Gothicka* (both Harvard University Press).

D.P. Watt is a writer living in the bowels of England. His collection of short stories *An Emporium of Automata* was reprinted by Eibonvale Press in 2013, and his novella 'Memorabilia' was published in *The Transfiguration of Mr Punch* with Egaeus Press.

Eugene Thacker is the author of several books, including the series *Horror of Philosophy* (Zero Books) and *After Life* (University of Chicago Press). He teaches at The New School in New York City.

Publication History

The Phantasmagorical Imperative and Other Fabrications
was first published as a collection
by Egaeus Press in 2014, limited to 250 copies

'The Phantasmagorical Imperative'
in *Sacrum Regnum Journal*,
eds Daniel Corrick and Mark Samuels, 2012

'Laudate Dominum (for many voices)'
in *Shadows and Tall Trees*,
ed. Michael Kelly, Issue 5, July 2013

'Holzwege' in *Delicate Toxins*,
ed. John Hirschorn-Smith, Side Real Press, 2011

Dehiscence, Ex Occidente Press, 2013

The Ten Dictates of Alfred Tesseller,
Ex Occidente Press, 2012

'…he was water before he was fire…' in *Shadows Edge*,
ed. Simon Strantzas, Gray Friar Press, 2013

'Vertep' in *The First Book of Classical Horror*,
ed. D.F. Lewis, Megazanthus Press, 2012

'A Harvest of Abandon'
in *BOOK*, InkerMen Press, 2011

'14ml of Matt Enamel #61'
and 'By Nature's Power Enshrined'
are previously unpublished

Printed in Great Britain
by Amazon